GAEA STAR CRYSTAL

AWAKENING THE TRIBES OF LIGHT

Book 1

by

Mariam Massaro

Published in the United States of America

ISBN 978-1-953904-03-4 (SC)
ISBN 978-1-955243-27-8 (Ebook)

Spirits of the Sun
99 Harvey Road
Worthington, Ma 01098
www.mariammassaro.com

Ordering Information and Rights Permission:

Quantity sales. Special discounts may be available on purchases by corporations, associations, and others. For details, contact the publisher at the address above.

For Book Rights Adaptation and other Rights Permission. Call us toll free 1-888-945-8513 or send email at admin@stellarliteray.com.

ACKNOWLEDGEMENTS

This book is lovingly dedicated to my parents, Pat and Marion Massaro who were absolutely devoted to each other and happily married for sixty-seven years. Together and individually, their loving attitude inspired me to be strong and fair, and to always believe there was nothing to hold me back, ever, to manifest my dreams. Their nine children, three sisters, five brothers, and I, have prospered in every way, thanks to growing up in such a wildly, wonderful, happy, loving, Irish Italian family. I am certain they are enjoying their celestial life together.

Gratitude to the Creator for the unending wondrous source of divine love and light, and to the warm nurturing Goddess, the divine feminine in all life, and to our beautiful Gaea Star, Mother Earth, who provides humanity with everything we need.

I am deeply grateful for her natural elemental beauty that nurtures me throughout this enchanting, uplifting, joyous life, where I wake happy to be alive for one more day in these richly fertile and serene magical lands of New England.

I appreciate the loving support from all my caring spiritual teachers and friends, Ashento, Dameron Midgett, Jesse Massaro, Charlotte, Teka Luttrell, Ray Taylor, Gail Krutka, Grandmother Diane, Paris and Pedro Fernandez, Nancy Crompton, Robert Fish, Freddy Arevalo, Charly Thom, Jay Lynch, Kuauthli Vasquez, Diana Noble, Sierra Bender, Robert Sherwood, Amanda Pollock, Lynne Massaro Davis, Diane McCormick, Gordon Michael Scallion, Cynthia Scallion, Cie Simurro, Robin Rooney, Dagen Julty, Sondra Lewis, Maya Apfelbaum, Jaia Wise, Martin Jones, Gabriel Howearth, Louise Finn and Barbara Robinson and Eve Christoph.

SONG CREDITS

Star of Water - Donnie Bartley

Ancient Mother- Robert Gass

Calling in the Elements, Pacha Mama,
Lyrics Co-writer - Sierra Bender

CONTENTS

PARTS, CHAPTERS, SUBTITLES

Part 1 - In the Beginning

Part 2 - Along the Way to Star Sirius Center

Part 3 - Star Sirius Center

Part 6 - Diyanna's Gardens

Part 7 - Onto the Labyrinth of Crystalline Light

Part 8 - The Labyrinth Ceremony

INTRODUCTION

The Gaea Star Crystal story begins with my explanation of how it all started rather than just leaping into the adventure. Our large family moved many times due to my father's military postings, one of which was southern Germany near the Zugspitze mountains. When young, I spent countless days happily exploring the magical German forests in the Alps, all of which inspired me to want to live in the country, on my own farm someday.

After high school in Watertown, in rural upstate New York, (the last place my father was transferred to), I left to travel freely, mostly hitch-hiking throughout the United States in the 1970's. Embracing the alternative back to the land movement, I studied natural healing, adopted a vegetarian diet and became a home birth midwife and organic farmer. I passionately learned about the Earth's medicinal plants, after personal herbal experiences, proved herbs worked to heal in gentle natural ways.

I lived all over the US, including the West Coast and traveled to India and Nepal. Eventually I landed in Western Massachusetts where I co-founded the Blazing Star Herbal School with Gail Ulrich in 1983, and an herbal products business, Isis Herbs. I chose the ancient, revered Egyptian Goddess, Isis, as I felt a spiritual connection with her. She is a powerful emanation of the divine mother, a midwife and teacher of esoteric healing arts.

I loved co-teaching herbal classes, but it was still necessary to meet my expenses through midwifery, after birth care and waitressing. I wanted to manifest a right livelihood to support doing what I love, joyfully and abundantly, without doing so many different things. So, I asked for spiritual guidance.

An astrological event, the Harmonic Convergence occurred for two weeks in August of 1987. It was heralded as a spiritual awakening for humanity to live more creatively and harmoniously. On the last day of this alignment, I walked through the forest, to a panoramic hill-top nearby, to meditate on this special day. I had a significant vision. Knowing it was important, I scratched it into my sitting pad and ran back through the woods to ask my artist housemate to sketch it. He agreed and gave me a visual rendition of the vision which turned out to be powerful to attune to.

A month later at a holistic health fair I was drawn to the booth of a spiritual psychic from New Hampshire, Gordon Michael Scallion, and his wife, Cynthia. When I asked him about the necklace he was wearing, which was similar to my vision, he said, "It is the Egyptian symbol of the Goddess, Isis." It made sense, why I chose Isis for my business name. She was and still is a guiding inspiration to me.

Gordon offered to create a special medallion using my design with gems that he ascertained were specific to awaken my inherent gifts. On December 12, he called, "The medallion was ready." I wore it home and was thrilled with the silver piece made with Shattuckite, a rare form of Lapis and Moonstone.

That night I dreamed of a formula, which I called, 'Detox Healing Bath Crystals.' It was an herbal and mineral bath to release environmental and chemical toxicity through the skin, which is the largest organ of elimination. Detox became a company best seller for years, even in Japan, where it became famous, until their FDA stopped the sales due to the word healing on the label and for its positive effects. Seems anything that helps is suspect to ban throughout the world in the quest to subdue natural medicine.

I designed a logo using my vision with Nancy Crompton, a local artist who bartered design work for being the midwife at her homebirth. She suggested I change Isis Herbs to WiseWays Herbals, since Isis was expressed in the logo design. I took her great idea and changed the name for the business and gave my rights to Blazing Star Herbal School, to Gail Ulrich, my co-founder.

I launched WiseWays Herbals with the new logo and thirteen medicinal and body care products, made in my home, in January 1988. I spoke at a lecture in Northampton on "What is the New Age" with Gail, on a freezing cold night. I displayed the new line with purple and white labels that Rudi Weeks, my husband then, painstakingly crafted from scratch as it was way before graphic design programs on computers. The partner of the product buyer from Cornucopia, a local health food store, saw the display. She suggested that the owner, Bud Stockwell, might be interested in the products. When I presented him the line, he asked, "What makes these any different from what I already have?"

I replied, "These are my ideas, from years of experiences. They are unique enough for your store." He and another product buyer, Patty Waters, from the Greenfield Coop, agreed to try them.

What a great feeling to launch a sustainable business after envisioning this dream. Developing a company with little experience entailed trial and error, dedication, hard work, late hours, and plenty of research to expand with new products.

That fall I presented the line to the buyer of Bread and Circus, now Whole Foods, who was a prior student from the Blazing Star Herbal School. She agreed to pick up the products if I used All Natural, her distributor. The owner, Paul Peckham, complied and still distributes our line after 34 years. That was the break needed to grow the company, into eventual national and international distribution.

For five years, I moved to expand my home business. I longed to get the oil mess out of my kitchen into a separate workspace and finally moved to the Stone House Farm, high upon a ridge with a great view, in Huntington in the middle of winter. There, in the cold basement of the castle like house, we set up the company's own workplace. What a relief to have my home back.

I started saving to manifest my dream of owning land and a bigger space for WiseWays Herbals. In January 1992, the Stone House Farm went up for sale and we were asked to move. Brr, it was cold, looking at farms in winter.

I consulted a psychic who said, "Stop looking, the farm is there. You'll hear on February 14th. Keep making the Radiant Rays Chakra oils." I liked that concept rather than searching all over with a young child in the freezing cold. On February 14, a former midwifery client called, asking if I wanted to buy their 1800s farm in Worthington, fifteen minutes north of my home.

I had delivered two babies there, a decade earlier. I loved its' peaceful beauty, forests, pastures and a misty brook flowing below the rambling house. It was a powerful, clear sign that this was my new place! Rudi and I decided to separate, so it was up to me to make the sale happen. I knew that I was being guided, so no worries.

I convinced the owners that I would raise the money to purchase it within a year and gave a down payment to show I was serious. They agreed on a lease to own contract and to our delight, Jesse and I, moved there in June of 1992. What a joyful feeling to be in our own home and adopt the sweet cat, Ophelia, they left and eat the delicious organic food from their huge gardens.

I focused on manifesting the funds to buy the farm. Thanks to my business contacts and friends, in August 1993, Singing Brook became our new permanent home.

What an adventure settling in. I loved every moment of the quiet beauty, reclaiming the house from disrepair and planting big gardens with organic herbs, roses and delicious fruit and vegetables, while managing the company. Over the years, new business additions, trees, shrubs, and Koi fish water gardens were added. It is satisfying to watch all the trees and shrubs growing tall and strong.

The natural serenity of this nurturing land always fills me with peaceful contentment. I'm often inspired to create songs and poetry during full moons, blizzards, thunder and lightning storms or crystal icy freezes. My dreams often impart messages, visions and healing remedies that I duly note in journals at my bedside.

When I wrote or sang my inspirations, I often felt a different energy other than my own. I never questioned that presence, even though my pen moved without guidance, with poetic, spiritual words that flowed like a gushing fountain of love.

I didn't realize I was channeling messages from an ascended spiritual master. I knew others did from reading their books. I kept this a secret until I connected with my celestial twin flame in 2003 in a dream while alone on a vision quest deep in the nearby woods.

In November 1998, I sat on a wood pile with my Manx cat, Fu Manchu, watching the colorful sunset. As pretty clouds drifted by, I heard a whisper, "Create a play, a lively expression of all that you feel at this moment of earthly serenity."

"Fu, look at nature's magnificent sky. I want to write a play to honor this spectacular beauty, to inspire others to preserve the Earth and her precious resources for future generations." I ran down the path with Fu following, to tell my son.

"Jesse, I was inspired to write a story to save the Earth. Do you want to help?"

"Sure, let's do it."

We sat in the kitchen, concocting "The Rainbow Crystals of the Earth" into an adventure story with seekers, who roam the earth searching for powerful wisdom crystals, that were buried when the Earth became out of balance. The faery, animal, forest and plant realms, unite with the seekers to find the crystals, helping to restore peaceful harmony. We envisioned an outdoor theater with performers collaborating in celebration of the majestic Earth.

Throughout the long winter, the story developed with many diverse characters. As I pondered the animal to represent the west, I looked out the west window and saw the answer; a large black bear was crossing the narrowest part of the brook. Now I knew where to build the bridge to access the forest on the other side of the brook. Four bridges have been built on that spot since 1999 due to Hurricane Irene and heavy rainstorms washing them away.

The play turned into a musical when new songs came to me. The first, "Calling in the Elements," was inspired while sitting at my stone fire circle, watching the evening sky. The wonderful aspect of original music is that anyone can contribute to the melody or lyrics, and it stays as part of the song forever. I often helped Sierra Bender, a yoga, fitness, and empowerment teacher, by leading lodges for her Boot Camp for Goddesses retreats. We embellished this song with new verses in the lodges and sang it with gusto on our hiking adventures.

Calling in the Elements

We call in the wind, the breath of our mother

Gaea, Gaea Star

We call in the fire, the spirit of our mother

Gaea, Gaea Star

We call in the water, the blood of our mother

Gaea, Gaea Star

We call in the Earth, the home of our mother

Gaea, Gaea Star

We call in creation, the home of our souls

Gaea, Gaea Star

"The Rainbow Crystals of the Earth'" was performed on Earth Day, April 24,1999, on a spring day with friends and others who came to build a sweat lodge for Charly Thom. He was a Karuk tribal elder from California, coming to lead sweat lodges. After finishing the lodge, we staged the play as a prayer for the Earth. We donned costumes and chose parts. I played a Goddess and also the parts not taken. I sang a few songs while Jesse and his friends, played the crystal seekers.

Elliot Tarry was our delightful storyteller,

"Eons ago, the enchanted Earth had magical creatures that roamed freely, not yet hidden by the veils of unbelief. Faeries danced in magical moonbeams. Elves played in the forest and regal unicorns pranced in lush meadows. Throughout the pure, fertile lands, peace reigned. Crystals were revered for their healing powers.

Simple ways of living, were replaced by the advances of technology, losing the inherent connection to live in harmony, in community, with a commitment to preserving Earth for future generations. Her purity became dangerously out of balance due to uncaring greedy people.

The concerned gather, hoping to find a way to heal this critical dilemma of the aching Earth before it is too late. As imbalance spreads, the crystals are buried for safe keeping by wise elders all over the world.

Hobiton, a crystal guardian, lived high in the mountains with his apprentice, Okemo. A great blizzard lasting for days, prevents Okemo's return from the village, where he went for supplies. After the storm broke, he climbs the steep pass to hear angelic singing,

Reborn, reborn, I am reborn,

I am returning to my sacred star, on wings of golden light.

He is surprised to see Hobiton, his master floating as a spirit in their cabin, having died in his absence. Hobiton asks, "Okemo, can you help restore the Earth's harmony?"

Okemo answers, "Yes, of course."

Hobiton says, "Then seek the key wisdom crystals, that are essential to unify the people. It is up to you as I am sailing to the heavens."

He fades in a white poof. Okemo sets out with hope, meeting other crystal seekers, animal and elemental spirits who all agree to help humanity save Gaea Star. They offer songs, gifts and prayers wherever they travel to."

We did a wonderful staging, to bring the story to life. A beautiful queen of the faeries fluttered around with huge golden gossamer wings, while her faerie helper, playfully sprinkled magic faery dust throughout the land.

The small audience became characters, as we tromped through the forest, to meet Grandfather Pine, elves and the brook's nymphs. As we emerged from the forest, a medicine man invited us to sit by a glowing fire, in front of his tipi, where he shared wise teachings and herbal tea. Rose Queens beckoned from the gardens and explained how to use their flowers essence's.

When the crystals were reunited, a celebration ensued with the crystal seekers doing a flamboyant sword dance to honor the four directions and the tribes of the world. Hopeful excitement for peace dawned for the Earth's nations.

Everyone agreed that the best part of the play was when a boy wearing a fox mask, read the fox part, with little enthusiasm. Just then a female fox, trotting down the road, veered into the upper driveway, coming to where we were standing in the field. We remained still and mesmerized, including a large dog, Thunder, that belonged to the Lady of the Beasts, who was one of the characters in the story. She whispered, "Thunder, stay," and he listened to her.

She had artfully arranged a cute collection of stuffed animals as her little beasts on a blanket on the ground. The fox sniffed each one before looking up, as if to say, "I see they are fake." She then went to her den just over the nearby stone wall, where she had four cute pups that often played in the gardens, much to our delight.

People wondered, "How did that happen?" The mystery of divine timing entered my life. Sometimes the line between what is real and what is make believe disappears, especially when the unseen ones in nature join in, as if they hear it all.

I'm sure this happens often, but it is not understood or believed except perhaps by children who never forget, that we are all from the same vital essence of love on this beautiful planet.

A few weeks later, life took an interesting turn when aspects of the story came to life. Charly Thom, arrived with a handsome fire keeper, Bob Fish. Smiling, he offered to do anything needed to prepare for the crowd coming. He completed my list by the next day, and asked for more with a wink, which made me look at this wild cowboy - a type I never dated.

After the weekend of lodges with Charlie, Bob persuaded me to be his partner and to wait for his return. He was going to participate in a native Sundance ceremony in California. Shortly after leaving, he called, asking me to fly to California with Jesse to support him in the ceremony. He had received two airline tickets by giving up his seat twice. It was like a rocket blasted into my life with full force.

Always up for an adventure, we went for the experience of a lifetime. We camped at the base of mighty Mt. Shasta with a magnificent view. It was truly amazing to pray with diverse people of similar hearts, for the well-being of the world.

After two months, Bob returned, barely escaping serious injury when his truck rolled while being driven by Charly's daughter on his way here. I had to send for his belongings that were strewn over the highway, including rocks from Mt. Shasta for more lodges for Charly Thom. What a way to begin a new relationship!

Charly came east to lead sweats at our farm for years. We happily shared in these native ways while raising horses, llamas, sheep, and angora bunnies, along with gardening, sewing tipi's and spinning, weaving, and knitting with my animals' fiber, while still managing the ever-growing Wise Ways Herbals.

"The Rainbow Crystals of the Earth" play was shelved and nearly thrown out, but I heard a voice say, "Wait, hold onto it. It may become a musical or a movie, someday." I stored it, since that was a wonderful dream to hold onto.

We sponsored elders from North and South America, who came to share the "Red Road and Green Way" plant teachings with our community. This spiritual path eventually led me to Colombia and Peru to study with shamans from the jungles and the Andes.

During these ceremonies, I discovered my true passion; singing songs which evolved into musical collaborations, honoring the beauty of Gaea Star, and our connection to our divine spirit.

The Vision Quest

It was a cold spring in late May of 2003 when a group from our prayer circles ventured deep into the nearby forest for a vision quest with Freddy Arevalo, a Peruvian shaman. The year before I planned to participate as a quester, but just as it was starting, I backed out as I was not ready to be in the forest alone.

Instead, I helped in the base camp, with food and bringing herbs into the nightly lodges to support the questers. It was a perfect preparation for me to feel brave enough to go on the next year's quest, as a prayer for my life. Knowing you are ready within your heart and mind is the first step in being alone on a vision quest.

After we did a sweat to prepare ourselves, we walked into the woods, where each quester was placed in their own spot with only necessary clothing, bedding, and a tarp to stay for four days and nights, just praying and fasting.

Immediately, a fierce thunderstorm burst upon us as we were putting up my tarp. I had to finish setting my site up with intense lightning cracking. I was grateful for my tarp, thinking, "Wow, what a way to begin. It's a good way to go, in the prayer, in the moment, in nature." I sang rather than be afraid and right then, I received the first of thirteen songs born on this quest.

Thunder Beings

Aho, aho, aho, thunder beings, aho

Lightning in the sky, changing the night into day

Shaking me to my core, with your mighty roar

Rain, rain, rain, rain

Restoring life to the earth, to the beauty of the plants

Moisture is in the air, wet dripping everywhere

Aho, aho, aho, thunder beings, aho

You purify my life, you cleanse my fears

You purify my way, you teach me

Aho, aho, aho, thunder beings, aho

I sang softly to not disturb the other questers, although no one could hear in the storm. To remember it, I took out a recorder which did not work. I realized I was not supposed to use it, but how was I to remember the melody? I devised a unique method by translating the melody into syllables that sounded like it.

For example, 'Aho, aho, aho, thunder beings, aho.' When I see these words, I sing them until the melody returns. The sounds of the letters carry the essence of the tune, which jog my memory. I remembered all the songs using this technique. It has helped when inspired with a new song and have nothing to record with. After returning home, the recorder worked. It seemed to say, "See, you had to teach yourself." It was an intensely empowering time, with hordes of mosquitos, no tent, and only a dripping tarp to try to remain dry from the continuous falling rain.

I had never been alone at night in scary sounding woods, far from houses. That first night I heard a cougar scream, and someone calling my name, but eventually I fell asleep and awoke grateful for being in the quiet of nature, undisturbed, to really listen and observe the serenity everywhere. Somehow in my sweet little sacred space, in the peaceful forest, I fell into a trance, spending time immersed in prayer, reviewing my life. After a few days, I adapted to thirst, hunger, cold and being wet, while lying on the uncomfortable ground, with tree roots. I knew it was good to manage this difficult challenge, as it was the hardest thing I would ever do on my own.

After days of aloneness, I was not afraid at night. I discovered the wonder of the majestic forest that I never noticed. Faces peered from the trees, and in the sky, inspiring a new song.

Spirit of the Forest

Hoye, hoye, hoye, ho ho ho ho ho

Spirit of the forest, spirit of the plants

Everywhere, your faces are looking at me

I am in the presence of holy creation

I am in the presence of divine spirit

I hear you in the wind, I taste you in the rain

I lie upon your gentle earth and feel renewed again

I feel renewed again

I am alone, seeking a vision, in the wonders of nature

In the wonders of your beauty, in the wonders of serenity

Mother Nature you heal my body

Mother Gaea you make me whole

Pachamama you heal my soul, Pachamama, Mother Gaea

I am in the presence of holy creation

I am in the presence of divine spirit

I align with my true nature

I'm awakening my courage and all my strength

I hear the owls in the holy forest

As I lie upon your gentle earth, I feel renewed again

And I feel renewed over and over again

In the wonders of nature, in the wonders of beauty,

in the wonders as far as I can see

Hoye, hoye, hoye, ho ho ho

On the fourth morning, miserable from the constant, dampness and dripping rain, I wrote, "I am cold and thirsty. I don't know if I can stay here another day, but I'll try."

Meeting My Twin Flame

That night I dreamed I was walking in a hallway next to a tall handsome blue skinned man with black hair and piercing eyes. We reached for the handle of a large wood door together and with his hand on mine, we turned it, to walk through the door, laughing.

I had never seen anyone that looked like him. He had several intricate tattoos on his chest and back that were multidimensional green and blue unfamiliar geometric patterns. There were beads, feathers and sparkling stars on the points of the design. The majestic ocean swirled with colorful living beings on his right arm. The beautiful golden sun, and the luminous white moon were shimmering and reflecting in rivers on his left arm.

"Hello, my sweetness, it is good to see you again," he said, smiling radiantly. I was speechless, as I did not remember meeting him. How could I ever forget such an incredible looking being?

He came close to look intensely into my eyes, saying, "My sweetness we have divine loving destiny."

Feeling his powerful energy embracing me, I took a deep breath to ground myself as intense warm currents flowed through me. I was stunned at my feelings for him so quickly. It was true love at first sight, and not easy to ignore. "Wow," I said, "you are very attractive, with profound charismatic, energy but I have a husband."

"Yes, he is fortunate for are a Goddess with great power. I will wait for you, as I am not of Earth and never will be again."

"I will certainly remember you. What is your name?"

"Steward," he replied.

I asked, "What are those unique tattoos all over you?"

"It is a strong prayer," he replied.

"Yes, it's quite a vision of elemental beauty," I answered.

We part with difficulty, almost hugging, but for some reason I just walk away. I told my husband about meeting Steward, as I did not want any feelings for him to interfere with our relationship. Still dreaming, Steward called my husband, to encourage them to meet, as one strong warrior to another, wishing to diffuse any source of jealousy.

He said, "Since I am not embodied in this world, I invite you to accept my energetic presence, to embrace my grand love flowing, and to know this divine love."

Later in the day, as I rested, but awake, I heard Steward whisper, "Lie on your stomach, I'll rub your sore back with your fingers." When I did, it felt so good to feel his love. Joy flushed over me when he said, "I am your twin flame. I will always love you."

He sang an incredible love song that I named "Let Me Love You." I memorized it and still cherish singing this romantic song. I have had the pleasure to sing it at three weddings, including one in Machu Picchu, Peru, as our wedding party was high atop a knoll looking at the surrounding panoramic vista.

Let Me Love You

Let me love you, let me hold you

Let me love you with my eyes

Let me touch you, let me kiss you

Let me love you with my heart

I will always be there in the morning

I will always be there in the night

I will always be there when you need me

I will always be by your side

Let me walk with you, let me talk with you

Let me love you with my mind

Let me laugh with you, let me cry with you

Let me wipe away your tears

Let me dance with you, let me sing for you

Let me whisper in your ears

Let me lay near you, make love with you

Let me love you with my touch

I am from your dreamtime

Look within and it is me you shall always find

Wherever you go, I'll follow, now that I've found you

You're the treasure within my heart

I'll love you forever

I'll love you eternally. I love you

On the last morning of the quest, Steward whispered, "Close your eyes for another vision as we walk." We enjoyed the vistas of stately western mountains and splendor along the flowing rivers. We rode horses past sacred temples and meandered through glorious gardens of exquisite flowers.

Steward said, "These are the times where we lived joyously in love on Gaea Star." He returned later in the day, to say, "Let us walk again." I saw ancient beings and golden and white animals, with unusual faces, dancing in a circle of women in ceremonial regalia.

One spoke; "We are grandmothers from the Star nations. You are a medicine healer from distant realms, Shoshoni Tonania, she who walks with the buffalo and owls. Use your voice, touch, eyes, heart and healing plants to walk this sacred path."

A beautiful woman wearing a long beaded white medicine dress, was drumming, singing a native song. The other women joined in singing and dancing in a circle around me.

Yani yatu heyo, yani yatu heyo, yani yatu hey hey ho,

Awu au heyya, awu au heyya, awu au hey, hey ya

Yahey, yahey, yahey, yahey, yahey, yahey, yahey, yahey,

yahey yahey, yahey, hey ya

I am an ancient one, behold from the stars I come,

a golden maiden of peace

So, take my hand to walk with me

upon this sacred ground in unity

Release your fears, release your cares

as you learn to share

This holy path of peace, upon this sacred ground

From the East and South, from the West and North

The holy path of peace

Celebrate mother earth, her healing plants

Holy fire, pure water, pure air

Seek your strength praying in nature, for a holy vision

May you find your power singing before me

Love each other day or night

as you walk in truth and light

Yani yatu heyo, yani yatu heyo, yani yatu hey o

Awu au heyya, awu a u heyya, awu a u hey, hey ya

What an honoring experience it was. I felt the support from these deep spiritual beings. I accepted their healing power song. I sang it quietly and wrote it down to remember it. I still sing it in ceremonies and performed it in the Gaea Star Goddess show, which evolved years later.

Steward returned later that day as I lay beneath the tall pine forest. He whispered, "Watch yourself breathe."

I closed my eyes, taking slow breaths. I saw balls of golden light growing larger, then floating away. "Does that happen whenever I breathe, warm golden energies of light flow out?"

"Yes, the human body releases energy like this all the time. It is good to acknowledge this, to pay attention to your words, for what you say has powerful effects."

Lulled by the soft rain, the stillness of the forest, the women's song, and Steward's special words, I easily made it to the end of the quest in a gentle trance. I was very proud to have overcome the challenges of the prayer. I felt changed forever by experiencing such an empowering vision quest.

Meeting Steward in that remarkable manner touched me deeply. After resuming my busyness, I did not commune directly with him like we had during the quest although I kept writing words of wisdom in my journals. Thinking of Steward as a celestial twin flame from a distant star, always gave me an uplifting warm feeling, and inspired several new songs.

During the quest, I brought a photo of a beautiful waterfront farm that was possibly for sale, '*To the right person,*' according to the Florida owners. They said we were '*first on the list*' when they were ready to sell. We wanted more pastures for our animals. What a perfect choice, since it was near my family in Watertown, NY. It was a lovely 1800s homestead with 185 acres and huge post and beam barns, on the Black River Bay, where it flowed into Lake Ontario in Dexter, NY. I always longed for a waterfront farm in Maine, but when Singing Brook farm turned up, I settled in Western Massachusetts and created a prosperous life there.

I placed the photo under my tarp on my altar to keep it dry. It was the first thing I focused on, to manifest the ability to buy it. I prayed often, as there is nothing to do on the quest except sit and pray, stand and pray, lay and pray, or sleep and dream.

Three days after the quest ended, the owner called asking us to come to New York to talk about the farm. We drove up immediately and to our joy, they agreed to sell the farm for a *'fair price'* which was an incredibly affordable *'deal of the century.'*

I had my farm appraised, to see if there was enough equity to not sell my home. What a surprise when the appraisal was exactly what was needed to buy the NY farm without selling Singing Brook farm. It had doubled in value in the ten years of owning it.

On August 15th, 2003, the same closing day for my farm in 1993, I bought the NY farm. We were thrilled to go to our new home that day. While looking out the west window, I saw two eagles flying in a love ritual above big pine trees by the water. We ran to watch as they magically mated, with enormous wings holding each other. They fell toward the earth until the last moment, where they split apart, flying into the sky to repeat the same ritual over again.

'Eagle Bay Sanctuary' became the name of the farm. The eagles nested in the pine and oak trees for years, right in view from the house where we watched them fishing the majestic Black River Bay. A few times there were two cute eaglets in the nest, a rare occurrence. They would look down unafraid, as we walked by to go through the woods to the waterfront area.

My partner, Bob, moved there right away, while I went back and forth between the two farms. I was planning to relocate once a new post and beam building was completed to move the herbal business too. My dream of waterfront living was slowly coming to reality, or so I thought. It was several years before the building was finished, which caused a strain on our relationship due to living apart for so long. My plans to relocate to Eagle Bay Sanctuary changed when we separated in 2006.

I still went for short trips, as I loved the inspiration from the serene waterfront. We held tipi ceremonies, sweat lodges and my fourth and final year of Vision Quest there. I loved the idyllic spot I chose along the peaceful waterfront to relax and pray.

It became a busy time, doing everything myself, with two farms, gardens, animals, the herb business, and music making. I knew I needed to slow down, to make life simpler, with more creative downtime, but I was not ready to make changes.

In January 2007, I met Dameron Midgett at a contra dance. Feeling an attraction, we soon became dynamic musical, spiritual life partners and enjoyed making a wonderful life together.

That fall, as I awakened, I heard, *"Revise 'The Rainbow Crystals of the Earth' to give to the world. Now is the time."* I found it on the bookshelf and started to ascertain what to do with it.

A new friend of Dameron's, Charlotte, offered to scan the play into her computer, since the original version no longer worked in my newer computer. She sent it back, excited. "What a great story! You should rewrite it into a screenplay. Can I send it to my friend, Teka? I'm sure he will like it too." She sent it to him. He loved it and wanted to become involved as the art director.

On December 31 as I rested due to a headache, I heard, *"Get up. Pay attention. Look at the starry sky."* I looked out the east window to see a glowing red star rising above the trees. It was Mars, closest to the Earth in many years. A green comet was also visible. Years later, I realized my headaches indicated a need to pay attention to Spirit. They stopped once I listened to the messages coming. I then heard, *'Change the name to the Gaea Star Crystal. Begin before the beginning, where the grand council, confers in heaven about Gaea Star.'*

Referring to Earth as Gaea Star, they continued, *'Express the angelic ones are guiding humanity to awaken to their true missions upon Gaea Star.'*

I was excited to begin the rewrite of the story that New Year's eve night with Dameron. We finished Act One at midnight, although it was revised seven times before completion.

I bought a sparkling blue notebook to write my ideas and songs in and put "The Gaea Star Crystal," on the cover. My creative abilities awakened deeper. When I wrote the messages from Steward, it was easier to understand his teachings. It was like holding a flying kite by its string, with the clues dangling in view. To access them I needed to pull down the string for the clues, to become tangible and easy to work with.

In January 2008, we celebrated our anniversary by skiing in the Vermont mountains. After a great day and delicious food, Dameron fell asleep, so I wrote. An idea came to introduce a love element into the story. I transformed the original character, Okemo into a star medicine woman, Ayalasha, who meets her twin flame, Steward as the eternal love of her life. Yes, that was good but was his name really Steward? It sounded so serious and not very celestial. When I mentioned Steward to a friend, she had said, "He must be a steward in heaven. I bet he has a different name."

Now was the perfect time to ask him. I wrote, "Steward, what is your name in heaven?"

I heard, "Ashento." I liked it. What a perfect fit. We checked the internet for "Ashento," for any info and to our surprise there were only two hits. One was the Erasmus Foundation quoting Dutch philosopher, Erasmus from his twelfth century *Book of Wisdom:*

"This time it is not to the great and glorious, nor they who ride hard
above the height of others, that I look for my land to be reclaimed,
not so. I have sent Apodura Ashentos over the tides; you have reviled
them. I have sent many messengers and you have destroyed them.
Small people of the Earth, the task is yours."

We wrote to this link but never heard back. The other was the Glade Foundation in England, which offered spiritual courses that included an Ashento level. I wrote to them asking what "Ashento" meant and explaining how I received it.

Ray Taylor's response:

"The seventh plane of light is known as the Zenith or pre-Ashento plane. To reach this level, the requirement to take lives on Earth would have long passed. The 'ordeal' is personal to each spirit, but on completion that spirit may be called 'Ashento, Ancient or Master.' They then have the gift of being free, roaming through all the dimensions of 'Home' and do not require permission. They have received wings. However, that is not the end of evolvement for that spirit, for when that spirit has attained perfection (which could take eons) then it might be permitted to approach the 'Crystala' one of the seven aspects of the Great Mind, which is a multifaceted pear-shaped crystal.

The Crystala will open, and that spirit will enter and then be one with the Great Mind. It has to be of utter purity; otherwise, it will be destroyed by the power. It is free to leave when it wishes, but it will then be given the title by the Great Mind to be addressed as ('Lord' and its name) and given its own "Rill of Power."

The irony or beauty is that when one no longer seeks power for its own end, it is given in the fullest measure. It is unlikely that you will find this information elsewhere, as it is the time for these teachings to be given and it seems that our foundation is to be one of the channels used. I am delighted but surprised that you found our website, for we are in the final stages of completing courses and then we were going to launch it with search engines."

My response:

"I am inspired by the 'Gaea Star Crystal story.' With permission, I want to use the aspects of an 'Ashento' to develop my 'Ashento' character and share a message of peace, compassion and love, while expressing our soul's longing to restore balance to Gaea Star."

His response:

"This will help your endeavors; religions on Earth have failed because they were based on the messenger instead of the teachings. Three thousand years ago (in our terms) a number of ancient highly evolved spirits were summoned to the Great Mind (God) and were told of lives that they would live on Gaea Star.

They would be known as the Crystal children, becoming the next leaders and helping to transmute the intensities. All of this will happen on Gaea Star due to their great wisdom, strength, humility, and love. It is a paradox that only the young and the old are told to take certain lives.

When the time comes, all of these crystal children, light beings, and their groups will combine powers for the new phase of humanity to evolve on its way. We are part of the Great Mind, created individually as eternal beings which is why in reality, we are all one.

However, we were not created at the same time. Consequently, we are all at different ages and levels of spiritual evolvement, which explains human behavior.

Religions will pass and be replaced by methods in which each individual will identify more with their own spiritual self and develop the latent intuitive (I prefer this word to "psychic") abilities which we all possess. Because we are a part of the Great Mind, we can of course, talk direct to God and do not need intermediaries.

In the meantime, as the world descends into chaos, healing will be needed. We decided to set up a spiritual organization that offered free healing and trainings in listening, helping and advisory skills."

We were impressed by his words and thrilled to commune with Ashento, such a high being of light. I delved into esoteric books from all over the world to understand more deeply the higher purpose of humanity.

In the *Flower of Life* by Drunvalo Melchizedek, *Clear Light Publishing, 1998,* I discovered that Ashento's geometric tattoo represented an ancient symbol of the blueprint, or Tetrahedron of the Earth's soul, known as the Tree of Life, the Merkabah or Metatron's cube.

The design indeed reflected Ashento's strong prayer for his love for Gaea Star as an Earth steward. I was on high alert, receiving, breathing, and creating this story in a totally unconventional, existential way. Books, music, and friends, all came to me with relevant information. It was as if the word was out in the higher realms and on earth that I was seeking answers and ideas for the ever-evolving story.

Crystals appeared in dreams; Satyaloka Quartz from the mountains of India, believed to enhance spiritual awakening and Morganite, the Pink Emerald, which enables one to connect with the angelic realm.

While in Maui on vacation in the remote area of Kipahulu, we were enjoying the panoramic beauty of an oceanside retreat center in the outdoor kitchen. A robust man walked up a steep hill carrying drums over his head. We laughed as Bubba was a perfect rendition of an exact character from the story. The next day, a friend said we should meet an artist who lived nearby, as he too sounded like a character. Since I follow any leads, we went on an adventure to find John in a remote area along the ocean. It took two tries before we found him, an older artist living in a rustic cabin, surrounded by his carved statues and stunning visionary paintings. Yes, he was a perfect emanation of Hobiton, the wise peaceful artistic elder from the original story.John and Bubba agreed to be in the movie. I wish we had filmed them right then, because as years pass it's harder to return to that magical moment with the same people, as lives changed.

We also met story characters in Western Mass, some of which have become my friends. I believe that we star in one another's lives and visions, without realizing it. How do we explain when you meet someone, who is so familiar and easy to get along with, that you immediately want to co-create and share lives together? You both feel the strong connection and how smoothly it flows into friendship, or love for a long time.

Was it another life, that we knew each other and agreed to meet again with a touchstone signal? Once we see each other, those far-off memories awaken within us. This time, there's no forgetting, since many believe, that before we came to earth, we chose our lives and now we are here to fulfill our spiritual contracts with these prearranged loved ones.

I finished the screenplay in July 2009, thanks to Ashento, Dameron and Teka Lutrell, the graphic artist who moved here from California to help rewrite the play into a screenplay.

Our friend, Charlotte, gave us a fascinating book on Damanhur, a spiritual artists' community in Italy, that built a series of astonishing underground temples, brimming with their incredible art. She suggested the celestial scenes could be filmed there.

After delays in connecting with her various contacts, I wrote to Damanhur directly, to ask permission to film there. To my surprise they agreed. After a year, plans were completed to go in March on a scouting, filming mission. Three friends wanted to join us after learning we were going. Our visit turned out to be a powerful haven from the harsh realities of this world, where creativity is encouraged as self-expression.

We had a creative artsy experience, where we dressed as celestial beings as we filmed some of the scenes in their fascinating outdoor temples along with volunteers from the Damanhur community. What pure inspiration to connect to such a kindred musical, spiritual, artistically positive community!

Their founder and teacher, Falco Tarassaco, or Oberto Airaudi (1950-2013), inspired the Damanhurians through weekly lectures, meditations, writings and unusual artistic creations. Their communities and supporting ones, now number over 25,000, in Italy and throughout the world. They believe that every day, one is to realize their true self in action by releasing their soul's artistic expression, or by being of service within their community.

I returned home inspired with a renewed awareness, to open to my creativity daily. I noticed a difference, as it became effortless to hear melodies and play instruments easily. It seemed as if the music was singing all along, showing that I was always tapped in, but I just had the volume turned down. Even ones that I never played, revealed how to bring out their sweet sounds, like the sitar, which I had not figured out how to tune or play it yet.

I dreamed that an Egyptian priestess, Shahiraba, was sailing down the Nile, singing a song about healing blue lotus flowers. When we looked it up, we learned blue lotus was an ancient temple flower used for centuries in Asia and Egypt for its sacred divinatory and healing properties. I picked up the sitar that morning, tuned and played the Shahiraba song with it. It was as if I knew the song from long ago in a different life.

During this time, Dameron, and I, recorded our first CD, '*Gaea Star Crystal, Awakening the Tribes of Light,*' in January 2009. Several songs from the '*Rainbow Crystals of the Earth*' story, were included. It was easier to create a CD than a movie, which was a daunting idea for us.

How do you get a screenplay into production? We decided to do it ourselves rather than waiting for '*the one*' to come along to manifest it into a movie. Friends say, I am a woman of action. Yes, that's true. I do it. When we realized how expensive and complex it is to make a movie, we took on filming it to maintain the control.

In the summer of 2010, we bought a digital camera, and with a friend, Diana Noble, we gathered actors and friends to film locally. It was fun and exciting to create costumes and stage a magical happening just like back in 1999 when we staged the first version, '*the Rainbow Crystals of the Earth.*'

Once again, we wandered the farm, fields and forests as faeries, wizards, spirits, villains and goddesses, with musicians playing. We filmed it ourselves even if we were novices. We did improv theater, in the glory of natures' elements, enjoying the magical mystery of the Faery realms.

It was challenging to use a script with children involved, so we set the intention for a scene and went with the flow. There were mystical moments captured with flashing crystals, dancing orbs and people in character freely expressing themselves.

That fall, we hiked in Peru's amazing Andes again. We made it to nearly 16,000 feet, where I dressed as Shalaya, a medicine priestess from the Gaea Star Crystal story, while Dameron filmed. I hiked higher and higher, in the midst of the mighty Ausengate peak, which is revered as one of Peru's sacred mountains. It was powerful to take in the almighty as a golden priestess in that astonishing splendor.

In 2010 I met Robert Sherwood after he came to work as a graphic designer for Wise Ways Herbals. His vast musical resume interested me. Months later, I dreamed I was learning piano from him. Since he is a master player, I asked for lessons. Something clicked as I loved singing while he played. He is excellent at knowing where I want to go musically without any effort, and thus began our long musical collaboration together. I never imagined it would lead to playing together in our Gaea Star Band, along with Dameron, Craig Harris, and others.

Through these musical inspirations, I created a live musical, the Gaea Star Goddess Show that was performed at the Academy of Music Theater in Northampton, Ma. and elsewhere for the next four years. The flamboyant show, expressed the colorful Divine Feminine, honored in cultures of the world; Pele, Inanna, Isis, Pacha Mama, and others. Each song was inspired from natures' lovely elements, dreams and travels to India, North and South America, and Hawaii.

We have recorded seven CD's and over 500 Gaea Star Crystal Radio Hour podcasts through Dreamvision 7 radio network as of August 2022. Thanks to Bob for his piano and engineering skills to create such excellent technically good music.

To celebrate the twenty-fifth-year anniversary of WiseWays Herbals in 2012, we compiled a trailer from our filming and used the song, *'Sail to the Realms'* from the first CD as the soundtrack. The faeries sing of sailing to Gaea Star to assist with the lightworkers mission to help humanity rebalance life there.

I submitted the film trailer to the Hollywood and Vine Independent Film Festival in June 2012. To our surprise in early December, I received notice that it won for the best trailer and was showing in a few weeks. What? How could that be? I was booked on another hiking trip to Peru, so I canceled it to go to Hollywood with Dameron to receive the award.

It was exciting to be there, to glimpse that scene. The trailer was shown in a small theater along with other winning creations. We were inspired by the unique films that won and made future connections for the filming of our movie-to-be. Sad though, to see how independent filmmakers still used violence, revenge and suffering as the themes for their movies. I believe that honoring the peaceful goodness of life through love and compassion is the only truth that will set humanity free and lead to harmonious living. We have to reconsider making art to change this troubled world, as violence is never the solution.

We enjoyed staying in a funky hotel from older Hollywood days. When we returned, the momentum for the movie fizzled out, as things sometimes do when life gets going. Although the film took a back seat, the feeling of the theme remained. It was like the baby I always wanted, always hoping to be born one day to gift to the world. I feel imprinted with this message to share through the creative process, to inspire beauty with colorful costuming, positive images, and passionate, uplifting music.

I wonder why we put down dreams, especially when they are halfway there, with encouraging results already. Then the day dawns when we finally say, "I am going to do this right now, to finish what I started, before I leave this planet." It took me a while to arrive at that point and now I have managed to bring it through even with the many distractions my full life brings.

First, I made peace with saying goodbye to the spectacular Eagle Bay Sanctuary, in NY. I knew Spirit was saying to let it go after the grandpa barns burned in 2010, only days before we went to Damanhur, due to a misplaced heat lamp for baby animals. What a loss of the buildings and precious items.

After zoning issues in retaining a small parcel, the way was finally cleared to sell Eagle Bay, although it was very hard to let my dream of living on the waterfront go. Exactly ten years after buying the lovely property, it was sold. One never thinks that a dream we desire may not always bring us what is the best and highest for our soul's well-being, and peace of mind. Often, lessons in life are difficult but essential for our growth.

I always loved the idea of a store/cafe along a scenic river, where I could express my artistic passions. So, with the upcoming sale, I found a place close to my home. It was a funky lodge in picturesque West Cummington, Massachusetts on a big river.

When the sale was held up for legal issues, I meditated to resolve it by invoking all of the beings, elementals, stones, and rivers, to release me as the NY owner and accept me as the new owner here on the river site.

The next day, my lawyer called, "Good news, I found the perfect lawyer who's willing to assist with the problem of the sale and he lives near you in Northampton." Sure enough, he cleared the legal way and I purchased it in March 2014.

There it was, an old lodge, on the mighty Westfield river, in an 1800's village, with an unusable rusty metal bridge in the back. At first, '*Rainbow Bridge*' was going to be the name, but I decided not to use that, after learning it was the term used to bury deceased pets online.

I like the word '*singing*' again as all rivers sing prettily, flowing on and on, whispering, roaring, and relaxing. I recalled that old metal bridges actually sang by humming when you drove over them. I checked online and yes, there were photos of similar bridges as ours and so the Singing Bridge Lodge name was born. I asked the town board if there was a way to restore the bridge. They agreed to repair it by the fall. They followed through by redoing it with donations from the local lumberyard, since the owner had fished off the bridge when he was young.

After renovations, the lodge/vegan cafe opened in spring of 2015 for Sunday get togethers. We built indoor and outdoor stages and a dragon stone pizza oven. I was the chef for the popular pizzas. After years of busyness, I closed the cafe to have more personal time. The lodge became a popular Airbnb site. We continued performing every Sunday with the Gaea Star band and musical guests - playing by the river and in the indoor music space.

I published the messages from Ashento in my first book, *Blessed by Light Filled Love, the Celestial Teachings of Ashento*, in 2014. When reediting it into an e-book in 2016, I discovered missing journal entries. As I was placing them in the newer version, I skimmed past an entry from 2012. I heard, *"Go back. Reread the entry."* I did and was surprised to see a dream I didn't remember, where I heard '*Stone Villa.*' I was running an artsy star nightclub, that was surrounded by stones inside and out, where people celebrated music in a warm, creative atmosphere, as a portal of love and healing for the earth. I realized that Singing Bridge Lodge was that building, with its stone walls, fireplaces, and a sunroom with a stone floor. It is indeed an uplifting refuge with food, music, friends, swimming as mermaids, playful children, and guests from around the world, all enjoying this peaceful pretty place.

After the elections of 2016, I had the impetus to rewrite the screenplay into a novel, now that the new administration was sadly destroying Earth's precious resources, exactly the Gaea Star Crystal story, theme. I still wanted to satisfy my desire to give the world this relevant story, which lives so deep within, to let it out, to drift like a pretty butterfly, high into the blue sky.

Writing delays set in until August 2018, when I moved through the blockages and wrote with clarity, going for it this time. Now I have a strong drive that inspires me, especially in the morning, before I do my busy things.

As I worked on *The Gaea Star Crystal Story*, I also rewrote *Blessed by Light Filled Love*. It was illuminating to see where life has led me since embarking on my creative and spiritual awakening path.

This is the moment to happily enjoy life, with no looking to the past as if you can change it.

I encourage all tribes to merge into one loving family, for we are one essence. Let's open our hearts and minds to realign with peace. May all nations rise up and reclaim loving ways in a celebration of life, free of stress and strife, in blissful harmony. May everyone be blessed with seeds of loving light to plant in the fertile gardens of their hearts. May we live in peace now that humanity entered the age of Aquarius recently. We are in for dynamic change, after the planetary alignment of Jupiter and Saturn, blazed as one star in the sky. An event which had not occurred in eight hundred years.

What a time for our country. The forces of light and dark are at odds. Those who care for humanity are rising up as powerfully as those who are desperate to hold onto their misguided beliefs of inequality and oppression.

Let's sail through this challenging time as we stand strong, shining our inner lights, breathing in the beauty and feeling love overcome all that holds us back.

Let's keep shining the light ever brightly to all beings everywhere.

We are radiant souls here on Gaea Star to learn to love and get along in all ways.

May our souls shine as peace prevails.

Mariam Massaro, August 4, 2022

GAEA STAR CRYSTAL

Awakening the Tribes of Light

Book 1

PART 1

IN THE BEGINNING

1

CELESTIAL ORIGINS

This story begins way before the beginning, high in the realms of heaven with radiant orbs of light sharing their beautiful aware presence with one another, just floating, drifting around, free of gravity, zooming here or there with wild energy in playful ways, making streaks of colorful musical filled rays across the universe. Then the orbs float slowly down, passing through rainbows, to land in a pristine rich setting.

A step stone path winds through a lush garden, bursting with abundant fruit trees and pendulous purple flowers. Tall selenite crystals stretch high, glistening white in the golden sun. A colorful, pulsating light illuminates a heart shaped doorway that opens into an airy gazebo. Clouds drift by, perfect to sit upon, while sweet music fills the air.

Several children playfully run up the path. Celestia wears a silvery turquoise dress and a pretty crown with seven glistening stars. She leaps onto a soft puffy cloud, and gleefully motions to Mira and Azul, to sit. They settle on the comfy clouds together. She says, "Isis was in my dream last night."

Mira, wearing a shimmering golden dress and a crown with five swirling galaxies, says, "She has a very special message."

Azul, wearing cobalt blue leggings, a golden shirt and a perky hat dotted with blue gems, nods, saying, "Let's sail into your dream to see what it's about." They draw in, closing their eyes. A silver orb flashes above as they dissolve into brilliant colors; Celestia into turquoise, Mira into golden, and Azul into lapis lazuli.

The three colors swirl into a rainbow that sails into the temple of the mystical goddess, Isis. She greets them arrayed in majestic shimmering gold, wearing a regal crown with a red sun in the center and arching horns. Her extended iridescent wings receive the sailing rainbow into her heart. Misty colors flow as the children then burst out smiling. Eager to be reunited with their beloved goddess mother, they crowd around her lovingly.

She speaks, "Dear ones whose hearts are pure and full of love, bless you for heeding my call. You are summoned for a journey of great importance, to a distant galaxy, for the great awakening is now."

Mira replies, "Isis, it is an honor to help shine through the darkness."

"Yes, we are ready to help wherever we are needed," Azul says.

"Then, children, we must leave right now. Please enter my red sun," she says while bowing down to release the red sun from her crown, where it then floats in front of them. The children nod in agreement, close their eyes, and instantly transform into a rainbow again, which swirls directly into the spinning red sphere.

"Sail with me," Isis says as she dissolves into golden light and streaks away. What an incredible sight; golden rays in black deep space, with the red sphere following, like a fire chariot sailing through the universe as a spaceship of love. Howling winds follow their path, harmonious Oms, sounding as ripples of colorful waves upon waves, flow on and on, with sweet ecstatic union. Everything they breeze by is reborn dramatically into shimmering golden light.

Flying through this deep ebony of space, a glowing blue turquoise orb appears with mists swirling. As they get close, the mists disappear revealing a new blue green planet of water, glittering like a starry diamond. The vibrations of this new wonder-filled world are vibrantly, fresh and pure.

Isis floats before this planet of water, bowing to receive the red sphere into the center of her crown, like a mothership opening for her smaller ship to enter.

In a sparkling burst of light, Celestia, Mira and Azul regain their body forms. They happily circle around Isis, excited to witness the birth of the new planet. They sing, *"Happy birthday to Gaea, Happy birthday Gaea Star, Happy birthday to you."*

The sweet face of Gaea Star emerges like a flower speeding up its flowering phase, sweetly smiling as the planet's blue-green mists swirl, dissipating in a puff as she emerges. She opens wide her arms, gesturing to the children to sit on clouds that suddenly appear. They settle on clouds of pure puffiness. A buzzing insect lands in front. Mira, who loves all creatures, leans in for a better view as it slowly bobs up and down.

"Oh, you're cute. What are you?"

Mira hears. "I am a creature of the silvery moonlight that touches Earth on the full moon. I am heaven on earth." It crawls up on her, looking into her eyes.

She says, "Oh, I love that, heaven on earth. Thank you for visiting."

Immediately a large white papery screen drops in front, as if to watch a movie. Gaea Star spirit, says, "I'll begin my story, but first lets' hear the Alaria angels sing." Just then a lovely band of ethereal angelic beings float around while singing softly.

Star of Water, oh divine star

Star of water, oh sacred star

Star of water, this holy being

The creator gave you, the power of creation

He ya na hey, nay oh

Star sun, oh divine star, star sun, oh, sacred star

Star sun, this holy being

The Creator gave you, the power of creation

He ya na hey nay oh

As the song ends, the angels drift by while Gaea Star speaks, "In the beginning, only pure joy, love and kindness existed in paradise. My children emerged out of love because they were sacred to me. I named them humans, for they were seeds of humanity, to sprout, bloom and evolve into their radiant forms.

They had everything needed to do this, even with the shadowy forces that work against them. Fear has gripped their hearts, causing them to live in doubt, with imaginary walls, that prevent them from seeing each other as brothers and sisters. The turmoil, and chaos is great with the greedy pillaging of my resources. It's hard to see my children, so lost in such an illusion."

She pauses as her mighty whales sing out from deep within her vast oceans, echoing their haunting calls throughout the universe, as if to ease her deep pain. The sea birds fly near, drying her tears with fluttering wings.

Gaea Star weeps, "I am a good mother. I provide enough for life to exist. Believe in me. I need your help to protect all that I am, my air, fire, water, and sacred earth, to prevent my demise."

Suddenly, a vast armada of diverse beings fly in from throughout the universe to show their support, with comforting reassurance that Gaea Star is not alone in facing this challenge. They join in singing with the Alaria choir and the whales.

Ancient Mother we hear your calling

Ancient Mother we hear your crying

Ancient Mother we taste your tears

O la mama wa ha su kola

O la mama wa ha su wam

O la mama kow wey hahahaha

O la mama ta tey kayee

Gaea Star swaying to the melody, says, "Yes, these songs are filled with love for my world. May all hearts bloom wide open, even the misguided ones."

The Archangels Send a Call

Then, from far in the distance, a brilliant golden ball hurtles at light-speed towards the gathered ones. Right in front of Gaea Star, it transforms into two luminous winged archangels. One is a dashing being holding a silvery sword of light. He says, "Greetings, precious Gaea Star, we hear the cries of your whales. We are all concerned for your planet." He looks at his companion, an angel in a peach robe holding a brass trumpet.

Gaea Star says, "Dear Michael, Gabriel, thank you for your concerned response. Yes, my planet of waters is truly in need of a great change for the well-being of humanity and the preservation of my resources."

He says, "I and the other archangels feel it is essential to send out a call for universal assistance to summon those willing to serve your cause." Michael raises his golden sword above his head and with a powerful wave, blasts out a brilliant holographic rainbow scroll-like message into the starry heavens as Gabriel blows her trumpet, which echoes dramatically through the deep space.

The archangels of light summon

all beings of the federation of intergalactic

multidimensional realms; all light workers

and keepers of the ancient ways of healing, love and compassion.

Please attend an important council on the Gaea Star project

at Sirius Star center immediately.

Mira, Celestia and Azul, jump up from the puffy clouds excitedly. Azul says, "Why, that's us. We need to go right now."

Celestia and Mira nod emphatically. "Yes," Mira says, "I'm ready to serve again. It will be a pleasure to see our old friends."

Celestia adds, "Yes, it's been a while since we were all together." She sighs as if thinking of someone. They close their eyes and swiftly transform into their colorful light bodies, again merging into a rainbow that follows the archangel's message, as it careens through space, calling in the forces of light.

2

THE RAINBOW BRIGADE RESPONDS

The Red Ray

Gabriel's rainbow musical message is whirling through deep starry space, into a galaxy surrounded by a reddish glow. The rainbow bursts like fireworks into the misty atmosphere of a red planet, with the red ray splitting off in a wide arc to float slowly down into a busy futuristic building project.

A fit young man, Kardichay, is standing in front of a half-finished structure, directing a crew near a spaceship portal dock. Nearby are rose gardens, bursting with lush roses. Several workers are singing as they gather the fragrant roses to place into baskets, while another worker feeds the petals into a distillery vat that is connected to an elaborate generator used to power the whole area.

Surrounding the gardens are piles of crystals, red minerals, and gorgeous stones that several beings are looking at. A statuesque mystical elder wearing a flowing hooded cape, with crystals and beads, is closely examining the specimens in her hands, and looks to see what is coming so quickly toward her.

37

The red ray streaks down like a comet, catching the attention of a rose gardener. "Hey, look at that," he says, pointing to the sky. Kardichay looks up in time to see the red ray coming directly into his heart. Then almost immediately a hologram with an intricate symbolic design lights up his chest, flashing rapidly.

He listens within to the message, then standing at attention, as if he preparing to go, says, "Goodbye my friends! I am called by the archangels. Please continue preparing the legion of light starships for their long journey home."

The mystic, having observed him, says, "Wait, Kardichay. I have an important keepsake for your journey." She walks over to place a specimen into his hand. It is a white crystal with deep red chunks imbedded within it. She holds his gaze briefly while closing her hand over his in a gesture of affection and says, "Please take this cinnabar quartz to use as a divining tool to access the realms you are traveling to. You may need the support."

Kardichay, touched, says, "Priestess Marsoula, it is a great fortune for your timely visit from Alay Lana, the temple of Mercury." He gazes at the mineral and then places it in his burgundy crystal pouch. "My deep gratitude for this insightful powerful gift."

"Thank you," Marsoula says, "it's energetic abilities helps to express the essence of one's divine life-path." She exchanges a warm hug and says, "Yes, it is so," and fades in a poof of red sparks. Brilliant red rays surround Kardichay, and he too disappears quickly, leaving a streak of red sparkling trails.

The red ray now flows into an enormous crystalline temple, crammed with a vast collection of crystals and minerals, in various shades of reds. Four giant rubies are perched on huge black tourmaline stones that form a square. Rionarta is instructing students as they stand around a silvery grid within the square.

A young person, Carmina, is laying horizontally, floating within the grid, a few feet above the ground. She opens her eyes, sensing something nearby. The red ray hovers above her in a tetrahedron pattern.

She says, "Hey, look. A red ray of light." Michael's face appears as a hologram and then fades away.

"Rionarta, Michael must have a message."

Rionarta goes within to listen to the message. "Yes, he is calling. I must go right now. Farewell, friends. I hope to continue our studies again."

Carmina, still floating, sits up, standing quickly. "Wait Rionarta. Please, I have something." She reaches into a small red pouch tucked on her side to retrieve a small black shiny crystalline stone. "Here, black tourmaline from our beloved planet. Its energy helps during times of imbalance. Carry it for protection and purification, for the challenges that lie ahead."

He takes the stone. "Thank you, Carmina, we are well protected when we carry this ancient healing mineral. I will cherish this, as a reminder of your sweetness."

She hugs him in a warm embrace, with apparent feelings for him. "Dear friend, take care, I await your return. It is hard to let you go. I know, we'll be together again. Stay strong for everyone. My heart is yours in all ways. Goodbye, Rionarta." She steps back as he touches her with one last affectionate caress.

Their eyes gaze at each other as he whispers, "Goodbye. In due light speed, our moments of being together will return."

He steps into the crystalline square grid, as reddish light swirls about him like a gauzy veil. Carmina and the other students watch mystified as he transforms in a blazing, bolt of red, like fireworks exploding into the sky.

The Orange Ray

The rainbow message zooms past stars and nebulas to explode again in a fiery blast, shooting off an orange comet that careens into a glowing orange planet. The ray bursts into the sky, showering down like lava onto an exercise area that is surrounded by massive very tall orange quartz crystals. An athletic man is energetically conducting a fitness class to driving upbeat music. His students are doing their best to keep up with his wild energy when suddenly shouts of surprise ring out, as someone in the crowd asks, "Hey, Lakul, what's that?"

Lakul looks up, responding loudly, "Well, look who's visiting - Michael, in a brilliant flash of light. Quite a sight, I must say." Although he is a master of his body-mind, he breathes rapidly to handle the intense energy and closes his eyes to read the message within his sharp mind. He reopens his eyes quickly, "Holy light power, Michael. I'll be right there! Carry on students. Keep on. Stir the fires of life from within. Remember, always breathe. I'll return, someday. Now watch this!"

He winks as he shoots up like a rocket faster than the speed of light. They watch stunned as he disappears into a spiraling fireball, flying into the distance in a streak of bright orange.

The Yellow Ray

The rainbow cascades over a small yellow planet, shooting off a fiery flashy streak that descends slowly to the planet's surface. The soft yellow ray unfurls itself and weaves through a mighty redwood forest to a secluded yellow crystalline temple where a young girl, Teesha, is painting visionary art on a canvas.

She watches as the yellow ray rises from within her colorful painting, flowing into her heart, whispering the message. She nods then rinses her brushes in a yellow container of water, dries them with a yellow cloth and puts them in a painted bag that she slings over her shoulder. She picks up a sparkling yellow citrine quartz from a window ledge, puts it in her bag, and waves goodbye to her friends who are playing in the distance, out the open window.

Teesha places her hands together in a prayer mudra while bowing her head as the yellow rays surround her. Off she sails with colorful yellow and gold paintbrush strokes trailing behind her. "Goodbye, Teesha," a friend says as they watch the yellow ray fade off into the distance. "Wonder where she went so quickly?"

The Green Ray

A lush green planet orbits around its sister, the yellow planet. It is encircled by the sailing rainbow, which then shoots a bright green ray from it. The light green ray meanders like a curling vine seeking a stronghold, into an abundant garden where there are clusters of large, green quartz all around.

The ray completely envelops a young woman with bright flowers tucked in her hair, as she speaks with delightful faeries nestled in the flowers. She smiles, feeling the pleasurable effects of the healing color all over her. "Faery friends, the green ray is calling with a message from the Legions of Light. I must go see what it's all about. May we dance and frolic in the moonlight again, someday."

The flower faces nod. An emerald-clad faery, with sparkling translucent wings whispers, "Oh, sweet Initamay. Please may I come along?"

Initamay says, "Why, Emeraldina, how sweet. Yes, let's enjoy another adventure together." The tiny faery flies to her shoulder, but you can hardly see that she's even there.

A cute purple faery says, "Dear friend, please take one of our apophyllite crystals to commune with us in the lands you may be going to." She flies over holding onto a stone that looks like a cluster of grapes. She must have sprinkled her magic faery dust on the stone to carry it so easily since it is nearly bigger than she is.

Initamay smiles while holding the crystal close and carefully looking it over. "Oh, thank you. It's so pretty, smooth, and shiny. I feel it's loving green energy. I'll carry this for sensing where you may be. I hope I always see your sweet faces and play and sing with you. I love you all."

They flit about as she puts the apophyllite in a pouch that she carries for special treasures just like that. She walks toward a young boy with a painted mime face as he lights a handful of powder while waving a sparkling crystal staff. Suddenly a green mist engulfs him in a poufy cloud as the green ray seeps into his heart area, exactly at the same time. He is surprised that his trick failed. "Oh, no, not again. What did I do wrong this time?"

"Ilanu, are you okay?" asks Initamay.

Ilanu tries to dust the powder off, but it just sticks. "Yes."

"Oh, good. Now what was the trick supposed to do?"

"Well, I was gonna pop into a green ball. I'm not sure. I guess it backfired. It wasn't my fault."

Initamay laughs, "No, it wasn't you at all. It was a green ray emissary from Michael summoning us. Remarkable how it flowed out of the flowers to seep into our hearts. Funny that you did the trick at the exact same moment. That's some timing."

He says, thrilled, "A green ray message? What did it say?"

"I don't know. I didn't read it yet."

Ilanu says, "Oh, let's check it out. I'll help."

He takes his magic magnetite powder from a pouch. "Hey, mister green ray, where are you? Hello, hu hu. I'm calling you."

He wildly throws it up trying to make it come back to life. "Hmm," he says as he watches it float away. "It's not working. I'll try again."

He tosses more into the air, but nothing happens to his dismay. Except, drifting all over him again. Initamay searches around with a listening pose, saying, "Hello, misty green ray, are you lingering nearby?" She sees something that makes her smile. She signals Ilanu to look at a stately tree towering at the forest's edge. There, where the branches begin, is a movement in the large leaves. The misty green ray slithers slowly down the sturdy trunk like a serpent in the jungle. Initamay smiles, saying, "Greetings green ray."

Ilanu replies, "Hello, news bearer, we're ready for your message." The green ray flickers, then the scroll drops in front of them.

> *All Beings of the federations of intergalactic*
>
> *multidimensional realms, all light workers,*
>
> *keepers of the ancient ways of healing,*
>
> *love and compassion.*
>
> *Please attend an important council on the Gaea Star project*
>
> *at Sirius Star center immediately.*

Initamay says, "I think we need to leave right now."

"Should I go like this, covered in my magic powder?" He tries to brush off the green powder, but to no avail.

Initamay laughs, "No, that's okay. I'm sure a little powder won't be a problem. I think it's important to get there - seems like a real concerned message."

Easily excited, Ilanu says, "Yes, I'm ready for a new adventure. A green ray calling card, clever. How did they do that? I want to learn that magic. Maybe I'll be his apprentice. I'm a good student. Well, my tricks have issues. Hey, how are we going?"

Just then the green ray changes into a large green eye that looks like the ancient geometric symbol, known as the vesica piscis. They stare at it until Initamay realizes why it appeared and says proudly, "Well, you asked for our mode of travel."

Ilanu laughs, as the watchful eye blinks, "Wow, a green eye. Super cool, what a fun tool. All right, I'm in, but you go ahead of me, my sweet sister, Initimi."

Initamay says, "Oh you and your silly rhyming. I'll go first, but only on one condition. Stay focused during the transport, nothing funny. Remember our training, to be successful, we have to focus our energies to move through the dimensions correctly."

Ilanu laughs. "Alright, boss. I will not cross. What do you think I'm gonna do? We're just flying through the universe, just me and you, hu hu?"

Initamay laughs, signaling to get ready while she centers herself by breathing in deep, shaking her body a little. Then she steps in front of the eye opening with Emeraldina nestled on her shoulder. She enters the eye, fading in with a puff of green. Ilanu starts to follow but he stops, going in and out, to see how it works. "This is the cleverest trick of them all. That is why I stall."

Her hand reaches from within the eye to take his hand as she calls from within, "Okay, Ilanu, enough examining. Come on." She pulls him into the eye.

"Oh, sorry, I wanted to see how it works."

Initamay says, "No, this is not the time."

They disappear in a puff of green. He says from within, "I am Ilanu, green eye. Show me your magic tricks, that make you fly."

Initamay says, "Stay clear, Ilanu. It's important. I mean it." The green eye closes up tight, zipping away in a green misty trail.

The Blue Ray

The rainbow sails through deep space, releasing sparks every so often. A glorious blue ray cascades from it, slowly drifting down into a bluish mist surrounding a temple floating on the ocean. Gentle waves are kissing the shore lined with coconut laden trees. Whales, purple and black dolphins, and shiny flying fish are frolicking in the pristine waters of this lush paradise. Nothing is in sight, only the exquisite, blue temple that rises out of the waters. The blue ray seeps into a library, swirling lazily around the numerous books, brimming to the ceilings. A stately, dignified, handsome teacher wearing a long royal blue robe holds a book as he engages with students. As the blue ray comes toward him, he nobly receives the ray into his heart and instantly a hologram with a brilliant star-shaped geometric design, emanates from his center. He knows immediately that it is a serious message from the archangels, as he is a seer of great intuitive depth.

He quietly speaks, "Michael, Gabriel, it is Ashento, responding to your call - always willing to serve in loving light." He turns to his students, "Goodbye, my aware students. As you see, I am summoned for an important reason. Please keep opening to the guiding grace of loving spirit in the temple of Lazure."

The surprised students watch as the piercing blue ray encircles Ashento. He rapidly dissolves into a luminous blue star comet that ascends, streaking into deep space. The students slowly close their books. One comments on his departure, "Wow, that was a powerful blue ray of light. I feel the force of love from its angelic messenger source."

"I will miss Ashento's teachings of the light," another says.

"Yes, he's a commanding blue ray of light," the last one says.

"May Ashento grace the meeting as nobly as he did for us," the first one says. They nod and remain to contemplate the immensity of what just happened.

The Purple Ray

The rainbow sails toward the atmosphere of a planet that is encircled by seven rings of purple. The rainbow casts off a vivid purple ray, drifting slowly down, past two bright full moons, that are perched high in the night. Two shooting stars streak like comets, across, as the purple ray meanders above an enormous lake with jagged snow-capped mountains rising in the distance. The purple ray winds through a lush garden to a bonfire where two regal horses with long manes and tails - one black, the other white, are grazing peacefully nearby.

An enchanting dark-haired woman, wearing a purple crystalline robe and an ornate star crown is plucking a small lute like instrument. She is singing to children playing on woven blankets near the fire.

A male accompanies her on a guitar, as she laughs and sings her simple, sweet song,

Oh, children of love, oh children of light, coming down from the stars

On a beacon of light, beacon of light, beacon of...

The purple ray lightly mists over her in swirling, majesty. A voice whispers, "Ayalasha, we have a message." A luminous hologram, which is the same design as Ashento's, instantly radiates from her heart, spinning and projecting a colorful ray of rainbow light in front of her. The musician stops playing, to come see what is happening. The message appears, shimmering as a white veil within the rainbow ray. Angels are sweetly singing as they read the words.

All beings of the federations of intergalactic multi-dimensional realms, all lightworkers, keepers of the ancient ways of healing, love and compassion. Please attend an important council on the Gaea Star project at Sirius Star center immediately.

She closes her eyes, breathing deep, to center, to contemplate the message. "My dear Tofal, Michael summons only when we are critically needed. I must heed the call to go when I am called. Thank you for caring for the little ones while I am absent."

He nods, "Yes, of course, dear, we will miss you, and await your timely return. Much love to you. Take care."

Ayalasha tucks her instrument inside her cape and goes to the children. "Blessings, dears, I have to go for a while. I'll hold you deep within my heart, with all my love. I await the moment when I will see your smiling faces again." She embraces them one by one, then gives a long hug to her partner, Tofal, saying, "I have no idea when I will return, only as my duties free me, but I will as soon as possible. I must make an offering prayer."

She stands strong in front of the bonfire, smiling at her family lovingly. Reaching into a medicine bag tucked inside her cape, she retrieves a handful of dried herbs. Holding them in her left hand, close to her heart, she breathes deep and says, "Spirit of the fire, spirit of above, below, and within, please bless my families' well-being and my travels to Sirius and beyond, if I am called elsewhere." The fire burns brighter as she tosses the dried herbs into the flames. The family watches as it flickers with captivating beauty, dancing a different tune.

Ayalasha breaks her gaze from the mesmerizing fire to says, "I am ready to sail. I bid you farewell." She pulls a purple amethyst wand from her bag, to hold like a beacon. She sings, *Purple ray, activate my Merkabah, to fly through the portal to Star Sirius."*

The ray returns, swirling around her amethyst to charge it up. Blinking like a strobe, it swirls into a violet flame, all about her and then into brilliant purple rays that circle around her in concentric shimmering light.

Ayalasha transforms into a purple twinkling star that ascends higher and higher until it suddenly streaks off like a comet in the same path as Ashento's blue comet. The horses watch her disappear and rear up, with their front legs extending high. Their curly manes and tails dangle as their massive wings unfurl magnificently. They gracefully fly off in the opposite direction into starry space.

The White Ray

The rainbow flies toward a silvery planetary realm. A white ray cascades from it, flowing into an ornate crystalline temple surrounded by stone walls and huge statues. A wizened bearded elder, Teladi, wearing a white and purple star cape, stands in front of his students in the midst of four intricately carved tall crystalline pillars that blink softly on and off.

The white ray seeps around the meditating students in through the pillars flickering white and silver rays. They open their eyes sensing something unusual while hearing angels singing. Teladi signals to receive the white ray into their hearts as it encircles all of them. He listens to the message and says, "Students, I am called by Archangel Michael, to go swiftly to Star Sirius, so please carry on, Azrael, in my absence. Be well."

Azrael stands tall, "Of course, Teladi, we'll continue with studying the teachings of ancient civilizations until you return."

Teladi replies, "Excellent, Azrael, one never knows when you may need to use this ageless wisdom. I must leave for Star Sirius. Please exit the crystal chamber as it is my trusty transport there."

Azrael says, "Yes, of course, goodbye, friend and teacher." He leads the others through the crystal entrance, while Teladi remains in the center.

He closes his eyes, places his hands in front as a prayer and says, "Adonai, I am ready to activate laser power scepters."

He taps the four crystalline pillars lightly. Instantly they change into vibrating, rotating rockets, with gigantic projectile points that form an open style spaceship. They each power up, with blinking lights and acceleration sounds to prepare to ascend.

The students are amazed as the ship rises through the temple, and blasts into space, leaving a trail of sparkling white stars. Azrael says, "He is certainly a wise one to create such a remarkable interplanetary crystal ship."

3

IN THE SHADOWS OF MARCON

In a barren desolate land strewn with debris of discarded vehicle parts from different eras, two men, are working on an old rusty spaceship with fading Marcon letters on the sides. Zosakel is tall, handsome, wiry and muscular, with blond hair and dressed in a frayed T- shirt and ragged jeans. His head is inside the front hood of the ship. The other man, Keme, is shorter and quite large. He is wearing baggy pants and a big hoodie as he stands nearby ready to help.

Zosakel says, "I think I got it, Keme. Hand me the cutters and the wire. I need to wrap a piece around this to fire the pistons."

Keme picks up a tool from a pile and a small piece of wire from a metal scrap heap. "Okay, here," he says, handing them to Zozakel's hand while his head remains under the hood.

"Thanks," he says, "this may be the ticket to get it to turn over. Then we take this baby to another faraway planet to gather what we can to sell."

He tweaks the engine as Keme looks hopeful, saying, "I'll be glad to get out of this place. There's nothing to eat. Good thing no one's watching us."

The engine starts, coughs, and stops again. Zosakel hurriedly tweaks another part to keep it going.

Suddenly a shadowy orb descends, to burst right near them. A thin older man with scant hair and dark beady eyes, wearing a tight-fitting jumpsuit, appears. "Well, my two thieving partners. Do you think we can't see what goes on down here?"

Zosakel quickly pops his head up from the whirling motor and hits his head on the top of the hood. "Ow, not again." He wipes his grimy hands on his jeans, saying, "Hmm, well, Slake, what do you want from us now?" He rubs his head. Keme looks surprised.

Slake speaks, "The Legions sent a message throughout the galaxies concerning Gaea Star - calling forces to Sirius. This demands the utmost vigilance as we have invested a great deal on that rich planet with our massive mining interests, which may be in grave danger if they succeed at restoring control. We need infiltration to ascertain what their plans are, and if possible, thwart their efforts and report back."

Puffing up his chest with a swaggering attitude, Zosakel says, "You know that we can do it Slake. Should be no problem."

Keme, still a bit shaken that Slake showed up right then, mumbles quietly, "Gaea Star, where's that? How are we supposed to get there? What are you really asking us to do?"

"It's okay, Keme. I know where that blue planet is," Zosakel replies.

Slake smiles, saying, "Good. Now that you have the Marcon ready, take this to help you get there easily. Put it on the engine for smoother running."

He hands Zosakel a dark shiny metallic rock.

He examines it closely, then looks at him, "Hmm, magnetic energy. This is just what we need. I always wanted a piece of this ore." He places the stone on the engine, and with the extra wire he has, wraps it tightly around it, saying, "Okay, Slake, what's the pay?"

Slake thinks briefly, saying, "A sizable reward. Nothing to be concerned about now. As you know I only deliver when you do. I have to return to headquarters now." He hands a small crystalline device to Zosakel, saying, "It's a dopant conductor communicator - the best way to stay in touch. Remember, turn it on."

Zosakel examines it, "Thanks. Yeah, looks easy enough to use." He puts it in his pants pocket.

Slake presses a button on a similar device that he takes from his pocket. A red light blinks and a serious face appears. He says, "Quadrant 44, I am ready." The face fades. A shadowy orb completely covers him and then he disappears quickly.

Keme immediately asks abruptly, "Zoz, are you sure about this? What did you get us into? Every time this guy is our boss, it does not turn out good for us. I thought we were working only for ourselves from now on."

Zoz says, "Yeah, I know I said that, but how about one last time? I heard about Gaea Star in a club a while ago. Seems it's a hotbed of many factions all trying to get her goods. Perhaps we can get in on the collecting. I mean, let's find what we can. Besides, the food is supposed to be fantastic."

Keme adds, "Well, sounds interesting, but I have a funny feeling about any job for Slake."

Zoz closes the cover to the engine now that it's running smoothly. He pats the top, "Great. Then let's go. She's running fine. Let's see what this baby does and where we end up." He jumps into the flight pit, fiddles with setting the coordinates as he speaks in front of the screen board, "Star Sirius planet, we ask to fly there."

The voice answers, "Affirmative, all set."

Zoz says, "Here we come."

Keme was not so fast in hoping into his seat next to him. Before he is settled in, Zoz hits the throttle and off they fly, a bit wild at first. Keme tries to get his seat belt on while Zoz is only focusing on driving the aged ship and does not care one bit about his belt.

Keme is concerned. "Hey, hold on Zoz. What the heck are we doing so fast? I didn't get a chance to figure things out!"

Zoz laughs, brimming with excitement, to have a new/old ship to fly. He is a man of action, learning as he goes - not the type to study things first or take precautions. The ship whizzes straight up into the sky. "Yes, we're going great, I like it."

Keme grips for dear life. "Hey. We're going too fast."

"No, we're fine. Hold on. Wee." The Marcon fades away. What a pair!

PART 2

ALONG THE WAY TO STAR SIRIUS CENTER

4

ARRIVALS

Countless beings are streaking toward the constellation Sirius, from all directions, in spaceships, rockets, and comets. Known as the Dog Star, it is the largest visible and brightest heavenly body, in the galaxy. Everyone is descending to the surface of the futuristic city of Sirius, which is unlike any other city on this dynamic planet.

The inhabitants are loyal, trustworthy beings, who cultivate great spiritual knowledge and have significant celestial navigation skills. The advanced progressive community feels it is a great privilege for their beloved city to be chosen as the meeting place for the gathering of the tribes of light. In honor of hosting this momentous congregation of high esteem, the city leaders, create a grandiose, festive, artistic, celebration for the participants before and after the historic meeting.

The Galactic Federation of Light sends a fleet of spaceships, to protectively patrol along with the city's own Green Alerts ships. Yes, it is necessary to maintain a watchful eye for the uninvited ones, who show up to try to figure out devious ways to pillage precious resources from all the free planets.

High in the majestic starry realms, the red, orange and yellow rays are flying from their planets. Somehow, they mysteriously align together, forming a partial rainbow destined for Sirius Star.

Just behind the rainbow is Ayalasha's purple star and Ashento's blue star, streaking as two comets, side by side, sailing to Sirius, in the same powerful trajectory. The flying stars, and other rainbows, descend into the twinkling night sky, like falling, sparkling, light rain, to land upon the planet. The largest rainbow lands near lush rose gardens where many beings are gathering.

The rainbow twinkles with shimmering iridescence and bursts into multiple brilliant colors all at once, releasing the travelers from their modes of light transport. They reacclimatize to their bodies by stretching and drinking rejuvenating water, which is full of life-giving properties.

The visitors look with awe at the city. The tall structures glisten as if covered in morning dew. Each has fanciful sparkling gems in geometric designs that flash and spritz out colorful rays in all directions, pulsating in distinct striations, to the sweet sounds of celestial music with angelic choirs singing in complex harmonies.

Sirius' epicenter is a vast complex of crystalline-shaped buildings with pointy spires and waving banners. In the middle, a statuesque temple with a towering turquoise spire rises high. It looks like a royal stone in a headpiece, from the long-ago golden eras of great king and queendoms.

What an unusual collection of varied rooftops with crystal-absorbing solar panels covering them. Each one, of course, is facing the sun to gain the most natural energy possible from such a complete free source of power.

Glistening crystalline stars float freely up in the air like balloons that have regrettably escaped from the hands of children. Numerous lush gardens abound in every possible area, with colored-bark trees casting their beautiful shade while very exotic statues and artistic creations, are decorating the beautifully planted diverse community grounds. It is a visionary treat for newcomers.

Rainbow Rays Emerge

Meanwhile, back where the large rainbow landed, Kardichay and Rionarta emerge from their red rays and hug warmly. Kardichay says, "Hello, Rionarta. We just flew as fast the speed of light with no time to observe anything."

Rionarta replies, "Hello, Kardichay. Nice to see you. Yes, we didn't even have a chance to view the asteroid field up close. It's the best way to travel now. What are you doing now since you went to work in the building trade?"

Kardichay replies, "Yes, it was speedy, with no negative effect on me, so far. It's great to see you. I'm happy in my element, designing with natural resources from whatever planetary realm I work in. I love every moment. Are you still researching and gathering crystals?"

Rionarta laughs. "Yes, they're my passion, always renewing and restoring me. I discover new ones all the time. I also teach magnetic crystal healing in the Rubelline temples." He looks to the massive structures that tower over the city. "Let's explore these colossal buildings. I'm intrigued by the crystals emanating. I don't know what they are."

"Sure, I'm in," Kardichay replies as they walk off talking.

The orange ray, still swirling in a fiery ball, suddenly blasts out Lakul. He is thrilled to land and is all set to go. "Wow, here we are in the midst of this fantastic cosmic collection of beings, impressive."

He looks around, grinning and realizes he is talking to himself. "Gee, I seem to talk to myself a lot. Looks like up ahead is where the action is." With a happy lift, he walks in the direction that the crowd is going.

The yellow ray flows down in a soft mist, releasing Teesha. She gasps in awe at the rich views around her, sighing and says, "Oh, look at all these colors – It's a living painting." She searches in her bag for her pencil to draw with and sits on a carved wooden bench next to a collection of fragrant, pendulous white trumpet-shaped flowers. She breathes in, saying, "Hmm, lovely. I'll stay until I am filled with the luscious scents of this beautiful, sweet flower." She nestles into the many blossoms sighing with joy.

The green eye, the vesica piscis, pops up near where the rainbows landed, with the eye closed. Once it stops vibrating, the eye opens and Initamay emerges slowly. She too is mesmerized by the surrounding greenery as she says, "Oh, it's so beautiful." She looks down first, since she does not want to step on anything living beneath her feet and then turns to watch Ilanu come out.

Her face changes to concern as she looks, expectantly waiting to see him emerge. He is not there, not anywhere. She holds open the eye to look in, nothing. She turns, scanning the horizon, no, not there either.

"Oh no, Ilanu. Where did he go this time?" She turns back to the fading green eye as it is slowly disappearing. Confused, she calls, "Hey green ray transport, where is Ilanu?" The green eye disappears without responding or revealing anything.

Concerned, she says, "Oh no, what did he do? We were traveling at the speed of light. He obviously tried a magic trick and could be anywhere. I'll head toward the center to see if I find him up ahead."

She walks briskly through the crowd, searching frantically as she is bumped by those who are not in the same space that she is. All of a sudden, in the air above her, a smaller rainbow descends, landing in front of her, dissolving into colorful light. Curious, she stops to see who it might be, just in case it was Ilanu.

Mira, Celestia, and Azul emerge, looking very different, then when they left Isis at her temple as children, right after hearing the archangel's message. Remember how they merged their colors into their rainbow light bodies to travel to Star Sirius? Well, instead of young children, they are now empowered, aware adolescent beings. They laugh at their new appearances.

Celestia says, "Wow, how did we change so fast?"

Azul proudly says, "Isis restored our shapeshifting abilities, to help us prepare for the journey to Gaea Star. She knows that we'll make a difference, this way."

Celestia says, "Well, you always were an expert at transforming to suit the occasion. This is one of those times."

Mira adds, "She invited us to witness the story of Gaea Star. It was up to us to join her cause, to willingly contribute in any way. How perfect that we're older and wiser, ready to go. I'm so excited to be in this incredible place."

They view the spectacular scenery of the vast city, that is brimming with diverse beings surging and walking to the center, with the gem-encrusted magnificent buildings towering above them. Colorful banners, representing the nations of the universe, are waving from the spires in the sparkling sky.

Azul, noticing something unusual, says, "Amazing, there are no transportation vehicles in sight."

"Yes, how can that be?" asks Celestia, "it seems that everyone is floating along, just fine. Or are they walking?"

Azul looks at the road, smiling, "Well, it's a slow-moving, light filled pathway, running on crystal light energy. Probably at no cost, just a pure harmless, carrier of all life."

Mira is taking in the sights. "I always wanted to visit this fabled city of beauty." Just then, she sees Initamay standing nearby, watching. She needed to rebalance herself for a few moments.

Mira says, "Initamay, are you alright? You look stressed. What's going on?" Celestia and Azul, come to see what is happening with her too.

Initamay, visibly relieved, says, "Hello, dear friends. I have warm feelings when I see you and recall the pleasant memories we shared in our brigade. I'm doing great, but Ilanu didn't make it through transport. I'm looking for him. Maybe he's up ahead."

Azul laughs, "Great to see you, Initamay. Stay calm. Ilanu's antics are nothing new. He'll turn up. He always does."

Celestia nods, agreeing. "Yes, he was probably just trying out a magic trick at the wrong moment and it backfired."

Mira chimes in, "Of course, that's what happened. Come on. Let's go. We'll find him." She hugs her with reassurance, taking her hand.

They walk along the lovely flower-filled avenue, not getting very far as they stop to gaze at the colorful flowers every few steps and almost bump into Teesha. She is absorbed drawing the exquisite flowers and does not look up. "Sorry. Oh, hello," she says when she finally looks and is surprised to see her old friends. She puts her drawing away to jump up, "Mira, Initamay."

Mira says, "Hello! How pleasant to see you, Teesha."

She replies as they hug. "I'm pleased we're together again and grateful we answered this critical call."

Celestia and Azul come from behind and hear their comments. Azul says, "Hello, Teesha. Yes, the archangels asked us to help unify the tribes in the beautiful realm of Gaea Star."

Celestia smiles, saying, "Hello, dear Teesha, priestess of the painting arts. How are you?"

Teesha responds shyly, "I'm great, thanks. Nice of you to say, Celestia. I still paint every day where I live in the peaceful realm of Torula."

Azul says, "I'm happy to be here too. We came after hearing from Isis and the Gaea Star spirit about the chaos there." They hug Teesha.

She says, "I'm delighted we're on another spirit-filled adventure."

Celestia is bursting with curiosity to see the unusual sights. She says, abruptly, "Sorry, but I'm so excited about the great hall. Let's go explore it before the meeting." They start walking.

Initamay, clearly not wanting to talk any more, says, "I'm moving on to search for Ilanu, so no stopping. See you up there." She walks on, pushing through the crowds.

Celestia tries coaxing Mira, Teesha and Azul to move quicker but gets frustrated as they're like turtles, creeping along since there is so much to explore. They're not in a hurry like she is, so she decides it's better to not force them, and stops to breathe and relax, thinking, *"Ah, now to enjoy the lovely attractions without rushing.'* She suddenly realizes there are amazing crystals and plants everywhere and is happy to slowly check them all out.

5

MASTER TELADI TO THE RESCUE

Initamay darts ahead, anxiously searching through the meandering crowd until it becomes too dense near the buildings, causing her to slow down. A voice whispers within, "Wait." She immediately stops, feeling something is about to happen. Her inner voice always leads her on the correct path. The years of training to be a rainbow brigade member, made her pay attention to what feels right, even if she doesn't understand what the voice is trying to say.

"Be alert," is an important message from our higher selves. It may be a voice whispering, "We are here, lending our support." Then it's up to us to do the rest. Sometimes that is the hardest thing to do, to stop, listen and wait, with no reaction.

Suddenly from above, a brilliant white ray with four crystalline rocket projections descends in front of her onto the path. The crowd scatters, scrambling to move away from where the powerful rocket boosters are landing. The shimmering crystal pillars cast off radiant white rays in all directions.

Slowly the rays disappear, revealing the wizard Teladi, sitting within the crystal pillars, still meditating. He opens his eyes and reacclimates to his new surrounding by breathing in and shaking his body. He looks to the stars, "Thank you, holy spirit. I am grateful for my crystal ship's safe journey." He does not notice Initamay nearby until she speaks."

"Hello, Master Teladi. How are you? I have not seen you since you journeyed to the realms of the Tishiyana Temples."

He bows, glad to see her. "Greetings, Initamay. I am well and still enjoy teaching others of your caliber. I think of you as one of my favorite students."

Initamay says, "Thank you. I miss your profound wisdom-filled classes. They were the best and most exciting. Right now, I'm concerned for my brother Ilanu, who has disappeared, lost in the transport to Sirius."

He laughs, "Hmm, so like him, isn't it? Let me search within the cosmos to ascertain that young ones, whereabouts." He closes his eyes - breathing in slowly. "Ah, yes, I see him easily. Thanks to the magnetite powder he is covered with, high lighting his energetic field. He's flying away in the wrong direction. We'll redirect his trajectory to Sirius. It may take a while, but he will return."

Initamay is relieved. "Thanks. I'm grateful you found him."

He glances to the side of the avenue. He sees a tall crystalline structure, flashing white. "Ah, exactly what I need to assist this action." He walks over to sit on a crystal translucent bench.

Initamay follows. "Is there anything I can do to help?"

Teladi replies, "Yes, please. Focus your healing energy. The portal is still open, due to the Central Federation's signals being emitted for landing area quadrants. We'll retrieve him by attuning to his magnetic field while relaying crystalline light beams."

Initamay says, "Yes, that's a good plan."

They become absorbed in the task amidst the milling crowd. She closes her eyes and laughs from what she sees within her mind, saying, "Ilanu is with the faery, Emeraldina, flying on his shoulder. I forgot she hopped on me as we were leaving. She is protecting him. Can't break thru to Ilanu. He is distracted by the incredibly fast mode of travel."

Teladi says, "Very good then. I'll commune with her since she'll be most receptive." He telepathically sends a greeting to her. "Hello, Emeraldina." They listen to see if she hears.

Initamay says excitedly, "She heard you and is waving sweetly."

Teladi says, "Green faery, we're helping you return to Star Sirius by sending a light retracking beam to magnetize with you. Once aligned, we'll set the course for turning you around."

"She's nodding in agreement," Initamay says.

"All right, let us begin," Teladi says closing his eyes to concentrate to begin the retrieval process.

The busy energy on the avenue slows, as if they are surrounded in a cocoon of healing vibrations.

He touches a tall spire. The crystal flashes brightly, casting luminous rays into the sky, like a rocket ship just launched.

Initamay meditates as Teladi guides Emeraldina. "Now, to generate the proper attraction for the new direction, open and close your wings seven times, as you perch on Ilanu's shoulder."

Emeraldina says, "Yes, opening and closing seven times, and I will sprinkle my magic dust around to help us fly away free."

Teladi says, "Ah, of course the exceptional potency of faery dust. Yes, after that will be the perfect moment to realign the magnetic power to reverse the trajectory to Sirius Star Center."

They concentrate. It happened fast. Emeraldina sprinkles her magic dust in the air then flaps her wings seven times. Suddenly there is a flash of white light.

Teladi says, "Adonai, it is so." He taps the crystals as they send brilliant white rays into the sky, like a tracking beam.

Emeraldina telepathically speaks with Initamay. "It worked, the rays caused the reversal. We're returning now. Thank you."

Initamay is thrilled. "It's successful. She did what you asked. They're heading here now."

Teladi nods, saying, "Yes, it is done. Thank you, Emeraldina." She flits her wings, smiling. He continues, "It was good fortune that Ilanu was covered with magnetite, a most energetic tool to attract one's desires. It made reversing the polarity quite easy." She waves as the images of her and Ilanu, covered in white misty rays, fade.

As they fly back to Sirius, Ilanu snaps awake, surprised. "We turned around. How did that happen, I didn't hear a sound?"

Emeraldina flutters to him. "Your sister, Master Teladi and I worked together, along with you. We were going the wrong way."

"Me? I helped? I don't remember anything," says Ilanu.

Emeraldina laughs. "You'll like this. The magic powder, all over you, helped Teladi to find us and reverse our course."

Ilanu says, "Wow, really? I knew I was lucky with spells, but with attracting magnetic powder. Cool, you're a friendly faery."

"Thanks."

This time he settles down for the return to Sirius. He doesn't try anything funny since he wants to be sure to get there quickly.

Initamay relaxes in relief, saying, "Teladi, thank you."

He touches her. "You're welcome. I'm always willing to help a friend. Now where were we? Ah, yes, onto the gathering, called by Michael, for the first time in ages. It is obviously something quite important that we're needed for. I must go see." He walks off briskly. "Why so many called, Michael? I hope to be of assistance."

Initamay, all smiles now, says, "Thank you. Thank you." As she watches him go, she smooths her hair, drinks water from her bag and is ready at last to enjoy the scenery, when Mira, Celestia, Azul and Teesha meetup with her.

Mira smiles, "There you are, Initamay. Any luck with Ilanu?"

"Yes, Teladi landed near me in his crystal ship. He tuned into Ilanu and found him flying in the wrong direction with Emeraldina, a faery. The magnetite powder, from one of his crazy tricks, was all over him. It helped to redirect them back here. They're coming."

Mira laughs, "That's awesome. I love Teladi. He is such a high wizard. What a blessing to meet him on the way."

Initamay says, "Yes, a real godsend indeed."

Azul adds, "Clever! What an amazing teacher. Yes, magnetite is a remarkable attracting mineral."

Teesha hugs her, "Great that he's okay."

Celestia agrees, "Yes, he'll be here soon. Come with us to see the art collection in the temples."

Initamay says, "Sounds good. I feel like a different person."

This time the pace the group sets out with, is perfect for all of them to enjoy the sights as they catch up on the years, they were apart. Initamay is thrilled to finally be able to enjoy this exciting adventure.

6

THE PORTAL DOCKS

In a little bit, Azul notices a large sign hanging on a crystalline post to the right. He stops to read it out loud, "The Ohana Main Portal Dock." He goes closer to the massive, intricate structure, and then signals to the others. As they come near, he says, "These are the first circular receiving platforms I've ever seen."

They crowd around to examine the impressive construction close up.

Celestia rubs her fingers on the smooth sides, saying, "I love the geometric patterns. It's the ancient Flower of Life design."

Teesha sighs, "Just looking at them evokes a serene feeling. It's fascinating how they overlap like flower petals."

Mira touches the edges. "Yes, the sacred symbol of the universe, implies all life originates from the source of eternal love."

Celestia laughs, saying, "Yes, I remember that from the many lessons, we had with all those years of incredible teachings."

Azul adds, "I love the thirteen overlapping circles and the old secrets hidden in these artistic and magnificent structures throughout history." They sigh, breathing in, to enhance their energy fields.

Celestia says, "Its' always pleasant to sense how we all come from the same universal spirit of love."

Mira nods, saying, "May we help everyone remember to live as one happy family in life."

Initamay looks at the flowers carved in the platforms, saying, "Yes, the flower of life, such an amazing symbol. They're like lotus flower petals, opening wide to the light." Mira, Celestia and Teesha crowd around to see them.

Azul says, "I'm checking this system out. See you later, at the building." He disappears around the back. Teesha takes out her sketch pad to quickly draw the different patterns.

Mira and Celestia walk around the petals, tracing the flower design. Initamay stops to listen, as if she hears something, "I hear a melody." She hums for a moment then sings,

> *The flower of life is the circle that continues on and on*
>
> *May we find our way inside the source of life*
>
> *As we wind our way home, oh yeah*
>
> *To where the circle flows around*
>
> *May we live to tell the tale of the circles dancing*
>
> *On the path to the light, oh, oh, the flowers of life*

Mira, Teesha and Celestia sing along, adding harmonies.

Teesha says, "I love it."

Celestia says, "Yes, how perfect, so sweet."

Initamay points to the lovely flowers growing on the sides of the platform docks. "Look, they're dancing, like faeries responding. They love your song. Keep singing, they may show themselves."

Mira is tickled, and says, "Oh, how beautiful." She hops down to see the flowers closer. She sings, *"Oh, oh, spirits are sweetly singing, as the flower of life endlessly unfolds in a circle, connecting us all."*

Initamay and the three are delighted to play with the faeries that pop out of the flowers. They are oblivious to doing anything else until Initamay finally comes to her senses to say, "The creativity here reflects the profound knowledge that resides on Star Sirius. Let's explore these docks. Hop up for a better look."

She steps onto the large dock that extends in all directions. The others begin to follow. Suddenly, from around the sides, Kardichay and Rionarta appear, so absorbed in talking, that Kardichay nearly bumps into her. "Oh, sorry. Initamay, well, well."

She smiles, "Hello, Kardichay, Rionarta. Glad we're all showing up here. Thanks to Michael."

Kardichay hugs her. "Hello. Pleased you're here."

She says, "Thanks. How's life on Ruby Star?-The planet of the red lightning crystals? I heard her pristine lands are being over harvested for them."

Kardichay responds, "Yes, the red crystals are overmined. Unfortunately, it's a problem everywhere."

Rionarta hugs her, saying, "Hello, Initamay. That's true, but luckily, wise ones hid what they could in secret temples for safe keeping."

"Yes," she says, "I imagine that other treasures are also being tucked away for the challenging times that lie ahead."

He agrees, "Yes, all over the universe, actually."

Kardichay and Rionarta notice Mira, Celestia and Teesha on the platform dock, checking out the designs.

Rionarta calls, "Hey, rainbow companions. What a marvel, this remarkable structure? We explored it thoroughly. We're happy to give a tour."

Kardichay says, "Hello, friends from my adventuresome past. It's been a long time since we were together. I have often thought of you." He says that while looking at Celestia, causing her to have a shy reaction from his sudden unexpected attention.

Azul walks from the side of the dock. He heard their comments and is anxious to hear about the design. He says, "I'm checking out the ingenious way the platforms move in and out to receive ships, with such flawless movement."

Rionarta laughs saying, "That may take a while, but if Demeclis is still here, he's the one, to explain the technical concepts. He just gave us a brief explanation."

Azul says, "Yes. Let's go see it then."

Kardichay says, "Yes, that's a good idea to ask him, since he's in charge of construction. He may still be at the back."

Kardichay starts to go but first smiles at Celestia. "Coming, Celestia, Initamay?"

Celestia responds, smiling at him, saying, "No, not this time."

Initamay says, "I'm going to take my time, no rushing for me anymore. I'm staying here to immerse in all the flowers here."

"Okay. We'll catch up afterward." He follows Rionarta and Azul as they walk, talking technical about the elaborate structure.

Celestia, with a wondering smile, shows her interest in Kardichay by how long she watches their departure. A warm exciting sensation flushes over her, causing her heart to beat rapidly. It is a new feeling within her youthful life. She stops looking only after five colorful women walk up to her carrying fragrant flower leis and luscious fruit cocktails in pretty carved, fruit bowls. They place the leis on her, Mira, and Initamay.

Teesha stops drawing the nearly complete, flower of life design and jumps up to receive a flower lei and says, "Thank you, it' so fresh and delightful. Hmm."

A greeter, Tela, says, "Welcome to Sirius. We are the Aloha Plumerias."

Initamay sniffs the fragrant lei, sighing with pleasure, "Wow, what an incredible lovely smell. Hmm, the fruit looks yummy, too. I am so hungry; I didn't even realize it." She sits to enjoy the wonderful fruit and flowers. "Thank you, these are so great."

Mira is also touched. "Fruit, my favorite. Thank you. I love it in this live fruit bowl, very clever."

Tela says, "Thank you, we love creating delicious living foods to nurture ourselves with the highest essence of aliveness."

Teesha staring at the leis, says, "I love these exquisite flowers. Where do you grow such fragrant ones?"

Tela answers, "These are from the Misty Mu gardens of the last Lemurian temple. I just returned from that delightful, lush land."

Celestia says, "Ladies, thank you for this delicious fruit, but I want to check out the brilliant gems flashing colors on the buildings. Glistening minerals always draw me. Are you coming?"

Initamay says, "No, I'll catch up soon." She wants to relax, to enjoy the fruit and flowers. No hurry, now that Ilanu is on his way.

Mira and Teesha, nod, smiling at the fruit ladies, as their mouths are too full to answer, as if to say. "We're sorry, have to go. Goodbye."

They follow Celestia slowly while relishing the fruit. She tries herding them like a mother hen with her brood, but it's too difficult, as they stop often to look at flowers, crystals or other objects that catch their attention.

Celestia gives up. "All right. I'm going to explore myself. Have fun. Meet you at the center." She heads off excitedly toward the buildings up ahead.

It's funny, they do not even hear what she says. Teesha is relishing the fruit and the flowers while Mira is humming and busily inhaling a delightful fragrance from huge purple flowers she spied hanging in clusters from the branches of a heavily laden tree. Suddenly, out of the corner of her eye, she sees lavender mistiness and then a faery, flies away quickly.

Mira perks up, "Hello, misty one, with the pretty wings, are you hiding? Teesha, come here. I saw a cute little faery."

Teesha goes to Mira as she stretches to the tree, filled with flowers, trying to coax her by saying, "Sweet faery, are you there?"

They peer into the tree where the huge clusters hang. Teesha says, "Yes, little one, we are your friends."

Suddenly a purple faery with a sweet, smiling face, flutters into sight. Mira extends her hand as the tiny one settles on it. Teesha, impressed by the faery, says, "Wow, she came right over. Hello, little faery, we're delighted to meet you."

Mira is proud. She is new to calling in the little ones, known as the fey. She always wanted to try though. She smiles. "Hello, tiny purple faery, you are so sweet."

The faery flutters, saying, "Hello, sisters of rainbow light. We are like sparkling stars that dot the skies, floating, hovering closely to the holy ground."

They're enraptured with the faery, as she flies about the flowers and the beautiful tree. She says, "Please, my new friends, come meet my companions."

Mira jumps at the chance, "Oh, that will be a delight. Come on, let's go with her." She waves to Initamay to get her attention. She looks and sees the faery fluttering about and goes to join them.

She says, "Hello, little purple one. What a flower of delight you are. Such happiness we feel from your sweet lightness of being."

Mira, Teesha and Initamay follow happily after the purple faery as she flies to a cluster of golden flowers, bending in the gentle breeze. She looks into the flowers, "Hello, Goldy. Please come out, I have friends to meet you."

A golden faery appears just like that, out of the petals. "Hello," she says, "it's a delight to meet you." Mira claps and squeals with pleasure while Teesha laughs joyfully. How exciting to make new faery friends.

Teesha says, "What a happy feeling of love abounding."

Initamay is pleased to see the two engaging pleasantly with the faeries. It is her favorite pastime. She was just a little girl, when she discovered her ability to see their sweet faces, whenever she admired the beauty of nature.

The purple faery is flitting about introducing her new friends to her family. She is certainly not shy as she is pleased to meet anyone new and loves the attention. Her faery friends feel safe to come out of hiding.

The Spaceship Arrivals

Meanwhile, an outlandish-shaped silvery spaceship with Regulus printed on the sides, descends slowly, releasing a burst of energy at the docking station. Wildly dressed beings spill out of the entrance, laughing and dancing.

They become so immersed in the festivities, that they fail to hear beeping from another sleek silvery blue ship, as it descends onto one of the platforms with the Pleiadean star formation painted on the sides. The dancers finally look up in time to move out of harm's way.

One says, "Hey, it's our friends from the Pleiadean community." They skip to the other ship to greet the newcomers.

Rays of light emanate around the large circular door of the ship. The door disappears, then boisterous musicians flow out, playing unique instruments. The groups are dancing, singing, and surging into the crowd that is amassing into great numbers, like a music festival.

Initamay, says to the faeries, after seeing all the exciting activity. "Little ones, it's a pleasure to meet you. I'm onto the next enchantment, to connect with these newcomers." The faeries, Mira and Teesha wave to her as she goes to mingle with the playful crowd.

Lakul, in the midst of the gathering, wants to connect with the musical action. He says, "Greetings, I'm Lakul. What a fabulous family of expressive musical light. Let's get one on for the unity of all life."

He is handed a carved drum and immediately joins in the drumming with gusto, creating an impromptu jam. What a celebration with all the talented free spirits, there.

A loud horn honks, like a buoy on the ocean, warning that a colorfully decorated hippie-style, odd-shaped bus, with Lotus Star Merkabus, painted on the sides, is arriving.

A sweet rose fragrance fills the air as it gracefully lands at the dock with a blast of golden light. The driver is not steering with a wheel; he is playing rocking music on a silvery lit up piano. Yes, that's right. It is powered by the piano music and has something to do with the fragrance of roses that is wafting out of the front end - oh, so heavenly fragrant. Can you imagine if all transportation smelled like sweet roses?

The piano player sings, "*Star Sirius Center/ here we are/ just dance off.*" The playing and flashing lights stop. More vibrant travelers of multi-ethnicities, emerge and join the festivities, loudly singing, their happy traveling song.

Lotus Star Magic Merkabus

Lotus Star Magic Merkabus

Flying through the portal of light

Flying through the portal of stars

Flower of light power, luminous light power

Musical light power

Celestial wonder, celestial beauty

Star Light power, Star Light power

Lotus Star Merkabus, Lotus Star Magic Merkabus

Tela, still sharing fruit, kisses and hugs, is near the Merkabus as it lands. After sniffing the rosy aroma, she asks the piano player, "Does the sweet fragrance of roses help to fly the Merkabus?"

He smiles as he plays a short ditty, firing up the lights with roses wafting again and says, "Yes, the music and rose oil from the Yasho gardens, power the Merkabus."

Tela says, "Wonderful. That's delightful, using flower aroma to generate energy to fly. I hope the Gaea Star inhabitants, harness natural ways of utilizing power for their energy needs, rather than keep misusing her resources as we have heard."

Lakul dances up just then leading the musicians. He is intrigued by the piano and the sweet rose air. He heard her comments, "I'm Lakul and happy to meet you. I like your concern. Beings throughout the universe need to hear that sentiment. Little do they realize how precious their natural resources are. Seems they do not care about their well-being. Who are you?"

Tela laughs. She loves being flirty with this handsome fellow. "I'm Tela. Thank you for your comments. This gathering is bringing souls from the far reaches, to Star Sirius. The others are up ahead." She points in the direction of the meeting hall.

Lakul beaming, says, "Well, Tela, I must be going. Hope to see you again. Lakul at your service." He taps her as he walks away, singing and dancing with more lightness, than he had before meeting her. She watches him leave with a lingering smile.

Arm in arm, Mira and Teesha go happily singing along the avenue. They pick up Celestia, and catch up to Lakul as he leads the dancing with gusto. He sings boisterously, *"We have an important date with fate, with beings of light, into the night. Oh, yay, yay."*

They stop to look at a bronze statue that moves, shimmering in the sunlight, as if it is real. Lakul pretends he is the statue, taking a pose next to it. The ladies do the same, laughing.

A flock of iridescent blue birds fly in front, chattering. Teesha says, "Look. Their blue is like Gaea Star's. Let's follow where they're going off too. I'd love to draw them."

Celestial and Mira say, "Sure, let's go." They follow after the birds that are still dipping in the crowds, as if to say hello.

Lakul happily dances through the packed crowds, singing joyfully and connecting with the parade as it gathers momentum.

The Marcon Near Crash Landing

Just as the frenzy of ships landing at the Ohana receiving dock seems to be settling down, the aging Marcon spaceship appears, having somehow miraculously managed to fly past the patrolling security ships. Oh no, it nearly crashes abruptly, landing with crunching. Luckily no one is nearby to see what happened. After a brief moment, a rusted door, kicked from within, falls off with a clatter in a cloud of metallic dust. Zosakel with Keme right behind him, trip over the door and tumble through the dust. They get up, a little confused from the speedy travel and try to pat off the powdery dust which does not come off too well.

Keme shouts, "Zoz! I said to let up on the controls before we hit! You never listen! We nearly did the ship and ourselves in."

"Keme, you're supposed to warn us when we're about to crash. Besides, we made it, thanks to the magnetic stone that helped propel us into the atmosphere. Well almost, here I'll fix the door."

Zoz picks up the rusty door and tries to put it back, but it won't fit. He looks up when he hears soft laughter and to his delight, sees the beautiful Aloha greeters walking toward them. He quickly hands the door to Keme. "Here you kicked it out. So, you fix it. I've got more important things to do now."

He hops off the dock, heading for the pretty greeters bearing flower leis and fruit. "Looking good! Aloha goddesses, this must be heaven!" Beaming, he opens his arms to receive their greetings. Then he strolls off, surrounded by the laughing ladies.

Keme tries to fit the rusty door on the ship's frame as he sees Zoz walk away. His efforts fail, so he drops it. Frustrated, he says, "Forget the door. It can wait." He hops off the platform. "Jeez, I'm glad we made it this far. Hey, Zoz, wait up." He runs off following after Zoz.

Minutes later, Rionarta, Azul, and Kardichay come from the back of the platforms after checking the system out with Demeclis. They are startled by the appearance of the aging ship, which wasn't there when they left for the tour.

Rionarta says, "Look at this aging contraption. What a sorry-looking ship to fly." They walk around it slowly, looking inside as best as they can.

Kardichay says, "I have an uncomfortable feeling about the missing drivers."

Azul adds, "Yes, their lingering negative energy is not in the highest, for sure."

Rionarta goes around back. "Well, whomever they are, they're up to no good. Probably doing something that we don't want. Let's keep a watchful eye for any characters, that seem a bit suspicious. I have already seen a few here."

Azul says, "I'll remember this particular energy field if we encounter them," as he touches the sides of the Marcon, getting powdery dust on his fingers which he too tries to brush off. "They must be nearby and easy to tell by the dust they wear. I'll keep a look out. They probably look different than most of the crowd here."

Kardichay says, "We lost Initamay and Celestia along the way. They must be checking out that party action up there."

Rionarta says, "Yeah, let's go. We have to get there anyway. I'm sure the meeting is happening soon."

Kardichay, says, "Alright, let's catch up about our past."

Rionarta agrees, "Yes, that's more interesting than noticing any passersby."

Azul agrees, "Yes, I imagine the meeting and what happens from there may prevent us from having time to talk. We may only have these moments. Where were we then?"

Kardichay says, "Yeah, we have a lot to catch up on."

Rionarta says, "Sure, sounds good."

They resume talking about the mysterious Marcon as they walk along the avenue toward the Star Sirius center.

A Dangerous Gust of Wind

Meanwhile, Keme is pursuing Zoz, until his way is blocked by a group of parents as they leave their children with two women wearing wild hats, standing in front of the Merkabus. Bella is large and colorfully dressed and holding up a sign, Joyous Bubbles Spirit Care. Miyah, her assistant, is wearing a more subdued outfit and carrying packs. Bella waves to the children, to clear the way for the crowd to relive the bottleneck. She is very conscious of keeping everything running smoothly and in order.

Keme is frozen, watching them in a flurry of organizing packs and gathering the unruly children, which is not an easy task, given their excitement. *"Not sure how to get past them,"* he thinks. *"Too many to move through, but I don't want to lose Zoz."*

Suddenly, a gust of wind blows the sign out of Bella's grip, flinging it dangerously close toward the children. Keme leaps forward, catching the sign before it causes any harm. He hands it to Bella. She sighs in relief, smiling, "Oh, thank you for your kind help just in time. I was concerned it was going to crash into my sweethearts before we even get started. For your heroic effort I have a tasty gift - my chocolate creme truffle. You will love it." She hands him a luscious sweet from a handmade basket.

Surprised, he mumbles, "Thanks," and eagerly pops the truffle into his mouth. His eyebrows rise, smiling. "Yum, what a tasty treat - delicious, very good." Bella, grateful for the appreciation, smiles back. Their eyes connect briefly. Keme, quite shy, looks down. He has not been around women for a long time, especially one who smiles nice and gave him such a tasty treat. Both are startled and have the same lingering thought, '*Who is this that sizzles something warm and fuzzy inside of me?*'

Bella keeps looking at Keme, but he does not realize it. Then she returns her focus to her job, rallying the children into action, with her great voice. She claps her hands, "Blue stars, crystals, indigos. Please, onto the Merkabus, one at a time. Daphne, the emerald dragon, is giving rides at the Misty Rainbows water park today!"

The children look in wonder. Did she say a real dragon to ride? Some have never even seen a dragon, let alone be on top of one. They enthusiastically whoop it up. It seems like it's a fun trip. Eagerly they form a crooked line but close enough for Bella. She lets them file past her onto the Merkabus.

"Oh, cool," says Aronsky as he jumps into a colorful seat that blinks to the rocking music played on the silver piano by the driver. He says, "Wow. This is awesome. A great ride." The kids file quickly onto the Merkabus and start dancing wildly. What a blast for all of them.

Keme still watching Bella, suddenly realizes that he's free to go. He says, "I better get a move on to find Zoz." He resumes walking in the direction Zoz went, with a big smile on his face. "*Wait,*" he thinks, turning to look at the Merkabus, that's ready for take-off, with the children, bouncing to the piano tunes.

Bella looks just then, waving and smiling. He waves and then he disappears into the crowd as the Merkabus zips away leaving a trail of rosy fragrance. What perfect timing for the two of them, that last lingering, pleasant look of appreciation.

Funny when you sail along the river of life, it often entails twists, turns and unexpected situations that change you forever. We never know when we may meet a new love for the first time.

Initamay walks up and does not even notice Keme rushing by, since she is so intrigued by the music and parade ahead.

Azul, Rionarta and Kardichay, are conversing, coming up the avenue, so they did not notice him going by either.

Finally, they stop talking due to a backup of the multitudes gathering up ahead. They realize it's time for addressing what is more important now - the activities that are looming right before them.

Kardichay says, "I want to find Celestia. See you in the hall." He weaves through the crowd, excited to go see her. He has not had a chance to be alone with her since reconnecting on Sirius.

Keme manages to make it past all of them, without being detected. What luck. *"Hey, there he is,"* thinks Keme. He caught up to Zoz, in the midst of the throngs watching the parade. What a relief to see him, even though he is still surrounded by the Aloha Plumeria ladies. Keme whispers, "Zoz."

Zoz looks away from the ladies and sees Keme. "Hey, Keme, good to see you made it. I wondered if you were going to find me after I saw all the yummy foods along the way."

Laughing and smiling, Keme says, "Yeah, I ran into a children's road-block." He does not mention the encounter with Bella. "This place is crawling with too many people for my comfort. Where are we heading?"

Zoz says, "I heard about a meeting in a hall up ahead. Let's stay with the crowd. We'll figure a way in without being seen. That's where the action is. I'm looking for the best time to do it." He is still arm in arm with the women.

Keme smirks. "Yeah, it looks like you're working really hard."

PART 3

STAR SIRIUS CENTER

7

FESTIVAL CONNECTIONS

Lakul is in front of the parade drumming robustly. He waves to the new arrivals, to step into the marching line. Initamay is thrilled to merge in with the lively dancing and singing parade goers. What a stunning sight to see everyone winding in a snake formation, toward the great hall. Massive tall crystals that line the avenue, blink and shimmer as the crowd passes. Lakul booms out singing.

Sing down the walls of darkness

Sing down the walls of fear

Sing out the light that shines from your heart

Sing out the light that shines from the stars

Dance in the light of spirit

Dance in the light of love

Live in the light of wisdom

Live in the light of love

Live in the light of peace

The parade stops in front of the Star Sirius building. The festive energy is coursing throughout the uplifted crowd. Many express admiration for the spectacular center with its sparkling spires, reaching high and waving colorful banners that represent all the nations of the galaxies.

The Grand Hallway

Lakul, always the entertainer, keeps dancing and singing exuberantly, with the happy crowd. He stops when he senses their energy shifting, to look up at the stately building complex. "Wow, impressive. Yes, it's true about the legendary beauty. Dear friends, let's see the inside. It must be as great as the outside appears."

He walks to the entrance, stopping in front of an archway with pillars imbedded with vibrant crystals in elaborate circular patterns. He runs his fingers on the smooth crystalline pillars, "Look at these gems. I love these dark red banded swirling crystals. What are they? I'll have to ask Rionarta or Kardichay. Oh, la, la, intriguing Egyptian eyes, that follow as you pass by."

He peers into the eyes which are exactly the same height. Wait, did he see that? The eyes blink, as if alive. He looks directly into them. He hears a voice, "Hello, Lakul, of the orange ray. We are pleased to meet you. Beyond the enchantment of this portal is a stunning hallway to enliven you and your tribe."

Lakul responds, "Thank you. I feel the spirit of the artist within. Yes, I feel the powerful artistry. I am excited to proceed into this magical arena of magnificence." He taps the portal and walks into the hallway, not noticing the crystal pillars flickering orange, then red rays in response to his touch. He is immediately enamored with exotic, sensually sculpted white marble figures. He chooses a sleek, muscular, stunning statue to stand in front of and then he strikes a similar pose, showing off like the statues and smiles at those who pass by and express surprise that he's actually alive - not a statue.

The hallway overflows with others exploring the artistic inspirations. Exotic flower bouquets are beautifully arranged in painted vases along the sides and are interspersed with unusual crystal clusters.

A geometric mandala design created with vibrant dazzling tile, is on the floor. The imaginative path winds down the hall to the far side. It ends in a golden star point in front of a massive wood door that has a crystalline star hanging in the center of it. The high clear ceilings are sprinkled with blinking stars, as if in the room. Comets streak by every so often beyond the glass ceilings.

Another Chance Encounter

Initamay is talking with parade participants in front of the building, when Zoz and Keme bump into her as they walk by. "Oh, sorry," Zoz says, nonchalantly, very transfixed by her beauty. "Hello, I saw you enjoying the parade."

Initamay responds with a faint smile, "Yes, it was fun to meet so many from the different realms." She is so excited like a child, by the sights, that she doesn't note his interest or his dusty clothing. It's apparent that she's concerned with other things when she says, "Excuse me. I have flowers to check out before my meeting." She goes to glimpse the nearby blooms. Even though she was supposed to be on the lookout for these two, she is so thrilled about everything that she fails to note their distinct differences from the happy crowd.

Keme holds Zoz's arm as he is stares at her, saying, "Zoz, come on, now. We have a plan. No funny stuff, no distractions."

Zoz glances at him, saying, "Yeah, all right. Let's go." He resumes watching her as she sniffs the floral creations. She sighs when she tries a stunning array of trumpet flowers and purple and white orchids.

Keme is relieved when Zoz finally turns back. He signals to Keme to be quiet, to follow behind without her knowing.

After making it through the flowers, Initamay passes under the red banded archway and into the grand hall where she is drawn to a stained-glass piece with a sun's face, hanging on a door. She says, "Wow, beautiful," as she runs her fingers along the sun's glass several times in a circle.

Suddenly, the door opens in, with a blast of wind startling her. No one else witnesses this, or so she thinks, as she looks to the left and right, but not behind her. Her curiosity leads her in. The door closes silently as the handle mysteriously fades away from the outside.

Zoz gestures to Keme to follow him to where he saw her disappear. The glass sun hangs on the shut door, with no way in. He whispers, "Where's the handle? Let's try to get in. This may be the perfect way to avoid scrutiny and security. I don't like checkpoints. They make me break out in cuffs you know."

Keme whispers, "Yeah, I remember all about that. Well, I saw her rub the sun's face in a circle. Let's try it."

Zoz says, "Go ahead, I know you'll figure out the trigger point. Oh, oh." Several beings walk by, looking at them curiously. They pretend to admire the stained glass. Zoz says, "Wow, this is beautiful."

Keme nods, "Oh yeah, very nice."

After the onlookers' pass, they smirk at each other. They are good at making up any silly story to fit the need at the moment.

Keme resumes touching the circle to trigger the door. "I know it's the pressure. I'm sure in a circle, I think. She did it slow and nice." After several tries, muttering, "Slow and nice," he completes the seventh circle. Presto, it opens in slowly.

"Finally," Zoz says, "I mean good work." They slip through the door which also closes behind them.

"It's dark in here."

"Quiet, Keme, we don't want to scare her."

He whispers, "Oh right, she's in here."

"Wait, don't move. Let me find a light."

"Okay."

Zoz fishes in his pockets and flicks on a device. "Aha." It lights up dimly for them to see a little, but it fades in and out. "These lights never last long. Darn junk."

They can barely make out where they are. It is a storage room full of large paintings and stained-glass art that is stacked all over the place. Zoz shines the light on a painting close by. "Wow, a real art collection. These will be nice to bring back."

Keme emphatically says, "No, Zoz, that's not why we came. No side quests. They backfire and always lead away from the plan."

Zoz laughs, "Not now, maybe on the way back. Art brings a sizable sum - a large stash. Cashola could come in real handy when we're done. Let's keep going. There must be another door out of this room, further down, if she's not in here."

They step over the paintings that seem to spring to life as they pass by. Interesting faces observe their sneaky energy, looking as if they know they are up to no good.

Keme says, "Gee, I feel like someone is watching us."

"Yeah, me too, so be careful. Come on. It's this way. My light has a few minutes, before it goes out." He hits the light to make it come on brighter.

Keme says, "Hey, wait, so I can see too." They are funny, constantly bickering like an old couple.

Suddenly Zoz stops. "Hey, did you hear singing?"

Keme stops. He hears pretty singing. "Yes, I do, up ahead. I bet it's her."

Zoz says, "Shh, let's go slow to get close."

Trying to be quiet is hard as the light is very dim and the room is chock-full of stuff, making it hard to maneuver around the random sized objects. "I have an idea. I'll go see. It's easier for one of us to get there without being discovered."

Keme adds, "No, not good. I don't have a light, remember?"

"Yeah. Right. Okay, follow me. Careful, no bumping into anything." They make their way quietly through the piled up loose stuff following her.

Zoz says, "I see her, up there. Oh, oh, she's near a door."

He's right, Initamay reaches for the door handle just as Keme knocks into a painting. Startled, she turns to see what it was as they quickly crouch to hide. "Who's there?" She listens but no reply. She thinks, *I must have loosened it when I went by. I'm glad for my in the dark training that lets me see the energy outlines of objects.*

Turning back, she opens the door to go into a brightly lit colorful room.

Zoz says, "Whew a close call. Now we'll go where we want to. Let's wait to make sure she's somewhere else. Then we'll sneak in, carefully though."

Keme whispers, loudly, "Okay."

"Shh," Zoz says.

Silvery Faery Nymphs

Meanwhile, back along the avenue, Teesha, Mira and Celestia emerge out of the crowd, absolutely awestruck at the massive architectural beauty of the front of the building. They pause at the crystalline archway entrance to the grand hall, to admire the brilliant red banded jasper crystals, the striking Egyptian eyes and the clusters of overhanging flowers that are hanging pendulously from the branches of several large trees.

Somehow, the trees are growing in through the building as if their roots are still connected to the ground and the structure is built all around them. A waterfall is gushing into a rocky pool along the side of the lush gardens, surrounding the buildings.

Celestia senses the powerful energy emanating from the portal. She steps back to attune quietly to it. Mira and Teesha walk away to not disturb her, to talk together.

Teesha smiles, sighing. She is always expressing herself that way, "I love the colorful flowers, hanging off the trees. They add the finishing touches. "Oh, look," she says, pointing to the mosaic floor that leads into the long hallway.

She goes to see it up close, leaving Mira to admire the waterfall, one of her favorites. "What a wonderful pattern," Teesha says, as she sits on the floor to view the tile work. "Mira, look, at this lovely mosaic with the complex matrix patterns. How each tile is so smoothly set."

Mira comes over, "Wow, nice, so colorfully put together."

"I'll going to draw these familiar designs, so I can remember them again," Teesha says.

Mira perks up, "I hear a sweet melody, singing. I'm going over to see where the trees meet the waterfall."

Teesha nods. She takes out her drawing book and pencils to become happily absorbed in sketching - her favorite pastime.

Mira hums while viewing the waterfall. She is curious and leans in over a pool that flows into smaller pools. Pretty flowering plants are growing on the edges and in the waters, along with glistening crystals, fragrant blue and pink lilies and fish swimming.

"What a thrill," she says as she sniffs a blue lily exuding an exhilarating fragrance. Near her are bumble bees, buzzing, lined up, as if waiting their turn to sniff the nectar of a stately pink Lotus flower. The bloom rises high above the waters, with its' roundish leaves dancing in the gentle breeze. Birds fly by, chattering.

"Oh, I love it, so sweet and pretty." She breathes in the fragrance of the Lotus, making sure she avoids sniffing it too close, in case a bee may be inside the petals and not notice her. They might be a little altered from taking in the delicious Lotus nectar. "I hear a melody." She makes up a song to honor everything she is touched by, naming it, "Flowers of delight."

Open our hearts, open our souls

Oh, may we know, the way to flow

Color us like the rainbow, color us like the trees

Oh, may we sail away into serenity

Oh, yeah, what a beautiful way, on this peaceful day

It's so lovely, lovely, everywhere, flowers fragrancing the air

Filling us with love

Oh, they're coloring us, painting pictures like rainbows in the sky

Oh yeah, flowers of delight, oh, happiness inside

Flowers of delight, flowers of light

Oh heavenly, heavenly, everywhere

Oh, they're growing everywhere you go

Flowing beauty, feeling love in the air

Waltzing in, coloring us like the tall trees

Oh, like the trees, so green everywhere

Oh, flowers of delight, oh, flowers of life

May we sail into serenity, filling our hearts with beauty

All around you feel the light of rainbows everywhere

Oh, flowers of delight, flowers of light, fragrancing the air

Oh, flowers of light, flowers of delight

Suddenly three silvery nymphs poke their heads out of the serene waters, to sing with her. Mira finishes, but they keep singing,

Oh, flowers of delight, in these magical waters

Oh, we're happy in sweet serenity

She smiles at their playfulness. They float up, slithering onto a shiny crystal in front of her. One says, "Hello, gentle Mira, please sit with us."

(Nymphs actually resemble sleek mermaids, even otters, and are often found in clusters, in pristine brooks, streams, rivers, and their favorite, lovely waterfalls.)

Mira gets close, "Hello, pretty ones. How do you know me?"

One of the nymphs, wearing a pretty seashell and a starfish crown, says, "On a glorious spring morning, Isis visited. She spoke of her celestial helpers that were coming soon."

The other nymph says, "She asked us to welcome and greet you."

Mira says, "Thank you, sweet Isis. I am grateful for her unlimited divine love."

"Yes, her gracious compassion flows in all of us," says the last one.

Mira says, "Yes, that is so." She settles on a sparkly crystal bench along the waters' edge to enjoy her new friends as she happily admires the lovely ponds.

Then, a painted turtle slides off a lily leaf to paddle to her. The turtle, holding her head up, says, "Hello, Mira, I am Painty."

Mira slides off the bench to get close so she can see the turtle.

"Painty, you're so dainty, with such a teeny, teeny tail."

Painty says, "Yes, I am, but can you find me?"

Painty bobs in and out as if in a hide and seek game, delighting Mira. She laughs and slips into the water by not paying attention. "Oops. Oh, well, the water is warm." She joyfully plays with adorable Painty and the nymphs. They are delighted to be cavorting with her.

The Enchantment of Petalite

All this time, Celestia was attuning to the intriguing crystal portal. After resuming her senses, she walks to the towering crystals and sees Teesha, still sitting on the floor drawing the mandala design. "Wow, did you notice all the red jaspers imbedded in the portal? They gave me a burst of powerful energy."

Teesha only nods, she is still absorbed in her design project and not easily distracted. Celestia realizes Teesha is probably not going to engage with her. She points up ahead, "Okay. I'm going to view those captivating crystals shining over there. I'm not sure which ones are doing that."

Teesha looks up, "I'll catch you when I'm done. Thanks."

Celestia walks to the front of a tall cluster of white crystals that glow and pulsate with throbbing, concentric rings. Enchanted, she runs her fingers on the crystals. "Wow, rainbow florescence quartz. I wonder why they light up?"

Funny how she too talks to herself when no one is listening. She knows that Mira and Teesha are too far to hear her. She is so enthralled with the dazzling crystal display that she does not notice Kardichay ambling up in time to hear her comments.

He quietly says, "It's petalite, a rare mineral known for its' strong energetic base conduction structure and magnetic activating capabilities which causes the bright resonation and far-reaching electromagnetic properties. Petalite is unparalleled in all realms."

Celestia laughs at his long-winded explanation. "Kardichay, thank you for explaining so well. Petalite, or lithium, reflects the radiant energy of the mighty sun and invigorates mental attunement, and conscious awakening to our destiny."

They stand silently admiring the stunning crystals as the intense energy between them builds. The quiet happiness they feel, from being so tenderly close, creates a warm pleasant sensation within them for the first time.

Finally, Kardichay says, "Let's check out the hallway. Looks like petalite is part of a crystal display from the whole multiverse."

Celestia nods as he reaches for her hand. She smiles, placing her fingers around his while beaming at the love feeling, bubbling between them. They meander throughout the hallway, admiring the countless crystals until the end where they discover a comfy couch to sit on. At last, a happy private moment to talk together.

Match Made in Heaven

High above the spires of the tall buildings, the purple and blue star comets of Ayalasha and Ashento descend rapidly, landing before the flowering archway of the meeting hall. Their colors merge into misty magenta, streaked with royal blue with intense sparks spraying. The crowd stands back, while watching riveted.

Azul and Rionarta are waiting for Initamay there, thinking she may appear, after going to seek out the parade. They don't know that she went into the arts room and is now ahead of them.

Rionarta gestures to clear the area. "Hey, make way. These must be masters of light blasting in from no telling where but certainly from distant stars."

Azul is impressed as the magenta, blue rays, shimmer. "Wow, majestic energies unifying with intense communion. Let's be aware of the powers rising here." He stands reverently as if awaiting a learned being. Slowly a figure emerges from the blue-magenta light.

It is Ashento, the teacher from the blue temple of Lazure, standing with eyes closed, as if meditating. He feels the energy of Sirius grounding him and opens them to gaze at the crowd and the buildings, taking it all in gracefully.

Rionarta is holding his hands together in a gesture of respect to him. Breathing in fresh air, Ashento steps forward, nodding to Rionarta, smiling. Then he looks to the heavens, "Thank you, great spirit, for my safe journey."

He takes off his blue cape and flings it over his shoulder, revealing a dramatic physical change to his body that he must have undergone during his light-speed journey to Sirius Star. It is a remarkable transformation, similar to the three angelic children, Celestia, Mira and Azul, at the beginning of this story. Remember when they transformed from children into teenagers after traveling in their rainbow light bodies to Sirius? They may all be masters of the ancient art of shape shifting.

(Shapeshifters are known to use supernatural powers to go beyond the boundaries of human physical expressions and appear or transform at their personal whims or desires.)

The misty magenta rays swirl about. Ayalasha, the priestess of the purple ray, emerges next. She too is in deep contemplation and takes a slow breath, while shaking herself to ground to the earth beneath her.

Now the drama unfolds, slowly, without them realizing. When she opens her eyes, she is surprised to see dashing Ashento, standing there, gazing deeply into her eyes. They are immediately transfixed by one another with palpable, passionate sparks flying. The onlookers are fascinated, anticipating the further reactions of these intense beings meeting this way.

Ashento, drinking in Ayalasha's serene majesty, says with a loving smile, "Hello, Goddess of the Purple ray. What a sweet pleasure to reconnect with your dynamic presence again."

Startled, she takes a questioning posture to study Ashento, scanning her memories for anything related to him. She stares intently, taking in his commanding stature, his light blue skin and colorful - tattooed body, long black hair and piercing dark eyes.

Azul, having witnessed their meeting, takes her silence to interject excitedly, "Excuse me, blue master. We are honored by you. I am Azul. Where are you from?"

Ashento says graciously, "Thank you, Azul, I am Ashento from the temples of Lazure in a faraway realm, where the blue ray mists surround us in relaxing wonder. I sense your blue ray essence. May we always connect with their healing rays."

He smiles at Ashento, "Wonderful, I'll look to experiencing your glorious energy in all ways. I am grateful to meet you."

Ashento nods smiling, then gestures with his left hand for the curious to come closer. He glances lovingly at awestruck Ayalasha. His presence towers over his admirers, one of which is Rionarta. They crowd around to marvel at the intricate blue-green tattoos on his body. Ayalasha watches with wonder, while holding Ashento's gaze.

Rionarta says to Azul, "Wow, that is fine artistry etched in his skin like that."

Azul replies, "Yes, amazing, his high blue energy is also powerfully profound."

As Mira was playing in the water, she saw magenta sparks, which caught her attention. She rises out of the water, saying to her friends, "Goodbye, Painty, silver nymphs. I must go see what is happening there. Thanks for the fun. I'll return soon. Love to you."

One of the nymphs, says, "Happy to meet you too."

Painty says, "Goodbye, you're a lot of fun, Mira."

"Keep on singing," says another nymph.

She waves and rushes over, dripping wet into the crowd that is gathering around Ashento and Ayalasha to see what is going on.

Teesha saw the magenta sparks flying when she looked through the long hallway to the entrance. The flashing rays were so compelling that she stopped sketching and rushed over to glimpse the action also.

She stands near enraptured Mira, as she is taking it all in. Mira whispers to Teesha who is equally mystified. "Wow, he's a royal sight to behold, isn't he?"

Teesha laughs shyly and then looks at Mira with surprise, "Wow, you're soaking wet. What happened? Yes, he is certainly an artful masterpiece. I'm sure behind those intense tattoos is a powerful story to tell."

Mira adds, "I fell into the pond playing with the cutest creatures there. Yes, they are amazing designs. I love the colorful ocean, purple dolphins, mermaids, whales and the little fishies swimming."

Teesha sighs, "I like the crystals, beads and dancing dangles. I want to paint it. Please help me recall what it looked like."

Mira says, "Yes, sure. I'll make a note within."

Azul and Rionarta return for a closer look at the swirling, breathing, as-if-alive figures on his chest. Azul realizes, "I understand what they mean. The colorful pattern, swirling in unity is a visionary prayer, in honor of the magnificent Gaea Star."

Rionarta nods, "Yes, we're in the presence of a masterful wise one."

Ashento smiles. "Thank you. Yes, it is my way of honoring all of Gaea Star's life."

The onlookers surround Ashento, preventing him from getting too close to Ayalasha. She uses the moment to steady herself after such an intense journey and passionate meeting with this incredible star being. Now she takes in the beautiful panoramic city, the diverse crowd, and the stimulating festival-like setting, brimming with so many diverse aspects in every direction.

Then Ashento's compelling energy reawakens her senses, to return to her inner thoughts. She has never seen anyone anywhere that looks like him. She ponders, *"Who is this being of such intensity that flashes and moves with radiant blue compelling luminosity? Am I dreaming this?"*

At last, she finds her voice to speak. "Do I know you? Have we met in a distant place that for some reason I don't remember?"

He breaks from his adoring fans to respond, "I am Ashento, my sweetness. I have longed to be near your exquisite light again. Eons ago, we were companions on lush Gaea Star as carriers of the light, in service to humanity, under the watchful guidance of Michael. Now, I dwell beyond the realms that you are familiar with, a long journey away."

Ayalasha's eyes widen. She is speechless, trying to access that far-away memory, that's deep, oh, so deep within. The onlookers remain absorbed watching their compelling interaction, as if nothing else matters around them.

"See, I knew their history was profoundly intertwined together," Teesha whispers to Mira and to those close by.

Azul says, "Yes, I heard about this first wave of light beings, way before we joined the rainbow brigade."

Rionarta says, "What an unforgettable way for them to rekindle their love. Yes, they are from that original enlightened pod of healing souls. Let's leave so they'll have a moment to be alone."

Mira says, "I like them. It's so romantic to reconnect with ancient love. I'm all for going on ahead. I see exquisite shiny statues up in the hallways." She takes Teesha's hand to walk away.

Rionarta says, "Sounds good. I want to see those crystals glistening ahead too. I'm sure they are rare."

Just then, the tall crystals shimmer warm flashes in the distance, as if calling, "Hello, daughters, sons. Come see me now."

Azul says, "They're beacons, sending out remarkable light."

The four excitedly walk toward the vast crystals to sense their radiant emanations close up. Rionarta says, " Yeah, I feel their strong qualities even from here."

"Yeah, I do too," Azul says, "let's stand in front to absorb their healing rays."

The four attune to the calming crystalline energy. Meanwhile, Celestia and Kardichay are still talking, snuggling in the corner of the hallway. No need to join the others yet.

A Strong Prayer

Ashento says quietly to Ayalasha, "The meeting hall is calling us soon. Please accompany me, my sweetness, with your delightful presence." He holds his arm up for her. She places her hand there, as if they were a couple. They promenade through the crowd into the hallway, where everyone clears way for the commanding pair to walk on the tiled path, that spirals into a sparkling star point. When they arrive at the tip of the star, they stand, holding one another, in front of the massive door with the gold star in the middle.

She speaks, "Thank you, Ashento, for your kind words and for answering Michael's call. I am Ayalasha. What is that amazing design on your body?"

Ashento proudly says, "A strong prayer." He comes close to connect deeper.

She responds to his intense energy by shifting, breathing and saying, "You are attractive, but I have an adoring love already."

He nods, staring into her eyes. "Yes, I believe you. He is fortunate to be with such a strong goddess. I'm waiting for you as I do not dwell within these realms. We have great destiny together."

Ayalasha touches his arm strongly and is about to respond, but suddenly, the gold star hanging on the huge door, lights up with twinkling golden light. An elderly angel floats through the star door to greet the surprised crowd. The door opens after her, to reveal a magnificent chamber with different rooms along the sides.

Smiling, the angel says, "Welcome to Sirius Star Center. I am Angel Ohm. We are not ready for your presence, so please enjoy our creativity rooms. Each is a pure delight to enrich appreciation of the creative arts. Enter everyone. Please mute contact devices and maintain a peaceful manner. The star door will illuminate when we are ready for you to enter the chamber." She then floats through the door followed by the crowd, thrilled to explore the intriguing rooms.

Ashento whispers, "Let's take a moment." She gracefully follows to a garden where they snuggle as long-lost lovers on a comfy sofa, with overhanging roses - perfect to talk privately.

PART 4

THE SIRIUS
CREATIVITY ROOMS

8

Enjoying The Art Rooms

The curious one's walk in to see what theme each room offers. An inviting temple is first with welcoming prayer flags waving at the entrance that represent the nations of Star Sirius.

Teladi is sitting in the middle, in his element, teaching meditation to fascinated students. "Now the actual purpose of mindfulness is to focus your thoughts, by letting them float by with no judgement. This settles the mind into stillness, with peaceful relaxation following." The students meditate with him.

Two red dragons, perched on either side of the entrance to the next room, breathe fire when someone walks by. Tables are flowing with craft materials to create stained glass, jewelry, beading, glass blowing, paper making and masks.

Initamay is sitting at a stained-glass table in front of a mosaic project, choosing pieces to add to this communal art. She entered this interesting room a while ago from the art storage room and perused the tables before anyone else arrived. She loves artsy crafts like paper making with materials from nature.

Rionarta and Azul, come down the hall and peek in. Azul says, "Initamay, there you are. We waited for you but gave up. How did you get here before us?"

She walks to the edge of the room to say, "It's funny. I came through the hall and saw a lovely sun, made of stained-glass on a door. After rubbing the face, it magically opened with a gust of wind. I walked nearly in the dark, around art creations until going through a door that led here."

Azul says, "Hmm, mystical and mysterious - so like you."

She agrees, "Yes, I felt the artists' energies. The paintings seemed to come alive as I passed by."

Rionarta says, "That's true. You can always sense the spirit of the person behind their art."

Suddenly there's a ruckus in the hallway. She says, "Whoa. What's going on out there? It's quite the commotion."

Rionarta says, "Might be in the next room. Let's go see." He laughs, saying, "It's a crazy painted clown bouncing up and down, luring visitors using mime."

Azul says, "Wow, it's like a carnival fun house, with jumping games, whirling gizmos, stuffed animals, magic tricks galore, all to satisfy those who like exciting fun."

Initamay laughs, "Oh, I'm sorry Ilanu is missing this." Just then she sees Mira and Teesha coming down the hall. They had stopped at the first room to feel, "The temple vibe," as Mira said.

Initamay signals to come to her. Teesha waves as if saying, "We're coming." They walk over. The clown bursts out in front, beaming, wearing oversized red polka dot boots.

"Wow, that's great, a fun house," Teesha says.

Mira squeals with delight. She loves clowns and colorful gizmos. "This is fabulous. Let's go in. We'll check it out for Ilanu." They follow the clown, laughing and whooping it up with the other fun seekers.

Azul, Rionarta and Initamay, smile and signal one another to explore the other rooms.

Next in stark contrast to the funhouse, is a dignified quiet library, where one can browse the vast collection of every book written throughout the universe.

Each one is easily accessible by scanning a large grid and touching the title that you choose, which then shows on a viewing screen. There are reading seats while you sip sweet-smelling beverages arrayed on a serve yourself table. The three keep on going, since reading was not what they wanted to do right then.

"Oh, how pretty," says Initamay as she touches a gorgeous intricate tapestry that hangs in the entrance of the next room. They see weavers working at large looms, while others are spinning fine threads with beautiful wheels. Some are preparing baskets of gossamer fibers for spinning. An adoring array of students surround Gandhi of India as he grins his wonderful smile while he spins fluffy white fiber on a small circular wheel. There is a lovely peaceful feeling throughout the room.

Upbeat driving music emanates from another room where beings are singing and playing with ornate unusual instruments. Lakul is beating a rhythm on two large drums as he boisterously sings, "*One, two, three, four. Yes, that's it, the planets are in synch with us. Come on, hit it.*" Everyone with an instrument plays while a few dance in the aisles.

The Integration Transmitter Crystal

Rionarta and Azul continue exploring until they are drawn in different directions. Azul goes to see flickering blue wavy lights, while Rionarta checks out a nearby gem collection. He exclaims, "Those are fine crystals and minerals from the universe." Azul didn't hear since he disappeared into the blue room.

Rionarta sits on a rose quartz bench where the enormous gems reach high into the open ceiling. He sighs with satisfaction, for he's in his element, the fascinating mineral realm. "I love learning about these powerful, crystal beings."

Kardichay and Celestia, still talking in the hallway, decide to explore the other gems on display. After examining the last of the towering crystals, he says, "Wow, an integration, transmitter crystal, the biggest I've seen. It's a mighty tool to access your higher purpose in the realm you exist in."

Celestia, touching it softly, says, "Yes, I remember. It's a master wisdom crystal, one of three to help with inter-dimensional communication throughout the centuries."

Kardichay adds, "Yes, bridging the realms of spirit and mental intellect."

Rionarta overhears their conversation, which draws him over to see what is so exciting. They are standing at the end of the impressive, crystal display in front of a large clear crystal. It is alone, perfectly flat, emanating silvery rays from its' three-sided triangular face in between two seven-sided faces.

Rionarta breathes in, saying in awe, "Amazing, I feel it's mighty energy."

Celestia comes close, smiling as she sweeps her graceful fingers along the sides gently.

"This is the perfect place for this wise crystal to help those passing by; to integrate what they have experienced and to awaken to their souls' destiny."

The transmitter crystal reacts to her soft touch by shimmering with a gentle wave of bright translucent light. All three nod, acknowledging the crystal's spirit.

Rionarta speaks reverently, "I'm sure this unique transmitter tool has telepathic powers and is a record keeper from the realms of all knowing."

He steps close, facing the triangle in the center, saying, "Grand wise one, we are blessed by your almighty presence. We seek your abiding wisdom regarding this meeting at the center."

Kardichay adds, "We promise to serve your crystal family with the utmost respect, especially if we continue on this mission to Gaea Star."

The crystal responds, by blinking when Celestia touches it. She says to the crystal, "The archangels called us. We came to help rebalance Gaea Star with our healing ways." She leans in as if to listen. She looks up, "Ah, it is a being of light and has a message."

She talks slowly, like she is channeling, as the crystal flickers rays of clear light.

"Shine brightly. Carry yourselves gracefully. Stay open to the goodness in all beings as you promote the true essence of love. We're here to help in every way."

Kardichay, standing behind her, says, "Hello, radiant being. You and your crystal family emanate the highest vibration of the divine essence of life. It is an honor to express our love for all nations wherever we go, with your guiding support."

The crystal responds by blinking rays of sparkling golden light that circle like wheels in many directions. Celestia says, "It is saying to come close, friends. Place your crystals within the triangle to access the frequency of awakening one's divine purpose, as you may forget."

Looking at each other, they reach within their bags to retrieve a crystal to place in front of the crystals,' triangle.

After thirty-three seconds, their crystals blink a translucent golden light at the same time, as if signaling the download from the crystal is complete. They pick up their crystals and hold them close to feel the crystalline energy within.

Kardichay smiles, "We are prepared for anything now. How could we forget who we are? It seems simple to be awake and aware, don't you think?"

Rionarta answers, "You never know. The challenges on Gaea Star are possibly quite intense. We may become separated and take difficult paths on the journey."

Celestia smiles, "Well, this crystal and our other ones will help us remember our starry origins."

She turns to the crystal. "Thank you, grand being of light, for your guidance. You have inspired us with hope." She touches it. The crystal responds by sending out dancing white light rays.

Kardichay says, "Thank you, Celestia. We appreciate your wisdom here."

Rionarta agrees, "Yes, we are blessed by your light and knowledge."

They also touch the crystal once more before they walk away. It flickers rays of light as they leave.

Art with the Masters - Salvador Dali

When Azul was searching for the wavy blue lights, he entered a room brimming with artists from all eras, busily painting and teaching. He became very involved there. He glances out the door, just as Mira and Teesha are going by after they had their fill of the crazy fun room.

"Hey, Mira, Teesha. Art masters, from long ago, in here to teach." They peer in with wonder.

Mira says, "Wow, yes I see."

Teesha sighing, "At last, artists so dear to my heart."

They enter, each going to the artists they are drawn to. Mira sees Salvador Dali, painting a panoramic celestial scene with double crystalline helixes, prominently placed at the center.

She says, "Hello, Salvador. I'm happy you're here. I love your unusual paintings and use of colors."

He smiles quirkily. "Ah, yes, thank you. Please be my guest. Avail me with your understanding of the visible excesses of human consciousness when it leaps into realms beyond the boundaries of comprehension."

She is speechless, then reaches for a brush from the table, dipping it into a brilliant golden color and swirls a twisting spiral right onto his canvas with a flourish. Laughing, she says, "Yes, this feels excellent indeed." She is soon exchanging colorful strokes with Salvador, as he paints wildly near her at the same time. Seems they are both extremely passionate about art.

Georgia O'Keefe

Teesha is intrigued by an impressive collection of brilliant flower paintings. She studies the flamboyant creations up close, saying, "Simply marvelous." An older gracious woman steps from behind a huge painting. Teesha recognizes her, "Hello, Georgia. I love your mixtures of colorful pastels, peach, purple, reds - all expressing radiant beauty, especially the desert flowers."

Georgia says, "Thank you. Please sit, my dear. Paint your appreciation, for that's the key to create wonderful expressive art, feeling it deep within one's heart and soul. Here is a lonely canvas, just perfect to receive your creativity."

Teesha takes the offer, sitting near Georgia to paint with her. She is blissful as flowers are her favorite to paint. She is very good. She is smiling at her blessed fortune to meet such a master of beautiful creations - one so dear to her heart.

Alphonse Mucha

The blue rays that drew Azul in were emanating from a visionary painting with gentle ocean waves in the center of the room. It has colorful rainbows, white birds sailing, portals with garlands of pendulous flowers, and misty waterfalls cascading into a quiet pool near the ocean. To his delight, there are gorgeous mermaids sunning on crystalline rocks, with golden light filtering through the rich green leaves of jungle plants growing everywhere.

"Ah, an Alphonse Mucha creation, with transcendental, uplifting, beauty of every element." He sits to absorb the living like soothing energy. He breathes it in slowly, for he is in no hurry and loves the blue tranquil effect of the painting.

Shady Ones Still Trailing

Initamay is lured out of the room when she hears enchanting gongs and harp music wafting down the hall. Just as she leaves, the back door into the arts room opens with Keme and Zoz peering in like two raccoons, casing the joint for a midnight food raid. Seeing that no one notices, they sneak in nonchalantly, pretending to look at the art displays on the tables.

Zoz sees masks by the entrance. "Let's check out the masks to get close to the front door. That's our free pass into the chamber." They pick up several masks, laughing as they place them on.

Keme says, "I like this one. It's my favorite - fire breathing, two - headed dragon." He pretends he is breathing fire.

Zoz looks around with a monkey mask on, and then quickly takes it off. "Keme, come on. The coast is clear." Keme takes his mask off and puts it down. They exit the arts room into the hall where they see orange lights flashing.

Zoz says, "Wonder what those blinking lights are for?"

Keme says, "Don't know. Looks like it's easy to get lost in the crowd. How about going near that door with the star on it?"

Zoz answers, "Okay. Let's walk like we own the place." It's true. With so many beings gathering, these unsavory characters blend in easily. No one is noticing what they're up to. They disappear down the hall, in search of a suitable hideout.

Temple Goddesses

Initamay follows the music down another hall until she sees exquisitely sculpted female statues, all dressed differently, standing in various postures at the entrance of another temple. As she enters, the statues move and one greets her, "Hello, green one, who communes with Deva spirits. Please enjoy our music."

Initamay smiles. "Thank you, beautiful living goddesses." Two of the statues, smiling radiantly, move from where they are to settle with Initamay on comfy, cushions. The chanting of the sweet music resumes with musicians playing unusual instruments. The mantra like repetitions are very calming as she relaxes in this peaceful serenity.

It was certainly an eventful day, filled with speedy light travel, losing Ilanu, reconnecting with friends, and seeing all the wonders along the avenue of the city of Sirius. She sighs, saying, "Ahh, I am in bountiful heaven. I hope Ilanu arrives soon as he is really missing all of this." She is in bliss from the ethereal music and finally lets' go of worrying about him to absorb the healing soothing music.

PART 5

THE GRAND CHAMBER

9

THE COUNCIL CONVENES

Deep within the great hall is a palatial circular chamber decorated with immense, brilliant celestial paintings, illuminated by light reflecting crystals. A white-haired being stands next to Angel Ohm just inside the star door. She points to the sky, "Metatron, look at the response of the multitudes, flowing in mass here in a show of loving support for Gaea Star."

As if on cue, the beautifully painted circular ceiling opens allowing streaks of light, similar to Northern Lights, to flood the area, making it easy to observe all the beings streaming toward the great hall. Metatron says, "Magnificent! Let the council begin!"

Angel Ohm raises her hand, sending a golden ray of light to illuminate the star door, which opens slowly. The crowd is excited to be summoned into the chamber – what a rare treat for sure.

Metatron flies to the center to join the archangels, seated in a semicircle. There is Michael, Ariel, Jophiel, Chamuel, Gabriel, Uriel, Raphael, Raziel, and Azrael. Their names holographically emanate below the golden auras about their heads. Angel Ohm takes a seat nearby. Archangel Lucifer, always a bit late, boldly strides in to sit with the archangels.

Spiritual masters of great renown from lives on Gaea Star are seated in the center, Maitreya, the happy Buddha, Kuan Yin, the Asian goddess of compassion, Ganesh, the elephant-head Hindu deity, regal Isis, and Yogananda, the yoga master. Lakshmi, the Hindu goddess of abundance is floating on a blue lotus flower.

Holographic imagery of arts and humanitarian leaders appear intermittently at the center, in an endless stream of loving faces. It is a rare assemblage of those who have served as supportive guardians for humanity on Gaea Star, the blue star planet.

Hundreds stream in, taking their seats in the vast chamber. Lively conversations abound with those who are newly reuniting at this gathering. Ashento and Ayalasha sit in the front. Celestia, Kardichay, Rionarta, Mira, Teladi, Teesha, Lakul and Initamay, leave wherever they are to join the meeting, when they hear Angel Ohm has summoned. They form a group to sit together.

Mira waves to Azul, signaling that she saved a seat, like Initamay does for Ilanu. She hopes he is arriving soon with Emeraldina after going the wrong way in the green eye transport.

The architecture and artistry in the chamber, as well as the congregation of such multi-diverse beings is fascinating enough to occupy one's interest for a good while.

As the attendees take their seats, Mira points out the blue and green holographic image of the Gaea Star planet rotating at the center, whispering, "Look at how pretty and radiant she is."

Teesha sighs, "Yes! She's a precious, rare gem in the galaxy." She observes Gaea Star closely, and then realizes what she's seeing and says, "Mother Gaea Star is with us. She's in the vision, alive, smiling at me. I love her."

Mira whispers, "Really, you see her? Where?"

Teesha points, saying, "Look beyond, into the colors, where they swirl into oneness."

Mira peers intently, saying, "Alright, I'm looking. Oh, yes, I see her there. Hello, mother, Gaea Star. We're glad you're with us."

Just then, Gaea Star's sweet green face, briefly appears as if she is showing herself to them. It seems that only Teesha and Mira noticed her as no one else reacts.

Well, actually Ashento and Ayalasha did see her, but due to their intense attraction for one another, they just keep smiling at each other. They know what has to happen, for Gaea Star's wellbeing and respect to be fully embraced. Perhaps it is better to leave things unsaid to allow the truth to be revealed freely.

Azul, even though he sits next to Mira, is so engrossed looking around that he didn't even know what was happening with Mira and Teesha.

Celestia says to Kardichay, "I'm enthralled with this gathering. We're part of a momentous meeting."

Kardichay nods. He chooses to observe silently, for he too is touched at the fascinating assembly of such high beings.

Lakul says, "We are certainly in the right place at the right moment. I feel real hope here. We are one family of love - yes, yes."

Teladi, always one to remain silent, laughs at Lakul's comment, saying, "We came to make a distinct difference in the shift that is looming ahead for humanity. We will need to stand strong, to hold the vision of oneness, working hard to break through the illusion of forgetting who, why and when, releasing the false premise of separation, once and for all."

Azul brings his attention back when he hears Teladi. "I'm hopeful we'll create positive change for Gaea Star, by restoring her beautiful harmony. It may not be easy."

Many nod rather than speak as the din of all the voices talking, makes it hard to be heard.

Metatron Begins

The crowded room is brimming with anticipation, excitement, and hushed murmurings, as if an award ceremony of the highest order, is about to start. Crystalline lights blink on and off as the crowd settles into silence. The mood is set with flickering candles and crystal lights shining brightly.

Metatron stands. He slowly and deliberately, gazes at every being in the room, to acknowledge each one, before he speaks.

"Welcome to all beings. Thank you for coming from so far on such short notice. Let us commence with a moment of silence to honor all faiths, all nations, all beings of loving light, in song for this momentous occasion."

A bell dings softly, relaxing the chamber, helping to focus, refresh and slow the excited energies into a quiet pause.

Metatron signals to Archangel Sandolphon, the director of the choir and orchestra, and Saraswathi, the Hindu goddess of the arts. She rises, summoning the choir and their guests to the center to assemble into three half-moon rows. The musicians tune up, then play an uplifting song accompanied by the choir.

Circle of light, circle of love, reaching towards the Source

Illuminate life with your presence,

your spirit, your love, your light

Circle of light, circle of love, reaching towards the Source

Feel your strength so deep within, the light, the way is clear

Flow through us now this current of love

Heal mother earth, heal Gaea Star

Circle of light, circle of love, reaching towards the Source

Light the way, light the way, light the way, light the way

Illuminate all souls with your light

Circle of light, circle of love

This is truly a significant gathering of wise, concerned and caring ones, from throughout the universe and beyond - all to create an encouraging difference on Gaea Star.

Crisis on Gaea Star

Michael stands as the music ends to say, "Thank you, for this powerful song. Gaea Star is suffering due to humanity forgetting their connection to the loving source of creation."

With a gentle fluid wave of his hand, he signals to Gaea Star as she rotates, growing bright and swirling into fantastic imagery of her peaceful beauty.

He says, "Please reveal your story."

Her sweet green face appears to everyone now. She smiles at Teesha and Mira, "Thank you, Michael. I love to tell my tale. Humans originally flourished in harmony on my earth, their planetary home. I provided all that is needed to live a peaceful spiritual existence, yet my whales calling, echoing throughout the universe is a cry that all is not well. There are many who do not care for my living essence anymore. Let me reveal the dilemma."

Misty clouds swirl about her and then lift revealing chaotic imagery of humanity acting without love for each other and technology swirling frenetically in negative proportions, disconnected from the natural cycles of life.

Gabriel rises to speak, "Gaea Star, thank you for showing these problems. It is quite evident to see how necessary it is to seek peaceful, thoughtful solutions to come to your aid soon."

Lucifer, agitated, says, "Michael, Gabriel, that is impossible! It is too late. The inevitable has happened. The Gaea Star project is failing due to free will, which creates delusions and separation from the source of love. The collapse is inevitable. Humanity is destroying itself by failing miserably to realize the results of their selfishness. Many are bent on disregarding the signs, as if they do not care, not one bit, for their own host planet."

Gaea Stars' mists swirl about then rise, revealing more images of suffering, wars, pollution, greed overtaking nature, seas swallowing homes, wildfires, violence, tribes fleeing unsafe lands, becoming refugees with nowhere to go. Chaos is abounding.

Michael says, "Gaea Star. We feel your pains with all of this. Lucifer speaks the truth. This imbalance cannot be denied."

Uriel adds, "It is free will that enables one to learn lessons in life and to create a meaningful existence."

Metatron adds, "Yes, it is this freedom that develops spiritual maturity, awakening the soul to awareness, to remember that love is the only answer."

Lucifer says, "However their egos implode with grandeur as they misuse the precious resources of Gaea Star. Unfortunately, it is the misguided belief they are separate and not connected as one spiritual family, which is the root cause of this destruction."

Just then, the troubling images fade as mists cover Gaea Star. As they rise, a vision appears of bulldozers clearing massive tracts of burned-out Amazon rainforests. A man and a child, watch from the edge of the jungle destruction. He is an honorable great leader, adorned in his traditional ceremonial garb.

Michael welcomes him, in his language, asking him to speak. The elder bows, then speaks, with his words translated through the Gaea Star spirit. She knows all things of her people and thereby can change the language for all to understand. "Yes, my tribes are deeply distressed. The oppressive ones are destroying the skin and lungs of our sacred mother for their own greedy purposes."

The child asks, "How can she breathe, Poppo? We need to help her. I'm afraid she will die."

The elder tenderly takes the child's hand. "Yes, my son, this is serious. She may perish unless the kind ones of this world and beyond heed our message to awaken her tribes, to pay attention, to what they are doing before it's too late."

The mist embraces them as they return to their forest home, holding each other gently, as if deeply saddened by the plight of their beloved land.

The mood in the room is somber and silent. Everyone knows the truth is spoken. Lucifer speaks again assertively, "The Gaea Star project cannot succeed, for the chains within their minds are severely imprisoning them."

Unseen chains rattle. A cold feeling and darkness descend on the chamber. The words, *"cannot succeed"* echo as frightening tigers, boars and screeching vampire bats fly, dipping and swooping, scaring the people. Voices rise anxiously.

Meanwhile, in the confusion, Keme and Zoz sneak in through a door, undetected to stand behind a pillar to watch. Zoz signals to him to not speak. He is right. The commotion is the perfect moment to come in without anyone noticing.

Michael stands, dramatically raising his sword. It glows with a brilliant golden blue light that dissipates the darkness. "Be still, fears and shadows. You are not welcome in this chamber of light. We send you away." The scary animals and darkness disappear immediately, dispensing the agitation in the chamber.

The Wise Ones Speak

Raphael speaks, "Council, remain at peace. The entire universe is watching Gaea Star for her unique role in shaping the destiny of creation." Countless eyes float in like a flock of birds flying invasively towards many of the beings seated, to prove the point. "We must pay attention to the havoc being done all over her planet." The eyes slowly fade away as Gaea Star revolves in serenity again.

Archangel Ariel stands, saying, "Be blessed with the sweetness of roses and lavender." She waves her hand, opening the top of a vial, releasing a healing aromatic fragrance that soothes everyone as it wafts throughout the tense chamber.

Many enjoy the uplifting pleasure. Lakul, invigorated by breathing it in, says, "Hmm, lavender opens us to the heavens. Its' sweetness heals all and yes, delightful roses to the rescue." He is invigorated.

Chamuel stands, "This is the moment. Humanity must foster a deeper connection to their spiritual selves in preparation for the Great Shift, for the earth changes are coming soon."

The mists envelop Gaea Star, then dissolve, revealing melting ice caps, polar bears searching for food, hurricane and flood devastation, and migrations leaving destroyed areas in search of sustainable homes.

Metatron signals to a male who rises. He nods, saying, "I am Vestara, from the Pleiadean star, Pleione. For centuries, our wise counselors offered teachings that fostered love and unity. However, the messengers were silenced to prevent their wisdom from helping, to keep humanity in fear. The denial of the truth of who they really are is the cause of this detrimental effect on Gaea Star."

He sits down as those nearby, agree by shaking their heads and murmuring, "Yes, that is so true."

Archangel Raziel stands, "When one overcomes the challenges of discovering their true self, dreams are manifested."

The negative imagery from Gaea Star is obscured again by mists that clear to reveal people of all ages and ethnicities actualizing their lofty goals in the arts, music, sports and politics. It is a bold display of the higher more positive aspects of humanity.

Gongs resound throughout as the Hindu master Yogananda, rises. "Humanity must become aware they are divine beings of love and light. If they retune to listen to their hearts' songs, awaken to their true essences and celebrate life with loving inspiration, then peace will engulf the world everywhere."

Lakul rises, "Amen. Thank you, so true, Yogananda. We will find the surest ways to awaken the tribes of Gaea Star." As he sits down, beings smile their approval near him. Yes, you can feel the hope in the air, with this impressive gathering of wise ones.

Kuan Yin and the Choir of Angels

As mystical gongs echo, Kuan Yin rises serenely, saying, "Yes, that is true. When all of my brothers and sisters cultivate compassion within their hearts, difficulties, sadness and chaos will disappear, clearing their lives forever." She waves her ethereal sleeves, toward the rear of the chamber.

Archangel Sandolphon gestures to the choir. The musicians bustle down to the inner chamber with their instruments, like an impromptu concert. A flute plays. The choir hums Om, until reaching harmony, then they and Kuan Yin sing,

Gather together in oneness

Gather together in peace

Gather together in oneness

Gather together in peace

May the feelings of love arise

May the feelings of love release

May the light within continue to shine

May the force of compassion begin to align

Beings of light, return to your center

Beings of light, prepare to reenter

Unity of pure light, unity of pure love

Pure light, pure love

Gather together in oneness

Gather together in peace, peace, peace

Smiling faces emanate loving feelings throughout the chamber, as the song ends. It is a splendid beginning for the momentous meeting.

Metatron speaks, "Thank you Kuan Yin, musicians, and choir for your heart-warming song. Indeed, gathering into oneness is essential for all souls who have forgotten that compassionate love emanates from deep within."

Rainbow Brigade Reunites

Michael says, "Yes. We seek to inspire humanity to understand that despite the negative illusions of life, they are loving beings within. Our council suggests the rainbow brigade, the caring light workers and stewards of their nations, form a mission to pave the way for this realization to occur."

Just then, above the revolving Gaea Star, an image appears of a group, all in similar attire. It is Azul, Mira, Celestia, Lakul, Teladi, Initamay, Kardichay, Rionarta, Teesha and Ilanu. A holograph emanates from their hearts, forming into one image in front. It is a sparkling rainbow star within a spiraling circle, surrounded by magenta, violet and golden light with feathers projecting out of the end.

Mira whispers, "Hey look. We're so cute in the front, there."

Celestia says, "Yes, I remember that wonderful moment."

Azul chimes in, "Seems like lifetimes ago when we joined the brigade to help preserve the well-being of the universe."

They glance at one another when suddenly their heart centers glow with the same symbol. They react as if they have never seen it radiate like that. It is a remarkable vision to witness.

Lakul stands, laughing, as he always loves the mysterious to take center stage. "We are ready. Let's rise up with renewed energy for healing the nations of confusion."

Azul jumps up, after he sees the glowing from within his heart becoming brighter - merging into brilliant rainbow light with the members of the brigade. They stand as if knowing something powerful is happening with them. He says, "We are energizing, as if we are already serving this very important cause."

Teladi speaks in an all-knowing manner, "Yes, we are reassembling our light forces. Michael knew what is needed for the betterment of humanity. We are activating, so be prepared, for the call may be soon."

Lakul says, "Okay, here we go on the wild flight to Gaea Star. I'm pumped for action. When do we leave?" He stretches as if he wants to be strong for what may be in the future for all of them.

Kardichay smiles. "Not yet. We're forming the energetic alignment to bring us to the forefront of the mission that lies ahead."

Celestia says, "I'm happy to help the cause of Gaea Star, at the request of Mother Isis, for she knows what is needed."

Teesha nods. She is drawing the glorious things in the chamber. It is the best chance to sketch what she can. "Any spare time is a new creative inspiration begun," is her abiding motto.

Initamay is enthusiastic to be in the midst of the many uplifting beings. "I'm grateful to experience this incredible adventure together. We make a good team." She hugs Celestia, Azul and Mira as nearby onlookers observe.

Archangel Raphael rises to address the chamber. "I agree with Michael. The rainbow brigade are wise esmissaries that will help humanity to realize who they really are, although it may take eons before accomplishing this. It is a daunting task to break through the shadowy grip overwhelming all their nations." Many heads nod, agreeing.

Metatron responds, "Alright then, it is essential that we approve. I ask the council to vote in favor of Michael's proposal by a yes or no. Laredo crystal, please appear."

Just then, small crystal orbs, float in, dropping in front of everyone, like an automatic voting device. They flicker. Some are surprised and others know what it is and exactly how to use it.

Metatron says, "The Laredo registers votes telepathically."

The chamber votes by lighting up their Laredo crystal with their thoughts. A positive answer is broadcast by a gold light blinking in the front, with a plus sign. It is obvious the voting is a favorable outcome. Smiles, and laughter abound with the result.

Upon seeing the 'Yes,' vote, Michael says, "Thank you council, for choosing the rainbow brigade, the highest option for all concerned. Let's act immediately as members of this fine band of gifted helpers are here. Brigade, please come to the council to share the skills you offer to aid this important mission." The brigade all stand at once.

Azul says, "We are prepared to heed the call." He is the first to walk to the center, Teesha and Mira go next, and then the rest of the brigade follow after them.

Many beings smile and look with wonder as these dynamic ones, weave through the crowded room with their holograms radiating from their hearts. Several stop the brigade to exchange congratulatory hugs before they arrive at the crescent council table.

Sinister Slake Finds His Cronies

Keme and Zoz, are bored hiding in the balcony behind a pillar. Since they're far from the center, they cannot see what is going on. Suddenly, Slake surprises them by popping up in front of the pillar they're leaning on. He signals to follow into the hall. They go with him. After he looks around to make sure the coast is clear, he says, "Good job, so far. Clever, Zoz, figuring the way in. Well done."

Keme and Zoz smile smugly. He continues, "Remember the sizable reward for thwarting this mission. Do not let them realize what your intentions are. We're counting on you to lead them astray. We plan to implement harvesting the planet's minerals for generating purposes. Stay in contact."

Zoz says, "Okay, boss, we'll do it." They quietly slip into the room, exactly where they were before.

Slake looks around to make sure no one is watching. He removes a small crystalline device from his pocket, and whispers into it, "Quadrant 444. I'm ready." Silently Slake dematerializes instantly in a puff of grey.

10

THE LIGHT WORKERS TALENTS

Azul's Peaceful Ways

The rainbow brigade assembles in front of the crescent table of the archangels. Michael stands, smiling. "Greetings, rainbow crystalla forces of light. The council and I welcome you. We thank you for bringing your good intentions here." He signals Azul to begin.

Azul stands proudly, "Thank you, Michael, council. I am Azul, emissary of compassionate communication, messenger of love. Wherever my light shines, people relax and listen. Peace is restored." He lifts his arms in an arc. Watery blue rays and healing fresh air flow through the chamber, calming everyone.

Archangel Gabriel smiles. "Thank you, Azul. We see your willingness to awaken humanity to their highest potential through the vibration of love."

He replies, "Yes, I believe only compassionate love will overcome suffering."

Gabriel nods. "Thank you, that is what they need to find their way home to that place within."

Mira, Sweet Singer

Azul glances at Mira. She smiles, thrilled to go next and says, "I am Mira. I hear gentle melodies of love and healing for all. Through my voice, I sing these divine inspirations." She waves her hands up, "Please join in if you feel called." The musicians and the choir reassemble and play along in support. She sings sweetly. Archangel Uriel and others join in. He loves to accompany uplifting music.

Restore, restore, restore the beauty of Gaea Star

Purify her water, purify her air, protect her ancient forests

Grandmother, Grandfather help us,

to live with purity, to love everyone equally

Unite as one people, come together as one world

Lay down your arms, to live as one in harmony

Restore balance, restore beauty

Giving Gaea Star a chance

She is the only Gaea Star we share

Beautiful Mother Earth, Gaea Star, Gaea Star

The chamber resounds with many singing, '*Gaea Star*' over and over again. Mira gives Uriel a warm hug, bowing gently, and turns to Celestia as the singing ends.

Celestia's Healing Light

"I am Celestia. I soothe those in need by sharing the luminous light energy of nurturing touch that exists throughout the realms, the stars, glorious suns, crystals, and all of nature's elements." She raises her arms up. Golden turquoise colors shower softly with feathery rays like soothing moonbeams, much to their delight, touching each one throughout the chamber.

Archangel Raphael, patron of healing, stands, "Celestia, we feel your pleasing energy emanating the golden light of love for all things. May humanity be blessed with your enduring touch."

"Thank you, Raphael. I love sharing warm healing energies as you do." He nods in acceptance. Michael waves to Rionarta to speak.

Rionarta, Crystal Caretaker

He stands proudly to say, "I am Rionarta, crystal caretaker of the seven realms. My knowledge of crystalline energies may assist in releasing the healing powers of Gaea Star." He reaches for a crystal wand from within his cloak, pointing it at the crystals in the room. Instantly, they glisten brightly, casting rainbows around the chamber. The colors swirl vibrantly in a dazzling display of geometric symmetry. An Om resounds, inspiring the choir to harmonize with the tone.

Michael gazes fondly at him, "Rionarta, impressive. I love how you demonstrated brilliant toning, and your unique skills in aligning with the crystalline vibration in the chamber. All of which is essential for the success of the mission to Gaea Star."

Rionarta says, "Thank you Michael. I am pleased to be of critical service there." He smiles as he signals Initamay to go next.

Initamay's Faerie's

Initamay speaks, "I am Initamay, plant medicine spirit teacher. Wherever I am, I commune with the faeries, that dwell in the living majesty of the many realms on Gaea Star. The little ones await our help to preserve her natural magnificence."

She takes a silver bell, ringing it three times. "Faeries, elves, please reveal your delightful selves." Instantly, faeries emerge from the plants in the room sailing here and there, surprising those who did not realize they were in their midst. They tinkle bells, singing, *Delight, delight, oh, what a live we live."*

Archangel Ariel joins in, as she is the protector of Gaea Star's wildlife and elemental faery realms. They keep singing.

We are from the spirit realm, lend us an ear

Put aside your troubles, gather near

Dance around faery rings, climb tall trees

Croak with frogs, hoot with owls

Quack with ducks, howl with coyotes

The faeries, and rambunctious singers from the chamber, mimic the funny animal sounds. Lakul especially loves to howl like a coyote.

Lighten up, lighten up, let your wings unfurl

We dance in meadows, in the full moonlight

Flowers are dresses, Foxgloves are hats,

Poppies, roses, tiger lilies, dutchman's breeches, too

We live in the forests, gardens and brooks

Here, there, wherever you don't look

Delight, delight, oh what a life we live

As the song ends, happiness permeates throughout the chamber. Everyone loved making the animal sounds which served to raise their energies.

Archangel Ariel says, "Initamay, thank you for sharing the delightful realms of nature."

"Thank you, Ariel. Faeries, please stay to visit," Initamay says. The faeries are thrilled, to flit about, joyfully mingling with the crowd. She goes to return to her seat when she senses something. She looks to the open ceiling in the center, hoping its Ilanu, finally.

Ilanu Reappears

Suddenly, a green ray blasts through the opening into the chamber, to land where the brigade is talking and holding the little faeries, sharing in their sweet delight. The ray flickers green briefly then transforms into green mist.

Initamay sighs with relief to see Ilanu appear out of the green mist, a little confused, with Emeraldina perched on his shoulder. She exclaims, "Emeraldina, Ilanu, just in time."

Ilanu looks embarrassed, after he realizes where he is. "Initamay, I'm sorry I'm late. You were right, the magic I tried in our wicked cool eye transport backfired, sending us to a distant galaxy. Thanks to this great faery, Emeraldina for helping Teladi and you turn us around. I'm just glad to stand on solid ground."

Emeraldina says, "It is my pleasure to return Ilanu. He is such a funny treasure."

Initamay says, "Thank you, Emeraldina for helping us out."

She says, "Why certainly." She flies to join the other faeries.

They sing, *"Welcome, Emeraldina. Here, there, delight, delight, oh what a life of light."*

Ilanu does not miss any chance to rhyme by saying, "Swell, it looks like we arrived just in time. Hey, it rhymes with who I am, a funny mime."

Initamay laughs. "Ilanu, welcome back. The council is waiting for you to express your talents for the Gaea Star mission."

"Sure thing, talents I bring." He quickly mimes a sequence of expressions about being too serious - something that never crosses his mind. He emphasizes the laughing aspects, like put on a happy face if you can, instead. He says, "As Ilanu, I invoke joyful mirth, inspiring the artist in all, to spring forth." A giant flower bursts from his hand as fragrant flowers float onto everyone with delight. He mimes their feelings, which causes the room to erupt in laughter. "Yes," he says, "that feels good. I bet you didn't know that it could." He has a wonderful jubilant effect wherever he goes."

Metatron laughs. "Well, son, you joyfully lifted our spirits. You inspire the child within to rise and sing the tune of happiness." He places a shiny gem in Ilanu's hand. "This is for your joyful work that lies ahead for you."

Ilanu is excited, "Thank you." He checks it out. "Wow, I love it. I always wanted a shiny rainbow gem, way back when."

"It's watermelon tourmaline, from Gaea Star, a remarkable rainbow reflective gem."

Ilanu says, "Yes." It is rare that he garners so much attention. He does a high-five handshake with Metatron, then proudly shows his gift to those nearby.

He senses Initamay trying to tell him something. She points to Teesha, it's her turn next. Ilanu understands and nods to her.

Teesha's Turn

He bows to Teesha, and rises up with a bouquet in his hand to give her. She takes it, sniffing the petals, sighing. "Oh, sweet. Thank you Ilanu." He bows again in an exaggerated manner. Presto, he brings a rose up to his heart while smiling at Teesha, who, by now, is blushing at the unfamiliar attention. The council easily sees what he is about, a clown magician - that is his renown.

Teesha, holding the bouquet and rose, addresses the council next. "As Teesha, I am inspired by creation's beauty. I paint the vivid colors of the force of life, of all creatures, of all things." She takes a rainbow fluorite crystal wand from her bag. Waving it, she says, "To my creations, in the ethers, please fly to me."

Several of her vibrant paintings fly through the open ceiling, landing in front of the council. Spectacular colorful rays swirl everywhere. The rays magically wake up the art, that decorates the chamber. The wonder-filled paintings dance alive, transformed into mini theaters that look like a three-dimensional showing.

One painting lands in front of Archangel Jophiel, the patron of the arts. She touches the panoramic scene. Smiling, she says, "Yes, Teesha, we see your creativity captures the sweet essence of the wonderful living vitality of the colors of the universe."

Teesha says, "Thank you, creations, please fly home now." She waves her wand. Her paintings fly through the roof, leaving a wispy trail of yellow rays. The chamber paintings settle down into being quiet paintings again. Every so often, they flicker colorfully as if remembering the magic, she invoked.

Kardichay, Master Builder

Kardichay goes next. "Hello to all. I am Kardichay, engineer of light energy technology. I utilize the vast supply of natural resources, in my building projects, including crystals that exist everywhere. This conscious ecological method does not harm the precious elements of Gaea Star or in other realms."

Archangel Raziel floats up, saying, "Kardichay, your talents are appreciated in many dominions. Please show your fine work."

Right then, a scene rises from the revolving holographic of Gaea Star, where Kardichay is carrying a shiny crystal while overseeing construction of a futuristic temple project. He maintains the living resources there, leaving trees in their natural state for side walls. Large crystals are placed strategically to generate energy, and solar panels fill the roofs aplenty to harness the solar rays.

Vestara from the Pleiades, stands, "Very impressive. What is the crystal you are working with?"

Kardichay responds, "Thank you. It is diaspore, my favorite tool for working with unseen, yet important energies that are inherent in all aspects of environmental building. Diaspore enables me to be clear, and adaptable to everything we encounter along the way. Through my efforts, buildings such as the Sirius Star center, were erected as naturally as possible."

Vestara nods, "Thank you for crafting with such attentive wisdom. May all nations use your example, of noninvasive technological growth to conserve their planet's resources, with minimal damage to the lands and waters."

Lakul's Fitness Powers

Kardichay nods, stepping aside for Lakul, who speaks in a deep voice, "I am Lakul. I teach awareness of the physical, to realize the body is a gift to treasure - a temple, to enjoy a long healthy life with. Yes, it is so." He stretches, showing off his handsome self, strength, and prowess - then does a limber move, ending with a loud huff. He looks at everyone with a happy expression. "All right. Are we ready to get up to groove, after too long-sitting?" He beats a rhythm on a drum from his bag. "Come on now. All who are able. Rise and shine. Let's stretch to the heavens together." He dances as he plays the drum.

At first, everyone is surprised, but a few stand, others follow. Ganesh joins in as he loves having fun. The musicians are revved up. You know how getting up to dance works. People are shy until someone makes the first move to venture out to the floor or volunteers for a demonstration on stage.

Many beings start to dance, doing their best. Soon the chamber is laughing, and moving to his upbeat energetic mannerisms, including Lucifer, who tries to keep up. Seems as if the archangels may lead a rather serious existence.

Finally, Lakul stops and exclaims, "Excellent. Didn't that feel good?" Beings nod, yes, they are exhilarated, due to his charismatic fitness energy.

Ganesh, all tuned up, enjoyed the dancing. He says, "Lakul you're a master of shifting energy to get the life force flowing. What a gift you'll bring to Gaea Star, to help motivate, and stimulate lives in positive ways." Lakul nods and hums as he dances to his seat while those nearby smile at him.

Ayalasha, Purple Ray Priestess

Ayalasha gracefully stands next, to speak. "As Ayalasha, I bloom hearts wide open, especially children of all ages, through the enchanted arts of music and theater. I love to inspire creativity, to awaken humanity from their deep slumber, to enable living in appreciation of the beauty and oneness with all creation."

She takes a beaded star rattle from her cape, to give to Ashento to shake while she plays on her ukulele like instrument. The musicians join. Purple rays encircle her, as she sings, *"I am the queen, queen of the heavens."* Images of happy beings, dancing and singing in flamboyant costumes, arise out of the revolving Gaea Star. It is delightful to see Gaea Star's sweet face peering out from her once again, pristine, green lushness surrounded with swirling blue waters. Ayalasha sings while Ashento touches her shoulder for all to see as he rattles a beat and hums along.

Dream with me, dance along your journey, home to the stars

It's all the same paradise from here to Gaea Star

Breathe in light, love and peace,

within your heart, within your soul

as you weave your web of life,

in paradise, in the universe

Surrender to the beauty within,

to the beauty above,

to the beauty of the fertile ground

Look around, look around

Nature's elements, wind, water, fire, earth

Pretty ethereal spirits dance around Gaea Star; the green earth, the light filled air, the warm fire, and silvery blue flowing waters. Its' as if they're faeries, touching everyone, gently, as Ayalasha sings the last line, *"You are alive, you are alive, in the wonders of Paradise."*

The elements fade as Gaea Star spirit sighs, "Thank you sweet Ayalasha. I am honored."

She smiles at Gaea Star, "You are most welcome. We love you, Mother Gaea Star." Such an uplifting serene energy now pervades in the chamber. Ashento touches her lovingly as she sits again. He is so pleased with her.

Ashento, Master Teacher

Ashento stands proudly, removing his cape as he glances adoringly at Ayalasha. A significant hush prevails throughout the chamber while those in the rear, strain to see why so many upfront are enthralled with his appearance. He does not look like anyone else. It is the fabulous geometric tattoos arrayed in symbology, all over his body that are causing the distinct murmurings. The air is rich with anticipation of what he is going to say.

Metatron says, "Welcome, Ashento. Thank you for presenting your incredible prayer that reflects the sacred pattern of the Tree of Life."

Ashento smiles, "Thank you, Metatron. Yes, it is a strong prayer for my beloved Gaea Star." He turns around to enable all in the chamber to clearly see the designs. The circular patterns revolve like Gaea Star. The stars throughout the design, sparkle and glisten in the light. Everything he is wearing looks so alive.

He speaks, "I am Ashento, teacher of esoteric wisdom of the high Crystalla. I share my knowledge to revitalize harmonious living on Gaea Star, the planet of blue waters where I lived so long ago."

A holographic image of his book, *The Teachings of Ashento* appears before the council and in the chamber for all to look at. A quote from the book, flashes at the center,

"As a messenger of spirit, be the hands, the voice, an example of love to shine, to reflect the deep abiding love that flows eternally from one's spirit into life. As you walk this peaceful path, share the light of radiance, of joyful happiness and true communion with Divine Source. Become a visionary way shower, a beacon of light in your community, as an open, expressive, positive, fully integrated being within."

There is interest in reviewing the book's content. Chamuel says, "Yes, we see your profound wisdom is far reaching." Many nod. Ashento smiles as he sits next to Ayalasha. She touches him in affection, with a smile of approval.

Teladi - White Light Bearer

Teladi speaks, "Thank you, Michael for summoning your dynamic brigade from the universe. Council, I am Teladi, master of telepathy and spiritual studies. Crystals of power, I call you."

Four crystalline pillars spring up around him. They are the ones that formed the base for his crystal ship. He smiles at everyone, saying, "The minds of humanity are veiled so deeply that they must relearn how to awaken to the truth, that they are masters of their own destiny." He closes his eyes as if concentrating within his mind.

Just then, several beings stand up in the chamber, looking confused and surprised, as if it was not their own idea. Teladi must have directed them as a demonstration of his telepathic ability. The first one speaks, "Adonai, the light is always shining within."

The other says, "I accept the teachings of spiritual transformation that enhance awareness of my true self." Both are stunned by what transpired. They sit and try to make sense of their experience, whispering with those near to them.

Archangel Azrael, patron to all teachers, stands. "Teladi used telepathic abilities to encourage these two to express what their souls know deep within. He is truly a master to assist with the esoteric aspects of human life."

Tall resonator crystals start humming throughout the chamber, a low Om tone, like the ancient vibration that emanates deep within the cellular fabric of all life. Everyone in the chamber breathes slower, becoming relaxed. The energy is silent and peaceful. Teladi says, "Yes, this is what all souls feel when the thoughts of the internal mind are put to rest."

Metatron speaks, "Thank you, Teladi for revealing such unique skills. You are gifted to lead the reawakening. We thank all of the brigade for coming forward. The council is fortunate to meet such an inspired, dynamic group, proposed by Michael. They may be the next wave of visionary light beings to embark on the Gaea Star mission. Brigade, please visit the Diyanna gardens while the council discusses further aspects of this mission."

Angel Ohm floats up, waving for them to follow. They go with her, excited for the next adventure of this dramatic day.

Lucifer's Element

Lucifer rises, "Excuse me, Metatron, council. May I add an element to aid the Gaea Star project? It may enable their success."

Metatron replies, "Oh, what is it?"

Lucifer answers, "Well, I have not come to any conclusions yet, as to what that may be, but in due time."

Metatron says, "Yes, all right then, council, please vote if you agree to Lucifer adding an element for the mission." The attendees vote telepathically blinking the golden lights in front of them.

Lucifer acknowledges the positive answer when it is visible, by holding his arms up. "Thank you, council, I shall go to meditate, to discern what the mission truly needs. I will return soon." He leaves the council, rubbing his chin, murmuring, deep in thought. "Now then, what do they truly need to establish the most favorable outcome?"

Hot on the Trail

Meanwhile, Keme and Zoz, tucked in the corner, have been waiting for action but since they are too far away to see what is going on down there, they are falling asleep. Zoz happens to look up just then and notices far below, the brigade going out with Angel Ohm. "Keme, looks like they're the ones that may be going to Gaea Star. She's with them too."

Keme asks, "Who?" He can't see anything either.

Zoz answers, "You know, the woman we saw on the road coming here and in the arts room. Let's go to keep an eye on them."

They slip into the hallway to stay close. As they walk, several beings pass by, talking. One says, "Now that they're going to the garden while the council meets, let's take a quick break."

Zoz smiles after hearing where they are going. It was too hard to understand what was happening in the center. He gives a thumbs up to Keme who nods with enthusiasm. He is finally starting to enjoy the job a little. Since Keme grew up on his grandpa's farm, he says confidently, "Feels like we're taking the fastest way to the outside. The garden is behind or on the side of the building. A back door always brings you to it for easy access."

For once, Zoz follows Keme. They slink down the hall, opening doors until Keme finds the right one. "Yes." They check if the coast is clear. It is. They go out and quickly crouch in the bushes to figure out what to do next, not wanting to be seen.

Keme whispers, "Let's wait here in case they return."

Zoz adds, "Yeah, they may go by, or we'll hear them up ahead." They stay for a while until they realize the brigade is not returning too soon. Slowly they set off walking in search of the brigade.

Part 6

Diyanna's Gardens

11

BOTANICAL DELIGHTS

Angel Ohm sings as she leads the brigade along a winding stone pathway with lush blooming plants adorning both sides. She flows beneath an ornately carved, reddish crystal-encrusted archway, which immediately flashes golden lights.

Teladi follows but this time, pure white lights zing out all over. He is not deterred. He continues walking into the gardens, saying, "Interesting, must be a direct result of the vibrational essence which passes beneath."

Rionarta goes next under the arch. Brilliant reds flash. "Fascinating, it must be imbedded with a magnifier crystal to amplify the energy generated by whatever walks under it."

Kardichay leans beneath the arch to see how it works. Red lights flash. "I see, it's rhodizite set in the archway to act as subtle energy detectors. The more rhodizite, the better. They enhance the vibrational components that reveal the true energetic essence."

Rionarta replies. "Excellent to know. Thanks." He looks beyond the pathway. "I'm going to see the interesting crystals ahead. There are some I'm not familiar with." Off he goes.

Ilanu is so excited with the unusual portal that he can't wait any longer, so he rushes by the others, to pass under the archway. When the lights flash green, he says, "Amazing, an energy reader. How does it light up?" He is enchanted by its mysterious magic, so he goes back and forth, to see how it works.

Finally, Initamay says, "Yes, Ilanu. It's cool, but we're waiting, so please get going."

He steps aside to let the others pass beneath the archway, calling out the different colors that flash, "Teesha - mellow yellow, Initamay - lime green, Celestia - rainbow gold, Mira - turquoise, Azul - blue, Lakul - orange, Ayalasha - violetta, Ashento - royal blue. How nice, what a clever device."

The brigade smiles but they are more interested in what lies ahead so they keep going into the garden. Only Ilanu and Kardichay remain.

He says, "Ilanu, this is a fascinating portal," as he closely admires the crystals and rhodizite in the archway.

Bursting with curiosity, Ilanu keeps setting it off by sticking his arm beneath it to trigger the green light response. He says, "I'm not leaving until I understand this. So, when you pass, it reads the energy, and different lights are triggered, hmm."

Kardichay, amused, says, "Ilanu, the sensors are packed with rhodizite crystals."

Ilanu asks, "Sensors, but how does it flash different colors?"

Kardichay replies, "Not sure. Let's check it out." He goes to the side to see while Ilanu gets on his knees to crawl around the base of the archway. He bumps into a cool striped cat with no tail.

"Meow," the cat says as it brushes against his leg.

"Hey, hello. Kitty, kitty. Where do you hail from without a tail?"

Cats are his favorite creatures. He loves how they're like tigers, which are next on his list. "You must be from the island of Man in the Irish Sea. I remember studying about Manx cats, that lived in the cool castles."

The cat likes him and keeps rubbing his leg. Ilanu sits on the ground petting him for a few minutes. Then the cat slinks into the jungle trees with Ilanu following, forgetting Kardichay and the mystery of the crystal archway. They soon play hide and seek in the trees - the cat being a tiger and Ilanu in sneaky pursuit.

Kardichay calls "Ilanu," after he disappears - no response. He gives up looking and ventures into the tropical surroundings. He is intrigued by a massive, towering tree with rainbow-striped bark. He thinks, "*What is this fine specimen with such smooth-colored bark?*

He sits beneath the long hanging leaves that are exuding a distinct menthol smell. "Hmm, such a great fragrance." The energy and agreeable aroma of the peaceful tree, relaxes him so well that he puts his head against the tree, closes his eyes, and falls asleep. He has had many eventful days recently.

Meanwhile Mira, Celestia, Initamay and Teesha, are thrilled to explore the gardens of colorful plants, abundant fruiting trees, flowing fountains, exotic birds, and sparkling crystals.

An ethereal angel looking like a ladybug, flows to them, smiling, singing, *"Welcome to Diyanna gardens, where all wishes for happiness and blessings, may blossom into fruition. Please enjoy our delightful play land."* She floats through a flower doorway, singing, *"Delight, delight, oh what a life we have."*

Teesha sighs, "Wow, a caring ladybug angel, to greet us in such a friendly way."

Initamay adds, "That's auspicious to meet her. She came to remind us that life is not meant to be serious, to lighten up, to play."

Celestia says, "All right then, let's go."

Initamay says, "Okay," and follows her along with Mira and Teesha. They sniff every flower, lingering for long moments to inhale the delightful fragrances which, of course, prevents them from getting far.

Initamay wanders away when she sees dried flowers ready to pick. She never likes to pluck flowers when fresh to let them be flowers for as long as they want too. She loves to collect plant materials for her pouch that dangles around her waist. She takes it off to fill it with petals and places it on a stone in front of her. Celestia waves to come see a beautiful flower. She goes over to see and forgets to pick up her medicine bag.

Celestia takes out a flat clear crystal to use as a magnifier. She bends down to peer into the inflorescences of the flowers, to see their artful creations. After checking out the beckoning flowers together, they walk off in other directions.

Initamay is enticed by pretty lilac flowers and leans in to talk to a few faeries she sees in there. "Hello, lilacs, lovely to see you." She waves to Mira, Teesha, and Celestia to come. They quickly go over as they know she really sees faeries.

"Look, can you see their lilac faces?" They peer at the flowers expectantly, but no one sees anything yet. "Go close. Look beyond what you think, you may be graced to see their sweetness. There." She points to a smiling face. "Hello, gentle one."

Mira peers into the petals closely. Delighted, she says, "Yes, I see her long eyelashes and sparkling tiny white shell earrings."

Teesha peers in too. "I see her. I love her turquoise wings."

Celestia leans in close to say, "Oh, yes, faery faces. Is there a faery in every flower? If so, I want to examine them again. How did I miss such cute faces?"

Initamay replies, "Well, try relaxing to commune with every plant, to see their living sweetness. They will happily show you."

Celestia says, "Thanks for helping me see their spirits. I wonder where these flowers are from. I'm going to look for a gardener to ask." She goes off in search of someone who knows the plants.

Mira, Teesha and Initamay are so involved in meeting the flower faeries, they forget about anything else until they are drawn elsewhere. Teesha finally takes a moment to herself. She is content to be in a lovely spot to do what she loves. She retrieves paper from her pouch and sits on a grassy pillow to sketch the flower and faerie faces using her colored pencils.

Mira dips her fingers into a gushing fountain, as she leans on an unusual multicolored rock. She sings a gentle melody to the waters, *"Oh, how I love the holy waters, they heal me so."* She closes her eyes and settles there, singing softly and soon drifts off into peaceful slumber. She could always easily nap if the situation was just right, and this is the perfect setting.

Lakul is vigorously doing a power workout near several orange trees that are bursting with fruit. He leans over to pick the closest fruit hanging, peels it, and pops a luscious piece into his mouth. His eyes light up. "Hmm, tastes as good as it looks. Orange, what a great ray for the body." He enjoys feeling energized by moving and stretching. An orange ray flashes deep in the trees, as if calling him, so off he goes to check it out.

Teladi discovers a quiet spot near the waterfalls complete with four tall crystalline selenite spires along the edge of one side. He sits in the middle of them, and immediately, bluish white rays, emanate and surround him. "Ah, a moment to replenish my body, mind and spirit." It is his favorite pastime, contemplation.

Ayalasha and Ashento snuggle on an ornate love seat crafted out of tree branches, plants and luscious roses, hanging luxuriously down. Ayalasha says, "Ashento, you said we know each other, but I do not remember where we met."

He speaks, "My sweetness, we are twin flames united through our divine spiritual birth together. Our paths led us onto different realms eons ago. That is when you forgot about me. Or did you my dear? Have you not felt the inner longing that I do?"

Ayalasha says, "Yes, I feel a warm, familiar love in my heart in your presence. Your energetic light is very powerful. However, my endearing spouse awaits my return."

Ashento responds, "Yes, he is fortunate, but you are a goddess worth waiting for." He reaches for her to snuggle close. She responds by tucking into his strong body. They remain enraptured until a cloud of magenta mist rises in front of them.

Vision from the Alaymytia Faery Realms

The wispy mist dissipates into a flickering vision of the two-winged horses, from Ayalasha's planet - the black and white ones - flying into the atmosphere of a planet, similar in appearance to Gaea Star.

They descend into a forest, to a clearing where faerie folk and an uncommon array of woodland animals are gathered. With a dramatic fluttering of their massive shiny wings, they land in front of a faerie couple, adorned in royal attire, wearing green-gold sparkly crowns. Everyone gathers to see what is going on, for the arrival of the winged horses is a rare event.

The black horse bows his regal head to the couple as his wild shimmering mane brushes the ground. He raises his head when the faerie queen touches his neck. "Lartimus, we welcome you and Ishima."

He speaks reverently, "Queen Oonalia, King Tubaiyo, our beloved Ayalasha, was summoned to Star Sirius for a universal meeting about the crisis on Gaea Star."

Oonalia, stroking his neck, says, "Yes, Lartimus, we heard of her departure. Isis prepared our kinfolk, long ago, to be ready to share healing love with our sister, Gaea Star. She is so in need of her people living with harmonious respect."

Oonalia calls out into the forest beyond the faery folk gathered. "Mystical guardians of the forest, legendary friends to all creatures, near and wide, we ask you to please come forward."

Rayanca and Luina - Unicorns

Two magnificent unicorns, a stallion, and a mare, walk slowly from behind the gathering. The little ones quickly clear the way for their large hooves. They come and regally stand before Oonalia and Tubaiyo. The sun light filters softly through the trees, highlighting their lustrous coats, like golden auras floating.

Oonalia speaks, "Dear Rayanca, Luina, revered beings, from deep within these magical realms. We ask you to escort us to our beloved Gaea Star, to inspire the humans who forgot who they really are, who forgot their wild spirits within, and that life is pure enchantment in their earthly, paradise of Gaea Star."

Surprised cries of dismay erupt among the kinfolk, after hearing these words. An elf says, "Queen Oonalia, King Tubaiyo, we will miss your guiding presence."

She responds, "Dear family, you know that we will return when love and lasting peace has returned to Gaea Star. We love our peaceful, beautiful, Alaymytia."

The concerned fey relax, some nod yes. Rayanca, and Luina commune by rubbing their spiraling horns together. He steps forward to speak, "Luina and I will love to join this noble endeavor to inspire unity and restore the precious balance on Gaea Star."

Yes, unicorns have the uncanny ability to communicate in the same manner as humans and faeries can, simply because they have the power to transform by shape shifting. If you remember Ashento and the angelic ones, Mira, Celestia and Azul, also underwent transformational changes when they flew to Star Sirius.

All things are possible when you believe in magic, and the Gaea Star Crystal story is full of amazing perceptions beyond our normal realities. This is the ancient art of storytelling, sharing timeless wisdom in a creative, engaging manner.

Luina steps proudly, tossing her mane and says, "Our presence may revive joyous lightness of being and the belief in the magical fantasy of life, seen and unseen."

Oonalia smiles. "Thank you for journeying with us. You live with majestic honor for life's wonders."

The mystical beings lovingly look at the faery kin, thinking of what it means to be also leaving their beloved family so soon. Rayanca says, "Wee ones, hop on for a last ride."

Faeries crowd around, clamoring for a lift up by the tall ones. It's funny since none of the little ones are big enough to reach. The unicorns are massive compared to the tiny kinfolk.

Rayanca and Luina know their limitations, so they lower their necks, bending their front legs as far as possible, while the elves and faeries climb on or try to fly onto their backs. They are teeny, tiny, and may not even know how to fly yet. Some bump into each other in a huffy puffy effort to get up there, but all in all, the fairy kin are laughing and happy. No one is upset if they accidentally get a wing or a pointy hat in their face or wherever.

Besides, who cares, when you're having so much fun? It is just such a thrill to be on the stately unicorns. Maybe they'll get to slide down their long spiral unicorn, since that is the most fun of all. Yes, the little ones are enjoying this last precious fun-time with their favorite, wondrous friends.

Rayanca and Luina happily prance around, very pleased to feel the kin enjoying their exciting rides. They'll miss the wee ones too. A little elf says, "We love your fun sprees. Hurry back, please, Uncle Rayanca and Auntie Luina."

Luina says, "Of course, we will never forget you, for you are within our hearts forever as our deepest treasures."

Rayanca says, "My dears, we'll return when it is possible."

A Great Change in Alaymytia Realm

Oonalia says to the horses, "Lartimus, Ishima, please watch over all of the forest kin during our absence."

Ishima bows her head as she swishes her lustrous tail. "We will care for our forest family as lovingly as you two did."

King Tubaiyo steps into the circle and raises his crystal staff to give a blessing. "Farewell friends. We lovingly carry you deep within. Please do join us on Gaea Star. Let's sing a farewell song."

The faerie kin respond to what just transpired. Voices speak all together. Anxiety, mixed with excitement. The changes are happening swiftly. For some, it is sudden. After all, they live peacefully in this dell, usually undisturbed, until recently when the veils between the realms began to crumble from the encroaching disturbances out there.

Three of the Fey gather close, a bright purple faery with sparkly crystals tucked into her dress, a slinky blue water nymph, and a green elf with a funny crooked hat and staff.

The purple faery says, "Of course we're coming after the festival of sweet blossoms is over. We love Gaea Star, especially her exotic flowers and magical crystals." She flits about as if she is gathering her things that seem to be all over the land and in the trees, just about everywhere. She mumbles in a strange language as if talking to someone who hears her.

The water nymph says, "I'll slide into the pure rushing rivers and exquisite waterfalls. I know they flow on delightfully."

The green elf hops and waves his staff, while trying to keep his floppy hat, from falling off, due to being off balance by a huge feather stuck in the side. He proudly says, "Yes, yes, that's us. We're not gonna miss the bus. Whizzing past the stars, to sail by Mars, to play on Gaea Star." How he loves to rhyme, all the time. It is so sublime.

Several other faeries comment, "Yes, we're coming."

"Right after we care for our mushroom and flower gardens."

"Wait for me, I have to go home to my family first."

An elf trio steps into the circle, carrying homemade musical instruments. They sit on tree stumps to play. An elf with a green flowing cape blows an echoing melody from his long wooden flute. The royal couple start off the dance first and then the kinfolk joins in. They dance as a light voice sings, *"Di di di di di di di,"* then they join in as the voice keeps singing.

Let's sail to the realms of Mother Gaea

on the path of the stars

Let's sail to the realms of Mother Gaea

on our divine mission

To awaken humanity to live in truth and love

To awaken the tribes of light, to remember who they are

Everyone hugs goodbye. What fun to be a faery and sing about going to Gaea Star. It's true. The faeries came to Gaea Star, to inspire imaginative wonder to all those that forgot its original magic.

Awaken, awaken, awaken tribes of light

Awaken, awaken, awaken tribes of love

Oh heya, heya, heya, heya Oh heya, heya, heya ho

We'll live in faerie realms of nature

her fire, water, air, and earth

We'll live in the forest, in the trees, in the flowers, in the breeze

We'll live with the birds, rivers and golden leaves

Growing gardens on Gaea with joy and inspiration

On to Mother Gaea, helping humanity, remember their way home

Through love, light, love only love

Awaken, awaken, awaken the tribes

Awaken, awaken, tribes of love

Awaken, awaken, tribes of peace, awaken

The expressive song ends with the haunting flute as a misty rain drifts in as if to say goodbye. The unicorns rear up with passionate enthusiasm for the adventure that lies ahead. Large opalescent wings emerge from them as they circle around for a moment and then fly to where the royal couple are waiting.

The faeries leap onto their backs, waving goodbye to their beloved faery folk. They look so tiny on the massive unicorns. Off they fly high into the sky leaving trails of rainbow light. The faery folk keep hugging and singing as they watch them sail away.

It is an auspicious transformation for the community and their realm. Yes, they knew this moment, called the grand shift, or the great awakening for humanity, was to happen someday. It was predicted centuries ago in many cultures, by the Maya, the Hopi, Nostradamus, and others. Called the eagle-condor prophecies, the end times of the Bible, and the dawning of the age of Aquarius.

The faery forest is pregnant with the promise of a new and better world for all, with hope to cast out the shadows of deception and greed, to lift the illusions that bind, with the understanding that love is the only way to forever transform Gaea Star.

Royal Fey & Unicorns in the Gardens

Suddenly, in a burst of radiant light, the mighty unicorns with the faeries still nestled on their necks, dramatically fly out of the vision to land right in front of Ayalasha and Ashento who were watching the scenario the whole time while on the love seat. Surprised, they rise to approach the unicorns where they stand, panting from their intense speedy journey they just completed.

Ayalasha says with wonder, "Oh, you are handsome, and beautiful and so strong." She reaches to touch Rayanca with great compassion, asking, "May I? Who are you?"

Rayanca nods, tossing his mane. "I am Rayanca, and this is Luina. It's a pleasure to meet you, priestess of the purple ray."

Ayalasha runs her fingers lovingly up his sleek white horn and then touches Luina's as well. "Oh, it's so smooth, regal, and mystical, just as the legends described."

Ashento is also taken by their incredible stature. "The magnificence of the stately forest emanates from you two, as if we are there in the beautiful stillness. Thank you for aligning with this noble mission to Gaea Star."

Ayalasha smiles at the faeries. "Welcome, nature's sweet loving friends. Thank you, for coming so swiftly from Venus, our shining star of love."

Oonalia says, "Hello, dear ones. Yes, we flew as fast as the light of love, guided by Isis, to unite with the forces of light for the healing of humanity."

Tubaiyo adds, "Yes, we responded, since Gaea Star, is our kin's home too." Initamay, Teesha and Celestia rush over, after seeing the burst of light from the gardens. Mira woke from her nap and ran there too. They crowd around the unicorns and the faeries, enthralled to meet and touch them.

Rayanca and Luina regally bow their massive necks, with their lustrous long manes and tails, touching the earth. What a sight for unbelievers of unicorns' existence. It is undeniable. There they are, magnificently standing, with wings still fluttering.

The four introduce themselves. "Greetings, I am Initamay. What a rare delight to meet you in these enchanting gardens."

"Welcome, noble ones. Thank you for coming from deep within the far-away realms of your forest. I am Mira."

"Hello unicorns and faeries. What a glorious surprise. I am Teesha. You emanate the serenity of the emerald forest."

"Welcome. It is an honor to meet all of you. I sense your wonderful devotion to this mission to Gaea Star. I am Celestia."

"Thank you. May we join you?" Oonalia says. Her and Tubaiyo fly off the unicorns. She lands on the hand of Initamay.

Tubaiyo lands on Mira's hand. She squeals with delight, "Oh, you are so sweet. Thank you for being here."

He laughs, "It is a pleasure to meet you dear, Mira."

Oonalia says, "Hello, to each of you. Yes, our beloved sister Gaea Star is the utmost concern for all of us."

Initamay, smiles, saying, "We are blessed by your royal presence, Rayanca and Luina. The faeries of Gaea Star will be delighted to meet you two."

Rayanca speaks, "Thank you. We serve the dominions of nature, wherever called. We hope to inspire the beings of Gaea Star, to open to living in harmony for all to benefit."

Luina speaks, "Gaea Star was our first home. We have come to help her."

Initamay responds, "Yes, what a profound gathering of those who love her to restore the balance for her unique nations."

Ayalasha says, "We share the earth, warm fire, fresh water, pure air, and healing plants with the realms of the Fey. The preservation of her precious elements is most essential."

Oonalia smiles, "Thank you, we are forever grateful. May you nurture her as you care for your home stars. What a unified presence we will make there."

Rionarta and Azul arrive breathless, with wonder, after running to the action. The bountiful garden and mineral collections had drawn them all over.

Kardichay was still sleeping under the branches of the exotic fragrant tree. He did not wake until an animal, perhaps a bird or squirrel, dropped seed pods on his head, as if to say, "Hey, wake up. You're missing the excitement."

He is sometimes slow to get going, but when the unicorns appeared, that was the push that prompted him to rush over to meet the unusual creatures.

The three are speechless, having never met such massive regal beings.

Ayalasha says, "They came quickly from Venus, the lovely sister planet, once they heard of the situation on Gaea Star."

Rionarta says, "Hello, I am Rionarta. Welcome. Thank you for coming to champion such a great cause."

Azul says, "Thank you. You will have a profound effect on those who have failed to live with loving intentions."

Kardichay says, "We are touched to see your devotion. Every being is vital to the success of this mission." Rayanca and Luina, nod in appreciation.

Meanwhile, two members are missing. Lakul was distracted exploring a cave, under a crystalline waterfall at the back of the gardens. He loves to investigate caves, especially to check out the stalactites and stalagmites. Once he went in, he kept going since he was following a luminous orange light that kept calling him. That's why he did not hear what was happening in the main part of the garden. He was so deep into the silence of the cave.

As for Ilanu, you never know what sidetracked him. He is hard to keep track of. The last time, he was playing with the cool cat in the jungle. He is still out of sight, as usual. Yes, he is easily diverted by everything exciting, and fun, fun, fun.

Is everyone accounted for? No. What about Keme and Zoz? Last seen they were pursuing the brigade before they got away as they went into Dianna's Garden with Angel Ohm.

Keme was proud when he picked the door that led down a path, saying, "We're close, this way." Off they went in hot pursuit of them.

Teladi's Grandmother Utawa

Teladi ambles up to meet the visitors and bursts into a smile, which is unusual for him. He recognizes the unicorns. Yes, their blessed appearance, rekindles a distant memory that went like this.

One bright spring day, when young Teladi walked with his grandmother, Utawa, through their sacred woods, they came upon a faery den that shimmered in the golden light of the morning dew.

The faeries were sleeping perhaps, for no one was there. It was the first time that Teladi saw the den. Usually, it was hidden behind the veils between the faery and the human realms.

His grandmother, Utawa, was a medicine healer, who knew the secrets into their realms quite well. She tossed out flower petals and a few crystals. "For the little ones. They reveal themselves only if they know you love and care for their home, mother earth. So, enjoy her beauty and give, give, give away, something every day." Instantly in a flash, a community of faeries appeared, filling the den with playing and gardening faeries.

"Yes, you see, grandson, the faeries were here all along. Life is the same. Everywhere one lives, the veils can easily be lifted through love, love, love."

Teladi reached into his pocket where he stashed the treasures from his adventures. He took out a shiny crystal from the riverbed - a long wand with a pointy end. He held it to his forehead, like a unicorn, saying, "I am the king of the ancient forest. I call forth the power of majesty to appear before me as your prince of magic."

Do you know what happened? Well, you can imagine the look on little Teladi when a misty rainbow appeared with two huge unicorns flying within it, into the den, to land next to Teladi.

Utawa heartily laughed with gusto. "Ahh, yes, you do have the gift, just as I dreamed. You are the one to carry the rainbow healing vision to the masses. They will need such wisdom. Teladi, let's meet the ones of majesty you called. Hello, noble rainbow carriers of light. I am Utawa from the village of Atelio."

Teladi stood proudly. "I am Teladi. Wow, you are so big and carry immeasurable magical energy."

Rayanca bowing with his spiral horn going up and down, said, "We know of your grandmother, from the crystal legends before the veils covered the lands. Hop on to journey through our forest with me."

Teladi looks to his grandmother for permission, and she, of course, nods approval. He lifted up quickly. It was very easy to get on, as all boys knew how to ride horses back then.

As they trotted through the faery realm, Rayanca introduced Teladi to faery and animal friends. What a thrilling experience, for such a promising crystal wizard to be. Sure to never be forgotten.

Teladi returns from reliving that pleasurable foray into the faery realm, back to Dianna's gardens, where the friendly unicorns are standing proudly before the rainbow brigade.

He says, "Hello, Rayanca, Luina. I greet you with deep pleasure again. Oh, so many winds have passed between us. They're too many I'm afraid."

Rayanca prances while Luina nods her head. They rub their necks on his shoulder, like a loving hug.

Rayanca says, "Teladi, you are welcome. The forest kin have missed you."

Luina says, "Where we are led in life, is often a mysterious graceful wonder. We hold you with admiration, Teladi. You mobilize the truth that meditation and love soothes all troubles."

Teladi is humbled by their majestic presence again. "Thank you. I am honored, Rayanca and Luina. Yes, humanity needs your powerful impact to remember their lightness of being. We will be a team of loving helpers to grace her lands."

The others crowd around to converse with the faeries and to take turns touching the unicorn's golden spiral horns.

Teesha says, "Oonalia, I love your colors and crowns. May I sketch you two?"

"Yes, of course," replies Oonalia.

Mira goes to Teesha holding Tubaiyo in her hand so she can draw him.

"Thanks, Mira," Teesha says.

Initamay says, "Here you go." She comes over with Oonalia fluttering on her fingers. Teesha is delighted and takes her pad to sketch all of them right then.

12

THE COUNCIL CHOOSES

After the attendees in the chamber enjoy a tea and fruit snack, they discuss Michael's suggestion for the rainbow brigade to go to Gaea Star. Metatron greets the council, "As you see this brigade of gifted helpers, are willing to go on this crucial mission. Are there any further concerns or is the chamber ready to vote?"

A being stands, "I am Ikabayo from Unaikota. We express our gratitude for Michael's dynamic brigade. We believe they are the perfect choice to reclaim the beautiful Gaea Star, before the crisis becomes totally out of control. No one else stepped forward to offer their services since they know that the rainbow crystallas, the brigade of light, are the ones suited to go there for now."

Many nod, agreeing without commenting while Michael, Isis and several archangels whisper about Ashento.

Metatron stands, "Council, the crystal vortex awaits your light again. Please vote yes or no for Michael's rainbow brigade for the Gaea Star mission." The council telepathically cast their votes when the Laredo crystal drops in front again. Most votes are yes. The brigade, holographically appears in the center like a group photo.

"Yes," says Metatron, "it is good to see the affirmative votes. This is fortunate for Gaea Star, as the council feels they will succeed in reawakening the essence of love there." Michael and the archangels, nod in agreement.

Metatron signals to Angel Ohm, saying, "Please, Angel Ohm, have them return from the garden."

She floats through the door, passing beneath the crystal archway which flickers a brilliant golden light. She goes to the ones clustered around the unicorns and the faeries. Smiling, she says, "Greetings, brigade. I hope you enjoyed the lovely gardens. The council awaits your return. Hello, Rayanca and Luina. It is a pleasure to see you ventured from the rainbow forest sanctuary of illumination and healing."

Luina says, "Hello. Yes, Angel Ohm. We were drawn to help reunite humanity, as one family of love."

Rayanca adds, "Yes, we are escorting our leaders of the Alaymytia dell since we all care about Gaea Star."

Oonalia flies to Angel Ohm. "We pledge to happily bless humanity with our peaceful loving delight. Tubayio and I will enjoy visiting these lovely gardens while we await further instructions."

Angel Ohm says, "Welcome, Oonalia and Tubaiyo. Splendid. Brigade, please, the chamber assembly awaits."

The group walks to the archway entrance, except, Lakul and Ilanu. Initamay starts to go but looks for Ilanu and does not see him. She calls, "Hey, Ilanu. Where are you? We need to go back."

"Lakul is not here either," Teladi says, "no sign of him. He's been gone a while."

Initamay laughs, saying, "I know." She whistles, then yells, "Ilanu, Lakul." Her piercing tone echoes all over the gardenss.

Ilanu pokes his head up, through a maze of vines at the base of a tree at the back of the garden. "I'm here. Sorry, I'm coming. Bye, cool cat, even if we do not chat."

His new friend, is hanging off a tree, having fun with him. He hops down to rub on Ilanu's leg and watches him run to catch his group as he says, "Hey wait, no leaving. I'm coming." Mister Cool follows him at his slow but steady pace. Ilanu is excited to meet the brigade gathered by the crystal archway. This time, he goes first underneath, and it flashes green. He says, "Hey, I forgot about the crystal sensor contraption. Wish I had time to explore this." He keeps stepping under, then out and back again. Everyone is amused by his antics, rather than be bothered.

The Cave of the Orange Ray

Rionarta reminds the group. "Lakul is missing. I'll call his sensor. It's a great tool for communication anywhere." He reaches into his crystal pouch for a small white crystalline point. Yes, it's a Natrolite sensor to access between the dimensions. Holding it close to his forehead, he thinks. *Lakul, we're called to return to the chambers.* The crystal flickers three times, each time, a little brighter. He returns it to his pouch.

Lakul was almost to the end of the cave, searching for the source of the orange light, when his sensor goes off in his pocket. Surprised, he takes it out to hold to his forehead to listen to the message. He says, "Okay. I'm coming. I was nearly there. Well, next time for sure. I hope I can find it."

He turns to leave, but hears a whisper, "Master Lakul, we await your return." Startled, Lakul turns to see who is speaking, but no one is there.

"Hmm, yes." He senses something within. "Spirit of the orange cave, I will follow the easiest path to return to your grace swiftly. Until then, my curious energy will always remember you."

He hears whispering, "Yes, that is true, Lakul. We know you are an honorable man of your word. As you walk the path out of the cave, pay attention, if anything drops. It is yours to cherish."

Lakul says, "Yes, I'm aware. Thank you. I know your word is true." He returns halfway through the cave when his arm brushes against the wall. It loosens something which falls with a plink.

Since it is so dark, Lakul takes out his sensor, which automatically lights up when you need it. "All right. What do we have here?" He shines his light on the ground. He sees a smooth reddish-orange glowing stone and picks it up to hold close to his heart. "Thank you, cave spirit for the blessing of this gift." He rubs the stone gently. Suddenly it flickers a warm orange glow.

A voice whispers, "I am Carnelian. I serve, inspire, activate, and impart fearless courage to tackle everything enthusiastically."

"Ah!" Lakul takes in a breath. "Yes, I feel your strength already. Thank you, Master Carnelian, I am at your service."

He places the carnelian in his pocket and walks through the cave, the jungle area, past the flowers and into the group as they stand at the portal, watching Ilanu light the archway with his antics.

Lakul grins with fascination at how the lights work, "Yes, that's cool. It's best to check it out, Ilanu. Righto, that's my motto."

Initamay taps Ilanu's shoulder, now that Lakul is there, they can proceed. "Let's keep moving my brother. We have a meeting to return to."

Ilanu blurts, "Okay, but I figured it out. The arch has rhodolite detectors, that read who pass by. That's why it changes."

Initamay laughs, "Sounds good. Did someone tell you that?"

"Well, yes. It was Rionarta or Kardichay. I helped to check out the site though. I think that counts, right."

"Ilanu, yes, that counts. I love how honest and funny you are." She hugs him and says to Angel Ohm, "We're all here now."

"Yes, then please follow me," Angel Ohm says. She smiles warmly at Teladi and turns to lead them to the meeting.

The Chosen Ones

They follow her as she flows, humming to the chamber. The door opens into the crowded room, and they go to stand near the council table. The din of voices stops - a hush settles in, so everyone can hear what is to be said.

Metatron commandingly addresses the group. "Congratulations! The federation council agreed that Michael's crystalla brigade is the first wave of light workers to journey to Gaea Star." A cheer of approval rings out resoundingly.

Michael stands, "My rainbow brigade, we recognize you are gifted messengers, capable of sharing your loving, peaceful, healing for humanity. Does the council have any further comments before they prepare to depart?"

Archangel Jophiel, rises. "Do not be afraid to stand strongly in your truth on Gaea Star as you fulfill your destinies."

Archangel Ariel goes next, "Congratulations. The challenges of life provide opportunities to comprehend the remarkable journey of awakening. Take care of each other and the precious life there."

Wise Ones from Bochuti

Suddenly, three silvery purple, winged elders, looking like they are from a realm of everlasting peace, mystically float to the center. They lovingly glance at every being in the chamber with gentle eyes and sweet smiles, causing a profound soothing effect.

One speaks, "I am Fayonallia, from the distant realm of Bochuti. We are pleased this council seeks the healing of the hearts of humanity. It is the first step to restore goodness and compassion there, for love is the highest, most agreeable aspect of all life, and is so necessary to exist peacefully in the universe." She smiles, sending out light-filled rays, then nods to her companions to express themselves.

Another silvery elder speaks, "I am Nepthytoka. Thank you, brigade, for engaging your precious souls for this noble cause. We share our radiant energies to inspire all of you to always foster loving encouraging actions." She too smiles at everyone warmly.

The last one raises her arms in an arch to the heavens, then places her hands together in a mudra. She hums in a serene voice and then waves to the musicians. Soon they and the choir, join her as she sings in an uplifting manner.

I am Amsinia, my healing music brings you home,

to your soul's birthplace, to the cradle of light

Oh, to the source of love, oh, oh, Amsinia

Graceful circles of light, oh graceful light

May you share these harmonies with the ones you love

With the ones who need to open their hearts a little more

To sweep away illusions, to float softly into their inner core

Amsinias' melodies, jingle truths to set you free

To remember who you really are, deeply within

Oh, sail to the realms of love, soaring ever higher

Oh, yeah to the light, to the source of love

To the home of your soul's birth

So deep within your core

where it's always loved your sweet soul

When you hear Amsinias' melodies

the healing tones will set you free, free, free

As she sang beautifully, the choir and musicians accompanied her. Many join in, creating a rich harmonic blending within the chamber, raising the vibrations higher. The celestial melodies transformed mysteriously into colorful brilliant orbs of golden violet light, floating, and drifting on all the beings, while some burst with bright sparkling colors, like a fireworks' show.

The colors change into vibrant, shimmering stars - half and full circles, triangles, squares, lines, arrows, and lights, floating randomly. Then they form into geometric patterns and shimmer in sequence to the melody which echoes throughout the chamber. The fantastic design hovers peacefully above the hall. A holographic design with a similar visionary pattern rises like the mists from the revolving Gaea Star. Her sweet face appears with a pleasurable smile of pure delight.

The crystals throughout the chamber glisten rainbows of lights whenever an orb passes. All of this is due to the powerful effects of the soothing ethereal music and luminous, electromagnetic designs drifting about. Even the wind arrived to join in lightly.

Metatron is pleased, "Thank you, Amsinia, remarkable. What a profound synthesis of the essence of all life."

Amsinia says, "Thank you. This essential arrangement of energetic vibrations is merged with the ancient truth, that we are all one, in ways forever linked." The three etheric beings float away from the center to rest in the upper chamber.

Ashento steps forward to enable everyone close to him to see the tattoo designs on his body which are quite similar to the floating geometric patterns. They flash blue, green, turquoise and golden rays of light, as if turned on for a night show. He smiles, saying, "Greetings to my family from Bochuti. Thank you for sharing your transcendent blessed energies. It makes it easier to sense the cosmic golden thread of love that weaves through all beings." They nod to Ashento.

Ayalasha gazes proudly at him. "Amsinia. Thank you for the beautiful song that sparked this wondrous vision. We will always remember it's celestial majesty." Her and Ashento sit together.

The rest of the brigade reflects how they were deeply affected by the Bochuti family. Lakul is stretching in a yoga mountain pose. Initamay is holding hands with Teesha, Mira, and Celestia. They still feel the graceful impact of the colorful meaningful creation. Teladi is deep in meditation, while Azul is mesmerized, reverentially looking up at the floating design.

Kardichay and Rionarta are marveling at the crystals in the chamber, that flash colors and emit low tones whenever an orb drifts by. They are curious about a collection of transparent blue-green glass stones that have bubbles within them. The stones are echoing tones as if singing a spiritual message with far-reaching effects.

Kardichay whispers to him. "These Aqua Lemurian crystals are triggered by the energy emanating from the floating geometric grids. The sounds they emit access Lemurian knowledge and help to stimulate intuition."

Rionarta says, "Oh, good to know. Yes, the crystalline reactive phenomenon is powerful. What an unusual collection of vibrationally energetic stones in this chamber."

Kardichay says, "I'd like to meet the crystal gatherers of these colossal gems that we encountered here on Star Sirius."

Ikabayo, the being from Unaikota who spoke in favor of the brigade at the meeting, overheard their discussion. He comes close to whisper, as if he wants privacy. "Light bearers, your mission is taking you to the mineral rich lands of Gaea Star. The crystal seeker who gathered the gems of Star Sirius, lives there. He is called the crystal stone man and chose to go to Gaea Star to preserve her spectacular crystals that were being overharvested."

Rionarta and Kardichay look at each other. Kardichay says, "Thank you. Ikabayo. We appreciate your support at the meeting. What was the crystal man's name?"

Ikabayo says, "Crystal stone man, is all I ever knew him as. I don't know any other name. He is an elusive shapeshifter, with many appearances. He is known to always appear after a golden mist and disappear the same way. Mysterious, yes. He has not been seen on Gaea Star for a long time, however. He disappeared when the crisis in over harvesting the crystals and other precious natural resources began."

Rionarta says, "Thank you. Ikabayo. We'll watch for him." Kardichay is about to ask him a question when Ilanu, who's chasing the floating orbs with the fairies and elves, bumps into them as they talk.

"Oops, sorry," he says as he rushes by them in pursuit of the orbs. It appears that is the end of the conversation about the golden mist crystal seeker. Kardichay wants to continue but Ikabayo waves goodbye as if he has to move on. They smile, walking away as well.

llanu is still trying to catch the orbs but every time he gets one in his fingers, it instantly floats away, much to his dismay. He says, "Gee. Slippery. How do they get away from me?" The faeries and elves fly or hop after the orbs but do not care about catching them. Being playful with Ilanu is their delight.

Angel Ohm floats to the front of the chamber and says, "Blessed beings from throughout the realms, we thank you for coming. We hold you dear within for accomplishing this task in a loving manner today."

Metatron agrees, "Yes, what a perfect demonstration of the loving support bestowed on this mission for Gaea Star."

Michael says, "Thank to the wise ones for all of your blessings."

Metatron signals to Michael. He nods and says, "Council, the momentous meeting is complete. Yes, thank you for your presence. We release all the unseen energies in accordance with the will of heaven. May it be so." He raises his arms in a gesture to open to all of creation. "Much love for this holy life."

Angel Ohm flies toward the top of the chamber, waving a crystal wand. In a sparkling spray of white and golden lights, the ceiling opens even wider to the starry realms. The geometric grids and orbs float gently up into the night sky.

The spirit of Gaea Star appears smiling and happy in the center - flashing blue and green. She says, "Thank you, dear ones. I am pleased for your loving attention. May the blessings of divine abundance and healing fill your lives forever." It's such a pretty vision as she floats into the skies above with angelic melodies following after her. Angel Ohm says, "All are free to move about or converse."

The crowd rises to discuss the profound meeting as the energies shift. Several gather around the brigade, expressing their congratulations for being chosen to go to Gaea Star.

Ashento's Different Mission

Isis flies to Ashento and Ayalasha, signaling to follow her. They look at each other and walk behind her holding hands onto the path that leads to the crystal entrance of the gardens. She gestures to a rose quartz bench in a secluded area. They sit upon it.

Smiling warmly, she remains standing to speak. "I'm sure you're wondering why I led you from the council and connecting with friends. I have important words for you in private. We honor you for being strong emissaries in your devotion to this high cause. Only one of you is destined to journey to Gaea Star."

Surprised, they glance at each other intensely. Their eyes say it all, but they remain silent, listening, still holding hands.

Isis looks at Ayalasha. "Priestess of the purple ray, we are pleased that you will share your creative, musical gifts on Gaea Star and assist in the awakening of the divine feminine energy."

Ayalasha takes her hand from Ashento, placing both together in front of her heart in a prayerful gesture. She nods in agreement, even if she has overwhelming feelings for Ashento after reconnecting with his powerful loving presence again.

'Oh, no,' she thinks, 'her rekindled beloved not going to Gaea Star.' She takes in a deep breath of pure life enhancing air, to try to settle the uncomfortable wave that flows through her at the thought of leaving his divine presence behind. Oh, how the heart and mind react when faced with the absence of someone we love. It is daunting, not what she expected, to be separated in completely different realms, her to Gaea Star while he remains in the heavens. A long-distance romance, with unknown duration, that could easily last lifetimes, calls for her courageous trust, to believe that they will reunite in love someday.

Ayalasha keeps all those thoughts to herself to say proudly, "Yes, Isis, I am honored to serve, to shine brightly, my reverent appreciation of the goddess, wherever it is needed. I wish to help with the healing and rebalancing of humanity by encouraging all beings to develop a peaceful loving heart through their creativity."

Isis says, "Yes, my daughter, you are wise in all ways. We believe you will walk the path of loving light, no matter how long the mission takes."

Ayalasha says, "True. It is a blessing to live. I hope to inspire the blossoming of a new humankind during this great change."

Isis gives her a long feather from her wings. "Here, Ayalasha, it is a gift, to use in ceremony, to attune to the lightness of the radiant force of divine love."

Ayalasha holds it to her heart, "Thank you, Isis. I will treasure this." She places it in her medicine bag and tucks it inside her cape.

Isis turns to Ashento to say, "Ashento, your spiritual pursuits lead you beyond the spheres of Gaea Star. The council asks you to remain in the celestial realms to continue developing mastery. You may serve as a guide, to the brigade throughout their mission to Gaea Star."

They exchange glances then nod to her words. Ashento breathes in deep, saying, "Isis, I knew this was a possibility. I accept progressing to different levels. My concern for Gaea Star, the nurturing planet of blue waters, and the rekindling of my love with Ayalasha is timeless. I await her return and pledge the utmost devotion in being a guiding spiritual mentor from afar."

They look at each other with adoration. Isis endearingly says, "Thank you, Ashento and Ayalasha for your understanding and dedication to each other, even with a lengthy separation. I must return to the temple to prepare for your eminent departure." She opens her rainbow wings to sail silently away. They go to each other and hug passionately.

Ashento touches her hair lovingly, "Ayalasha. I'll miss your sweet presence. I am sorry I will not enjoy the blessings of life on Gaea Star with you again, but you are with me eternally."

Ayalasha sighs. "Ashento, you are in my heart forever. Yes, it's far away - what a challenge for our love. I will never forget you. My heart will always long to be with you."

He smiles, squeezing her hands in a burst of love. She smiles too, sending love through all of herself, as they hold each other's gaze. He has lived lifetimes on Gaea Star and remembers facing the challenges and the times when the veils of illusions overcast past promises from the heavenly realms. He does not say what he is thinking though. It may not be true. Perhaps she will remember him in the midst of her life there.

They breathe in slowly until they become a radiant force of unified, masculine and feminine forces. They connect in that sweet precious way for a few moments until Michael's commanding voice calls out loudly even from where they sit on the rose quartz bench.

"Rainbow brigade, please go immediately to the labyrinth of crystalline light for the farewell ceremony and departure instructions. We have sent word to your loved ones and home keepers that you are not returning until your Gaea Star missions are successful. Please keep these plans to yourselves."

Ashento and Ayalasha stand quickly and are speechless at the sequence of events that just transpired. It is difficult to grasp they have so little time remaining together. They recall when they first saw the archangels' message to gather on Star Sirius. Then coming from so far, so fast, and dramatically reconnecting with each other there before the great meeting building.

Ayalasha's mind races. It's hard to believe this is happening, separating before they enjoy a loving life together on Gaea Star. Ashento takes her hands, looking into her eyes, while walking quietly. They stop to smile, to breathe in deeply, letting the breath out, and shaking their bodies a little. Ayalasha says, "If we are experiencing this situation, then we are prepared to handle the decision before us."

Ashento says, "Yes, to accept our destiny, of being apart, for however long it takes for humanity to wake up to living in peaceful harmony. Let's choose a touch stone, a sign for you to help remember that I am here in spirit, loving and guiding you and waiting forever for your celestial return."

Two sparkling stars whizz by in golden trails across the sky. She points, "Look, twin stars sailing by."

Ashento says, "Yes, my sweetness, that is our sign."

Ayalasha says, "Ashento, you are unforgettable. I'll be on the look-out for our streaking touchstone in the skies."

They hug and walk toward a light in the distance that is from the torches of the labyrinth of crystalline light where a ceremony is to be held for the departing rainbow brigade.

PART 7

ONTO THE LABYRINTH
OF CRYSTALLINE LIGHT

13

THE CRYSTAL ARCHWAY ALARM

Angel Ohm floats about the chamber while most of the brigade talk to friends even though they heard Michael's request to go to the ceremonial site. She waves to follow her. Excited, they assemble and walk with her past Diyanna's garden to a different path that leads to the labyrinth, where the lights are flickering in the distance.

Ilanu says to Initamay, "Sis, we're on another adventure, sure to be a treasure filled pleasure. Wish that cool cat could come. I liked him. He's a lot of fun - one of our kin."

She replies, "Well, you never know, you may meet a cat to share fun with when we get there." She suddenly stops with a stricken look, "Oh, no, I left my medicine bag in the gardens. I have to go back. I'll meet you and the others at the Labyrinth. Ilanu, please stay with everyone. Do not leave. No funny acts, okay?"

He laughs. "For sure. No worry, just hurry." She turns to rush back there, dodging several beings who want to congratulate and talk about her upcoming trip.

She just waves goodbye rather than engage. "Sorry, I have to get something really fast before the ceremony begins."

Off she runs quickly. Yes, that's one of her strengths, racing through the lovely woods on a beautiful day with the sun and wind in her hair. She's really focused on getting there swiftly.

Meanwhile, Keme and Zoz are walking on the garden path, trying to be unnoticed. Zoz comes to the crystal portal first, and without hesitation, steps beneath it, with Keme right behind him. The lights flash dark then light on and off rapidly, going through all the colors as if it is overloaded. A high-pitched tone beeps a warning that has not sounded before that startles them. Zoz says, "Oh, no, Keme, we triggered something. Come on. Let's go. We can't draw attention. Hurry, someone may hear the beeping."

He takes off running, with Keme desperately trying to keep up. "Hey, Zoz, wait up. No one's here. What's the rush?"

He says, "True, but someone may come along, especially if they hear this. We're not waiting to explain ourselves."

Keme is not as agile and fit as Zoz. They run like thieves caught red-handed through the gardens, into Initamay who is so intent on getting there, that she does not see them. She bumps into Zoz, abruptly with a crunch, surprising them both.

She says, "Woops. Oh, I'm sorry, I didn't see you." She looks at him - this time, seriously. "You two again? Strange that we keep running into each other. What are you doing here? Are you following me for something?"

Zoz steps back, smiling nervously, trying to figure out what to say, as he knows they're not supposed to be there. "Well, I'm glad to see you again. Ah, we were." Just then, the cat that Ilanu played with, Mister Coole, slowly ambles by, as if he is coming to see what's up with them.

Zoz thinks quickly and says, "Oh, there he is. We're nature lovers and just wanted to check out this cool cat. He's like the ones we've studied elsewhere. We're curious about him."

Keme nods, "Yeah, this rare creature indeed." They lean to pet him, but he's not interested in their touch. He eyes them rather suspiciously - the way cats do and saunters away, as if to say, "No thanks, I have more important things to check out than you two."

Zoz says, "Oh well, at least we got a good look at him." Keme nods. Zoz looks at her. "Who are you? Why the rush? Weren't you one of those down in the front, in that meeting room?"

He knows they met by the parade, then followed her through the sun door into the arts room and beyond, but he keeps that to himself. No reason to alarm her.

It's Initamay's turn to respond, but remember she is not to discuss the mission. "I left something in the gardens. My friends are waiting for me." All the while, they look at each other intently.

Zoz is intrigued by her powerful beauty. Smiling and winking, he says, "You are just who I love to meet, so a - how about it - oh, I mean would you like too?"

Initamay smiles, as she wonders who this handsome mysterious stranger is, but she has no time to linger. "Well, it's nice to connect but I have to go. They're waiting for me."

Funny, she did not notice their ragged appearance. Even though she had run into them a few times, she did not question that fact. She was concerned about her missing bag which was far more important, and she also wanted to return to the labyrinth ceremony before it begins as being on time is essential for her.

Zoz says, "Hey, wait, going so fast? How will I find you?"

Initamay laughs, "If it is meant to be, we'll bump into, I mean connect again. Life is full of surprises, that's for sure." She touches his shoulder, and then rushes into the gardens. She sees her bag on the rock, just where she left it. "Oh, yes, it's still here. How forgetful, I'll never do that again. My treasures are so dear and helpful." She picks up the bag, puts it around her waist and heads back in the opposite direction.

Zoz places his fingers where she touched him. "Whew, we made it without being discovered. She is ravishing. Wish we talked more. She is going to Gaea Star. Let's follow them. They must be leaving in a ship somewhere ahead. We may not have much time. Looks like they're gathering up there before taking off."

Keme says, "Zoz, good thing she left. No need to get hooked in with her. Let's stick with the job we have to do now."

Zoz says, "Well, our job is to keep track of the ones going to Gaea Star, and you're right, that was too close for comfort."

Keme agrees, "Yes, we were quick to come up with something believable though, if I may say so."

Zoz snorts, "Okay. Don't be so proud of yourself. I saw the cat first, remember?" They walk away, mumbling, until they hear voices behind them. Zoz signals to be quiet - to follow. They quickly sneak into the bushes to hide and are relieved to be out of sight.

Last Goodbyes

Ashento and Ayalasha walk by, still enraptured together. Ashento says, "My sweetness, let's walk the garden path to have one last moment on the rose seat before we separate for lifetimes." She nods silently, for she cherishes every instance to be near his powerful, radiant spiritual presence.

They meander through the luscious plants, taking their time, until coming upon the crystal-encrusted archway beeping loudly and blinking wildly. Surprised, they exchange concerned glances and look to see what triggered such a reaction.

Ashento closes his eyes to sense the energy. "Hmm, someone without good intentions. This portal detects all energies within the body-mind. So be careful, my sweetness. There are many, who do not want the mission to succeed, for the resources of Gaea Star are in high demand in the universe. Trust only what you feel from the depths of your heart when you meet anyone. Look deep into their eyes, to see into their souls - you will know if they are from the light."

Ayalasha says, "Thank you. I'm not frightened. I always feel the blessings of spirit. I will go within to commune with loving intentions, with those who are in alignment, with our journey."

Ashento looks around the portal area but does not see anything. "The energy has shifted as it is quietly pulsating. Let's pass beneath it now." Together they walk hand in hand through the portal, which this time, reflects an intense magenta, purple, blue hue of radiant light in all directions.

Two sparkling stars shoot out of the crystals in the arch, streaking across in a blazing trail of rainbow light. Laughing, they delight in the appearance of their symbolic touchstone, the twin stars racing through the skies and cuddle happily on the love seat, sharing their love.

Zoz and Keme peer out from the bushes when they sense it is safe. Silently, Zoz signals to follow, crawling through the large plants as fast as they can without making noise. Once back on the path, Zoz says, "Let's head in the direction that lovely one took. It is where the action seems to be."

Keme says, "Ah, yeah, right, it's always that way with you."

"Oh, come on, you know I'm right. She is leading us to where we need to be. So, lighten up, I have a sense about it."

"Okay, I'm coming." They walk a little bit faster, bantering about who has the best ideas and so forth until they fade off into the distance.

Oh, Great Lover of My Soul

Still cuddling, Ashento says to Ayalasha, "My sweetness, the stars celebrate our divine union, even in our separation. I'll sing or whisper messages to guide you. Here is a song as my departing gift." His deep voice resonates as crickets chirp, birds peacefully call, and the soft wind, blows gently, whistling along, as he sings.

Oh, great lover of my soul, oh great lover of my light

You live within me to my sweet delight

Oh, great lover of my soul

I long to sail along the rivers of life with you,

drifting in a wooden canoe

All my love, all my love, flows to you

Oh, sweet love, to lie with you, where the sun shines golden

Your sweet perfume on a summer night is pure delight

From the glory of the seventh realm above, glorious heaven,

I'll send you my radiant love

shining so blue, my rays of love, rays of love

Oh, great lover of my soul, oh great lover of my light

You are within my heart

I'll follow you forever

I'm waiting for you in realms of heavenly bliss

Forever, I am waiting, oh great lover of my soul

Ayalasha is touched by his intense voice singing romantically, evoking passionate feelings within her heart. Tears stream down her face. She feels longing for him already, even though they are still together. She says softly, "Ashento, that is beautiful. The words are exactly how I feel. I am truly sorry that we cannot enjoy our rekindled love that dwells so intensely within our hearts. My sweet lover of light, I will wait for you." They embrace tightly, as several roses fall from the arbor into their laps as gifts of love. Yes, even the flowers know that the moment of separation, is coming soon. Oh, how difficult it is going to be to live in such different far away realms.

Will Ayalasha spend lonely moments, wondering why she has not met her true love yet? Will Ashento's spiritual pursuits fill the emptiness of his lost love with his twin flame? Are they a testimony that eternal love is true? Only experiences of life and beyond reveal the answers to those questions.

Ashento says, "My sweetness, we will be together in divine celestial union, in a distant realm ahead. This trial of separation will bring us even closer. On Gaea Star, you will encounter opportunities to get it right as you learn your lessons, and sail into the treasure deep within your graceful, awakened soul, where peace and my loving presence dwell forever."

Ayalasha nods to his words, leaning to him for a final comforting hug. They meld warmly into pure divine love, in the silence of the intense moment.

A red headed woodpecker loudly taps on a tree while birds flutter close to land on the branches above them, singing, *"Lighten up, lighten up, let your wings unfurl."*

Ayalasha says, "Why, they sing like faeries."

Ashento laughs. "Yes, as we heard, they are with you always, in the plants, in the rivers, in the breezes." He releases his embrace to stand up, as if it's time to go. "Come, my sweetness. They say life is to celebrate in all ways. Departure is near. Let's proceed to the ceremony grounds."

She stands, taking in a deep breath, "Yes, I feel that too." She gracefully takes his arm in loving warmth, to walk to the labyrinth grounds. She carries herself calmly as if her heart is being pulled by spirit – centered, at peace and one with him.

As honorable high beings in dynamic love together, they cause a ripple, a commotion of the earthy elements as they pass by. On the lush land, the wind swirls into spiraling balls of wispy tumbleweeds of magenta light, while flocks of birds fly here and there. The faeries that were singing, now dance and flit about, excited to see the happy couple coming near.

Ashento stops, turning to Ayalasha. "My sweetness. I have a gift." He reaches into his cape to retrieve a shiny pouch. "Here, please, take this." He places it in her trembling hand, as they smile adoringly at each other. Oh, how she gazes in anticipation of a treasure, while Ashento intently watches.

As she undoes the laces of the pouch, she says, "I am so touched by your act of love." She takes out a small item wrapped in a golden fabric. Rainbows and gold light flash from it, surprising her, while she unwraps it. When it is completely uncovered, she gasps, "Oh, it is lovely." She brings a silver glowing stone close to gaze at the etchings inscribed on the front of it.

"Thank you, Ashento. I sense mystical qualities. Why does this precious mineral glow like stardust?"

He touches her endearingly, gently caressing her hair. "It is platinum, my sweetness, a precious metal from Gaea Star, a symbol of eternal love that stimulates the connection to the cosmic energy of the universe, enhancing communing with me when you awaken."

Ayalasha holds the shimmering piece close as she listens. "Ashento, I will hold this dear to my heart. What do you mean when I awaken? I'm not going to fall asleep or ever forget you, that I am certain. I'll remember the light-filled pulsations of this stone."

Ashento responds, "My sweetness, at the meeting, you heard that one may forget who they are and why they came to Gaea Star. You are chosen for this mission, to share your inherent talents for the betterment of humanity. As lives unfold, however, the divine contract may be forgotten, as material life becomes far more important. Some may not cast off the illusions of all that plagues Gaea Star. You will have the opportunity to realize your divine connection. Embrace each day with the awareness that you're the one, to direct your life into positive action. Disregard those trying to cloak the essence of goodness or the power of love.

The body is the dynamic tool for the manifestation of life. Use it wisely. Believe that everything will right itself, for all is meant to be in balance. There is nothing to despair, only to pray, attune and unify with humanity and reaffirm that life is wonderful, as you glide along your sacred journey home."

Ayalasha is stunned. "Wow, Ashento, thank you for so many astute words. I hope I remember all this wisdom."

He says, "My sweetness, when we reconnect through our spirits, we will exchange these messages and many more again."

Ayalasha leans on him, feeling his deep connection, "Ashento, I'll miss you so and will never forget the purpose of my starry origin."

"Yes, my sweetness, I know you feel that. However, it may be a long time on Gaea Star, surrounded by ones who have separated from spirit within their minds and hearts. The secret to becoming aware, is to always be compassionate and connected to love, to slow life down, to listen to nature, as she sings through the winds. The spirit of our love will shine through in the healing energy of her pure radiance."

Ayalasha sighs, "Yes, I'll remember your endearing words. I will be filled with warmth when I think of you holding me so close within your soul, for eternity." He nods, with a warm loving smile.

They hug. What a precious moment. She reaches into her cape for a purple starry bag and places the platinum inside it. Suddenly, they hear bells ringing, coming from behind them. They turn to see what it is.

The Tribal Elders from Requayo

It is an unusual sight. A colorful tribal entourage with an elderly couple leading two llamas are slowly ambling up the path. The llamas carry stuffed packs and are decorated with bright headdresses. Ayalasha and Ashento stand surprised. The female elder says, "Greetings, from the far highlands of Recuayo. I am Andaluchiya and this is my husband, Ritoyo." He nods with a smile.

"Welcome, Andaluchiya and Ritoyo. I am Ayalasha and he is Ashento." They hug one another.

Andaluchiya says, "At the request of Michael, we came to bless those who are chosen to share their radiant light with our beloved Gaea Star."

Ayalasha says, "I am one of those selected and Ashento is to be our distant star guide." She exchanges glances with Ashento.

He smiles warmly at Ayalasha, then speaks, "Thank you for traveling from so far to share your graceful knowledge for all to benefit – It is a noble action."

Andaluchiya translates to Ritoyo as he does not speak the same language. He beams a heartwarming smile as he gestures for them to come to meet their llamas. They are cute, wearing dangly earrings on their pointy, banana - shaped ears, besides the pretty bobbing headdresses crafted from their spun fibers.

They go close, enabling the llamas to stretch their long necks to first sniff Ashento's face gently, with their whiskers tickling his chin. He laughs at the funny feeling as he says, "What a pleasure to meet these loving, sweet animals. I know your tribal family dwells untainted in remote mountain regions and your community fosters ancient traditions, of living simply and always honoring the spirit within."

Andaluchiya translates to Ritoyo. He acknowledges his words by smiling as he holds the llamas who are interested in meeting Ashento. They rub his arms, for pets. He laughs, sensing their desires, and strokes the soft lustrous fiber on their long necks.

Ayalasha giggles when they gently touch her face with their softness. "Andaluchiya, please tell us about these loving creatures. How did they become part of your tribe?"

She smiles. "Thank you. They are a legend in our lands. Wise ones say that eons ago, they were brought from a distant star to give comfort, strength, loyal friendship, warm fiber for clothing and to carry supplies up and down our steep mountains."

She translates to Ritoyo. He relays his thoughts. She turns to Ayalasha. "Ritoyo is a high shaman of our tribe and would like to offer his deep understandings." She translates as he speaks.

"Llamas are guardians of the sacred rainbow and the fifth element. They are sweet loving beings that inspire caring, joy, telepathic communication, and unifying with the universe, with the great cosmic force of all things."

Ayalasha speaks, "Thank you for explaining. Perhaps they are meant to grace the highlands of Gaea Star."

Andaluchiya smiles. "Yes, they are destined to walk her sacred grounds. We offer these peaceful loving friends, to journey with the brigade to Gaea Star, to be cherished there, as we do."

Ayalasha laughs, excited, "Oh, what a blessing to send these gentle beings to those in need. We'll make sure they land in the best place for their well-being."

Ashento says, "Thank you. We are blessed by this good fortune and will envision their delightful presence benefitting humanity. Let us go now. The sendoff ceremony is due to begin." He and Ayalasha happily bond with the colorful tribe as they walk along with their llamas.

14

The Magnificent Labyrinth Entrance

Bright sparkling, crystalline torches illuminate the ceremonial area, creating a mystical setting for the momentous occasion. Countless beings are surging in like rivers of water, coursing over the ground after a heavy rainstorm. Friends, teachers, archangels, and council members are all gathering to say goodbye to the brigade before embarking for Gaea Star.

The Merkabus, filled with the bubbling children, flies in close to land next to Michael. He smiles and then starts swaying to the rocking, piano tunes that are blasting through the windows. Nearly every child is dancing in the aisles or standing on their seats as they flash colored lights. What a wild ride for the caretakers, Bella and Miyah. They had their hands full. Bella is holding on for dear life to a post near the door with her hat and curly hair all askew.

Miyah, obviously exhausted, is sitting in the front, letting Bella take charge in her commanding voice. "Children, we have arrived. Please file off slowly, one by one. Watch out for each other. Oh, great fortune. I see visitors from the faery realms and a real delight, the regal unicorns are here!"

The children joyfully shout, as most have only heard about the magical creature, even in these realms. Their majestic presence had already disappeared from inhabited areas long ago. Leaping off excitedly, they disregard Bella's words, and go racing over to the unicorns as they proudly prance about. The children form a huge lively audience around the beautiful creatures.

Ilanu rushes over to take a place in the line that formed to pet the stunning unicorns, but then he notices the green elf. "Hello, green elf. Am I in time to greet the one who talks in rhyme?"

The elf steps to Ilanu with an air of puffed-up importance, even though he does not reach past his knees. "I am Verdalon, with always time to make a rhyme. How did you know that I am the one to chatter with, so? Oh, ho, ho, ho. Alright, then, let's have a go."

Ilanu, thrilled to play rhyming games, asks one of the children in the line, "Hey, save my place. I'll be back, in an ace." He says to Verdalon, "Oh my, do you have wings to fly?"

Verdalon hops around, "Save my place, in an ace. I do fly, with wings of light. Save my place, in an ace, wings to fly, in light."

Ilanu is confused, "Hey, wait. Does that count? Fly with light, is that what it's about?"

Verdalon, still jumping up and down, says. "Why, yes. Who cares? What's with all the airs? How we create words, so many birds, does it matter if it makes silly chatter?"

Ilanu realizes he has met his match. He excitedly responds, "Have you any mystical crystals in your pouches, of no slouches?"

"Why, yes. I do, in fact, more than enough for you."

They are soon so absorbed in outfoxing one another in this game, that they forget everyone and anything else.

"Mints, hints."

I'll give you two cents." On and on they banter back and forth.

Meanwhile, the soft loving manners of the unicorns must have had a calming effect on the boisterous children since they're actually being orderly in taking turns to pet or ride them. They nearly kneel to let the little ones try to hop on their massive backs. Of course, the faeries make sure no one falls off. What a fun experience for all the children, one they will never forget.

After their turns, the children go play with the faeries who are delighted with their happy company. They missed being with children since it is so difficult to interact in the human's domains because, sadly, many do not believe in fairies. It is an ominous sign that life is changing everywhere when the veils of unbelief appear in their magical realms as well.

Meeting the Llamas

Suddenly there is a distant tinkling of bells heard coming from down the path. A little one says, "Oh, what is that?"

Another responds, "I hear bells." The children turn to see what is making the pretty sounds that are becoming louder from around the bend. What do you think they saw? What a total surprise that no one expected. It's the tribal musicians walking, softly drumming and chanting. Behind them, are Andaluchiya and Ritoyo walking with Ayalasha and Ashento who are thrilled to lead the llamas they have fallen in love with.

Ayalasha is wearing a colorful woven hat and Ashento is draped in a soft poncho. They match the llamas whose pretty head dresses tinkle with bells. The tiny crystals tied to the sides of their packs are glittering. The rest of the tribe is coming behind them.

"Oh, look. What are they?" Aronsky, a child from the Merkabus, exclaims. With joyful shouts, those not in line, rush to greet the new arrivals with curious wonder and awe, as they have never seen such regal creatures either.

Ayalasha stands protectively in front of the llamas, smiling, "Hello, dear ones. Take care, no rushing. First, I have a story about these wonderful creatures." They immediately relax even though they're so exhilarated about these new furry, friendly animals.

She continues, "They are llamas. Their tribe is from the mountains of Requayo, from a distant star, so far away. They are not used to so much attention, so please walk lightly and talk softly. Like tippy toe really slow, but they're friendly and give sweet kisses if you are gentle when you approach them."

The wide-eyed children nod in agreement. Some say, "Oh yes," and look thrilled to meet the new animals. They can hardly contain themselves, but they listen to Ayalasha since she has an endearing ability to make children feel special while teaching them to act with graceful caring for all life.

She smiles, saying, "Thank you for your calmness. I'm sure that these wonderful caretakers, Andaluchiya and Ritoyo, will happily introduce you to Ausan and Cusi." She scratches behind their ears while she looks at the elders and says, "Thank you. It was a pleasure to meet your wonderful tribe and lead the llamas. We must go to the ceremony to prepare for my departure. I hope we meet again."

Andaluchiya says, "Thank you, you are so very welcome."

Ashento says, "Yes, I love your tribe as well. I will fondly remember the friendly llamas. Goodbye to your family."

They give the llamas affectionate rubs and receive last whiskery kisses from both of them. Ayalasha returns her and Ashento's ropes to Ritoyo. Then they walk toward the labyrinth that is illuminated in the distance by flickering fire torches. The peaceful children pet the llamas under the gentle guidance of Andaluchiya and Ritoyo.

Crystalline Torches of Illumination

The labyrinth appears as a sacred, energetically powerful ritual space in the misty moonlight. Winged angels float up, holding brilliantly shining crystal torches. They move like wispy feathers in a magical parade to light the other torches that line the labyrinth and along the entrance. It is an enormous masterpiece, a seven-circuit design that invitingly spreads out with immense crystals of all sizes and shapes in a geometric pattern all together.

Each circular pathway is highlighted with candles and crystal glowing lamps that resemble healing salt blocks. A small fire is glowing in the center, with four crystal pillars rising high above.

Archangel Sandalphon and Saraswathi, the goddess of the arts, walk up with the Alaria choir and musicians. They shimmer in white, gold, and purple raiment as they carry harps, lutes, flutes and drums to where eleven, star children are assembled. They are also wearing glistening, star outfits and star crowns. Saraswathi signals the music to begin. She leads the song,

Children of the stars

we are all from the same light

We are all from the stars

It's the same light inside of you and me

It's the same light in all of us

The blue stars, the goldens, the indigos and the crystals

And the pixies, the faeries, the sprites and little green elves

When the faery kin hear these words, they fly over, flitting here and there, with Emeraldina landing on a star child. How pleasant to see the interaction and sense the happiness of the faery kin who are thrilled to mingle with all of those gathered. Soon the whole crowd joins in singing.

Children of the stars, we are all the same inside

We are shining bright inside, dancing and singing on this night

Children of the stars, we are all one family

We are all one family of light, one family of love

As the choir finishes the song, an ethereal melody emanates from other musicians, as they play on the left. All at once, thirteen drummers appear, beating a tribal rhythm on handmade drums. Soon, flamboyantly colorful beings are dancing to the upbeat rhythms and playing on a fascinating array of instruments.

There are two giant drums, crafted from a big tree branch that fell right there. The tree, the drums came from, still towers high above everyone. A small wood ladder is built in between the drums to be able to reach to the top to play them. Several small ones climb the ladder to take turns dropping a large wood baton onto the drums in a slow rhythmic manner.

The baton is bigger than they are, but they figure out a way to help one another, to lift and drop it with a deep resonating echo. It's so powerful they're almost shaken off the ladder by the intense vibrations. Of course, that makes it more thrilling to try to stay there while laughing and holding each other. "What fun," they say.

Lakul, having discovered those drums, is waiting for a turn to play them. He is vigorously dancing a wild routine, singing loudly, *Yes, music is our spirit busting out, singing, oh yeah, love that bass tone, sounds like we're in the cave of the all-knowing.*

He has all the dancers and their children, getting down, shaking their bodies. It is a scene of joyful abandon. Azul is dancing wildly with Rionarta. Even Teladi is moving, a bit controlled, but with a smile. Lakul gives him a big thumbs up.

Meanwhile, some of the brigade go near the labyrinth entrance. Celestia smiles shyly when she sees Kardichay glancing at her with a lingering warm look. When he reaches out his hand, she accepts it. She is pleasantly surprised at the flush of excitement within her, whenever he is near. They are excited to be together for the unusual adventure. Their future is promising. He takes her to a quiet spot, to snuggle and talk about their remarkable experiences so far.

Initamay rushes up, breathless, from running back to retrieve her bag. She sees Ilanu near the unicorn line, playing with Verdalon. She whistles for him rather than try to weave back through the dense crowds. He looks up, miming an *"Oh, no,"* face. He was so involved playing with Verdalon that he forgot about his turn with the unicorns. Initamay is insistent by waving with a stern look. At first, it does not appear that he's coming since he wants his turn to ride the massive ones, but it's really past the time for his turn anyway.

Ilanu mimes back, as if to say, *"Oh, all right, coming."* He turns to Verdalon to say his last rhyme, goodbye. "Oh, I must be going as my ship is flowing, all the way, so far away, on through the dark sky. Oh, I wish I could just fly."

Verdalon smiles. "Yes, it is the time. Now is the last rhyme. Goodbye, so you can fly."

He reluctantly leaves to go to Initamay. She is impatient, since she wants him on time, at the labyrinth, for once, to not miss walking through when they're supposed to. She knows Ilanu. After all, she is his sister and has cared for him since he was young, after their parents went on a brigade mission and never returned.

Mira and Teesha rush there also, when they finished having their fun ride on Rayanca, at the same time. It was "Super cool," according to Teesha. Her and Mira have become very close. They are happy to arrive at the impressive labyrinth entrance together.

Mira says, "Wow, I've never seen a crystal labyrinth. It's so pretty, mystical and elaborate."

Teesha responds, "Yes, it's an extraordinary creation. What an experience we're having Mira. I'm honored to share this incredible adventure with you."

Mira squeezes her hand. "I hope we stay connected through thick and thin. I heard we may forget each other - I don't think so."

Teesha looks deep into her eyes, "Of course, that won't happen with us. We'll always remember each other. I love you." They embrace closely.

Mira says, "I love you too."

Teladi slowly walks up, still shaking to the drumming that he left behind. Now he is onto a thoughtful prayer. Everything has a time and place, so he never rushes.

Rionarta is intrigued by the milky quartz sentinels, standing with ceremonial presence at the labyrinth entrance. Along their sides, castle-like projections rise high. As he touches the crystal pillars, pure white rays of healing light emanate brilliantly, causing Kardichay and Celestia to stop talking to come see what is causing the dazzling light.

"Wow," Kardichay says, "it's a variety of clear quartz - the highest of the high. An energetic mineral to illuminate white light."

Rionarta touches them gently. "Yes, they are positioned to emit high frequency light energy, to help the labyrinth walkers gain a deeper understanding of their spirit."

Celestia goes close to study the crystals, complex structure. She strokes one on its' side. It flashes brightly in response to her gentle touch. She says, "It is a messenger crystal. See how the markings, are etched in the crystal, making it look like a code of ancient information within its' temple-like repositories? I will search the Akashic hall of records, by asking within."

She closes her eyes to go within, to glimpse what these great energy beacons of such radiant light, could be. After a few moments, she slowly opens her eyes, "Yes, it is cathedral quartz, rich with esoteric wisdom. Perfect for those souls who seek to reach their highest spiritual potential and to unify as a community."

Kardichay nods. "True. Many use this quartz for inspiration and for interdimensional communication with the brotherhood of light, the archangels and high beings of healing frequencies."

Celestia says, "We are fortunate to experience their extraordinary energy beacons before walking the labyrinth."

Rionarta says, "Yes, we'll see clearly into our own destinies."

Kardichay nods, as he touches the crystals. They flash in response as well. He smiles, breathing in deeply and says, "We are grateful for their presence."

The three stand there, taking in the powerful crystal energies, peacefully, enjoying the incredible place of magnificent wonder.

15

UNSAVORY DUO SHENANIGANS

While all this is going on, Keme and Zosakel are sneaking up the path, after finding the way past the gardens. They still hide in the bushes occasionally and pop out at the edge of the path to check if the coast is clear. Zoz sees the crowd near the labyrinth and says, "I can't tell what they're doing but it's a good time to try get close. No one is looking our way, as long as we stay quiet."

Keme who can't see well without glasses, says, "Okay, but where are we going?"

Zoz says, "Shh, too loud."

"Sorry. Zoz, but do you think we can sneak into somewhere that we don't even know yet? What about all the people everywhere?"

Zoz speaks gruffly. "Stop worrying. We made it this far without being discovered. Why don't you believe we can do it? There's gotta be a transport ship nearby. We find it first, then we'll hide until they go in and figure out how to sneak in after. It's simple, there's no other choice. Lets' go find it. Follow me. No talking."

"All right, but why did I get involved with you?"

"Come on. You're here so what else are you gonna do?" Zoz says gruffly.

Keme retorts, "Well, I'm hungry, for a big meal." He thinks, *'Hmm, that tasty chocolate treat from Bella. It was so good. Wish I had another one. Wonder where she ended up with all the kids on that funny-looking bus?'*

Zoz laughs, "Is that all you think about? We'll eat to our content once we get there. I promise, so come on."

Off they go, warily walking. Zoz spies what looks like a launching pad over to the far right of the crowd. He gestures to follow him since no one is there. He sees up ahead, at the ceremonial grounds, blazing torches, flashing crystals, angels, elders, and a big crowd. It's too hard to make out what is happening since he can't see well either, as night is descending.

They sneak up to a large metallic structure perched on a base of clear quartz crystals. Four tall crystalline pillars rise up around the sides. There is an iridescent clear chamber in the center. The entire vessel is softly shimmering.

They go around back to hide in the shadows of the pillars. Zoz is smiling, proud his hunch is right. "See, what did I tell you? Wow, what a piece of work. Wonder how it flies? Now we wait. We'll have a sizable reward if we get on board. Remember, what Slake said? Stay with the group, keep them from doing what they want. So, come one, let's hang in there."

Keme says, "Okay. I hope it works."

Zoz says gruffly, "Shh. It will if we make it that way. We have to try." They sit to wait and then Zoz says, "At last, a rest. I need a quick snooze, a power nap."

He closes his eyes and immediately falls asleep, snoring loudly. Keme tries to wake him, but all he does is grunt, move a bit and snore louder. He finally shakes him awake, saying, "Stop snoring so loud. Everyone will know where we are." Zoz nods in a groggy daze, then resumes snoring louder.

Keme laughs, thinking, *"Well, no one is here, so I guess it's okay for a few minutes."* He settles down and falls asleep also. After all, it was an exciting undertaking so far. Funny how they both are snoring away until a powerful gong echoes resoundingly, to signal the beginning of the ceremony. Startled by it, they nearly fall on each other, since they were leaning on the pillars, snoozing.

Zoz jumps up, ready for action. "Hey, what was that?"

Keme wakes up but is much slower to react than Zoz. He says, "Sounded like a loud bell. Let's go see. Maybe we'll find a quick snack and then get back here to hide before anyone else comes."

Zoz answers, "No way. Not right now."

Keme is adamant, "Why not? Zoz. It may be a while."

Zoz shakes no, but then changes his mind. "All right, we'll have to look like we're part of the crowd though. No talking, just watching. Then, we hightail it back here before they board the ship to leave. So, stay near me, Keme." He goes off briskly.

Keme perks up, trying to follow Zoz into the crowd.

They each hope secretly they might run into the two women who crossed their paths, capturing their attentions - Bella for Keme and Initamay for Zoz.

When they get to the main area, Keme sees the Merkabus parked, so he veers that way without saying why. When he nears the bus, he sees no one there, although now he is even more excited and hopeful to run into Bella. He thinks, *"Hmm, she must be somewhere close, maybe wherever the kids are."* He looks and sees children surrounding funny looking, camel-like creatures, the llamas, in the distance, and wonders what they are. He yells, "Hey, Zoz, I'm going to see what those furry critters are over there, okay?"

Zoz is so distracted by the beautiful women in the crowd that he just nods okay. Keme walks against the surging beings. As he is looking for Bella, her voice booms out, "Children, time for the ceremony. It's up ahead." Keme recalls the loud gong noise waking them up. That must have been the signal.

Bella is walking toward Keme holding the hands of two children. She is listening to the littlest one as she says, "I like the llamas' pointy ears and tickling whiskers. They're my favorite."

The other one says, "Mine are the big, beautiful unicorns."

Keme steps in front of them, saying, "Excuse me. Hello."

Surprised to see him, Bella smiles, "Hello, my knight. We meet again. Are you going somewhere? Aren't you here for the sendoff? Come along. We're going the right way." He turns around with that invitation, enthralled to walk next to her.

Keme says, "Actually, I was just looking for a quick bite to eat. Thought I might find something over that way."

Bella laughs. "No, only llamas and unicorns are over there."

He says, "Oh, too bad. Unicorns, really? I thought they were only a fantasy. Never heard of llamas. Where are they from?"

One of the girls looks at him, saying, emphatically, "For your information, unicorns are real. Yes, because I sat on one."

The other girl says, "llamas are friendly, furry, fun and give great kisses." They laugh.

The first one says, "Yes, they kissed us so softly."

The other says, "It felt funny, how it tickled my chin."

Bella stops to let go of their hands and reaches into her big bag that hangs off her shoulder to bring out a small bag. She says, "Care for snacks from our trip? They're still good and tasty."

She hands the bag to Keme. He smiles in approval and is oh, so very happy to sample more of her delicious snacks. He says, "Yes, yes. Thank you. Just what I wanted. Hmm, these are good." He munches the snacks with gusto. He is so absorbed in walking with her, that he forgets what he promised Zoz, who is now looking for him, quite concerned for his disappearance.

He thinks, *"Alright, where did Keme go? Last I heard, he was off to see furry creatures. Now what the heck did that mean? "*

Trying to sort out which direction to go, he hears sweet melodic singing coming from behind. He turns to see a bevy of silvery, slinky torch bearers floating by, laughing, enjoying each other's company. He follows them, distracted by the beautiful feminine of which he favors above reason or responsibility, as you can see from his actions so far.

When he ends up near the labyrinth entrance, he is startled to see a strange sequence of circular patterns on the ground. He thinks, "*Oh, no, what I am doing here?*" Realizing he detoured from his important task, he turns around to disappear into the crowd, hopefully without being noticed. Then suddenly Initamay appears, coming toward the lit-up labyrinth.

Now what is he going to do? Beings surging from the other way, are bumping into him. He turns around to move in the same direction rather than be an obstacle. Perhaps this may lead to being closer to her. Yes, we see how he is rather changeable. He becomes uncomfortable as it doesn't make sense to go too close to the main gathering area. He's supposed to be incognito and here he is out in the open. So, he decides it's best to get out of there quick and turns around.

Just then, Initamay moves to make room for the surging crowd and sees him. She says, "Hello, hmm. Funny how you keep turning up wherever I am. Lovely spot here, especially all the showy, sparkling crystal lights."

Zoz is torn, as he wants to speak with her, but it's not the right place for him, way too much attention with all the goings on. "Hello, again. I came to get a good look at this site. I've never seen a design like that. What is it?"

"It's a labyrinth, used for spiritual and ritual purposes."

Zoz says, "Thank you, that's nice." He's not really interested in an explanation. He just wants to talk. "What brings you here?"

"Sorry, I can't talk with you. I'm going away soon. In fact, I have to go. Goodbye." She quickly leaves, without enough information for his satisfaction.

He's surprised, watching her move away, while people walk by and bump into him. Finally, he stops staring as he thinks, "*I better find Keme. I bet she's leaving on that colossal spaceship back there. What a twist. I love my interesting job.*"

He rushes against the surging crowd to return to the transport ship before anyone else does. Just as he gets around a large group, he runs into Keme, as he walks with Bella and the children and says with emphasis, "Keme, I've been looking for you. Come on. We need to go."

He walks past Bella, stopping ahead, to wait for him. He looks to Keme as if to say, "You heard, come on."

Keme quickly says to Bella, "Excuse me. What's your name?"

She smiles. "Bella."

"Good to meet you, Bella. I have to go with my friend. I'm Keme. See you again. I hope. Thanks for the snacks."

Bella says, "Yes, nice to share them with you." She waves goodbye with a cute, happy look at Keme, which makes him blush.

He reluctantly walks to Zoz who says, "Well, I see that was not a llama."

"I did go to the cute furry things over there, but we left them."

"Hmm, Bella. You just met her on the way here?"

"Yeah, after you left with the fruit ladies, when I was looking for you."

Zoz laughs. "Ah, my sweet Aloha Plumerias, heaven sent."

Keme snorts. "Where did you go? I couldn't find you, so I just kept walking."

Zoz says, "I went to see that labyrinth all lit up. Quite a design, but let's keep moving - talk later - to get back to our hiding place before anyone comes. Any moment someone may arrive."

They do not reveal their feelings for the two women that caught their attention. They know its' not a good idea to be distracted by them when they have a job to complete.

Interesting when truths are not spoken, hiding our secret feelings of attraction or passion within one's heart. How likely is it to become involved with these two anyway? Aren't these just temporary encounters, only for the moments, right then?

Yet, those warm lovey feelings that make us wonder and fantasize for a deeper, long-lasting connection are hard to walk away from because our hearts and minds keep feeling, thinking, and conjecturing, even if the connection is improbable and may never repeat again, all to love, or be loved.

Zoz and Keme concentrate on making their way back, maneuvering, quickly around the surging crowds. Zoz is relieved when they see the transport ship looming in the far distance, still flickering on and off.

He says, "Come on. Let's sneak up to see if the coast is clear."

Keme follows as they crouch to make a quick run to get to the back door. No one is there, so they settle in, glad to rest at last, with no further distractions. They breathe in, sighing, and each relive thinking fondly about Bella and Initamay and wondering what the future brings in that regard.

What are they going to do on Gaea Star anyway? They didn't plan very well for anything. They even left their ship, the Marcon. They're just following what Slake told them to do without thinking of an escape plan. They should be thinking more about how they are going to follow the brigade to Gaea Star and what they are going to do if they succeed.

It seems fairly common in the world of thievery, that one thinks of taking everything that one can at the moment. Then get the heck out of there and ask questions later.

PART 8

THE LABYRINTH CEREMONY

16

THE WISE ONES BLESSINGS

Michael and the other archangels are standing in a semi-circle near the labyrinth, overseeing the gathering crowd. He holds his silvery blue sword up high, over his head. It glistens in the moonlight. He says, "Welcome to all. Thank you for joining us in honor of our beloved Gaea Star. For those that did not attend the earlier meeting, I'll give a quick summary of the proceedings.

Recently haunting whale cries were heard throughout the universe, from Gaea Star, prompting the meeting on Star Sirius, to seek a resolution to the crisis of the pilfering of her precious resources and life out of balance there. The council selected members of the crystalla rainbow brigade to undertake a mission to restore harmony on Gaea Star and to inspire humanity with their inherent talents. Brigade, please come to the labyrinth entrance."

The members weave through the crowd, to the majestic entrance, although many offer encouragement and congratulations on their way passing through.

Metatron greets them with a friendly hand hold when they are assembled. "May your new lives be successful in all ways. Wisdom bearers, please share your blessings and words of encouragement." A distinguished group of elders, walk up with flashing crystal staffs, carrying baskets filled with gifts and plants.

Ganesh speaks, "Beings of light, if the challenges of life become too intense, seek the stillness within, to hear the wisdom of your inner spirit. Accomplish all you desire by standing strong, never wavering in your intentions to manifest your true purpose."

He steps aside for Lakshmi, the goddess of abundance, as she floats up gracefully. "We celebrate your acceptance to embark on this mission to the rich planet of fertile waters. The lifetimes it may take to fulfill your destinies, will be worth it. Believe you are always loved, and abundance is your birthright. May you share orbs of love with the suffering of Gaea Star." Holding her hands to her heart, she then casts out gold coins from her fingers all over. Little ones happily run to snatch them up.

Lakshmi steps aside for Archangel Gabriel. She raises her shiny trumpet to the skies, blowing a long blast, to echo in the full moon light. She smiles, saying, "Listen to your heart songs. They lead to the place of meaningful purity. Celestial guidance flows to you, only when requested."

Kuan Yin floats up serenely. "I restore the vibration of love when I hear the cries of all souls in need. If the shadows of darkness cloud humanity, please foster loving compassion within. Honor the wisdom of the ancients. They know the way home. Here is a song from the gentle wise ones, to hold within your hearts."

Listen to the elders, listen

Listen to their wisdom, listen

Listen to the grandfathers, listen

Listen to the grandmothers, listen

Listen to the shamans, listen

Listen to their healing gentle ways

You are all my blessed ones, om, om, om

The Crystal Star Children

Isis appears in golden rainbow splendor. She gracefully leads eleven crystal star children to the labyrinth entrance. She gestures for the brigade to form into a half-moon and then for the children to begin. Each child walks to the brigade and chooses one of them to stand in front of. Their wonderful smiles and gentle demeanors, reflect their happiness in being chosen to have this special honor.

Michael, upon seeing what the star children do, stands behind Rionarta. He gestures to the archangels, to do the same. Uriel understands right away. "Yes, let us each align with a light worker, to serve as their spiritual guides from afar." He flows behind Mira, as her patron, to inspire her with new ideas and wonderful music. She is thrilled to be one of the first chosen.

The other archangels align with the remaining members, Jophiel, the patron of artists, chooses Teesha, while Metatron, protector of children, slides in behind Ilanu. Gabriel, as the messenger of communication, chooses Celestia, while Raphael, as patron of healing and restoring peace, chooses Azul.

Azrael, patron of teachers, chooses Teladi, Ariel, patron of wildlife and the preservation of the environment, chooses Initamay, and Ganesh, courageous remover of obstacles, selects Lakul. He grins with thumbs up. Ashento stands beside Ayalasha, touching her shoulders as she holds his hand and gazes at the star children.

Archangel Raziel, changes into a vibrant rainbow that arches over like rainbows do. Then one end of the rainbow, lands behind Kardichay and bursts into dazzling rainbow lights and instantly transforms into smiling, Archangel Raziel.

Kardichay is amazed. "Wow, thank you. Yes, Raziel, I love you and all rainbows."

The Guidance of Isis

Now that the selection is complete, Isis says with her rainbow wings, fluttering. "Beings of light, this extraordinary labyrinth is a powerful ritual site. Please release all concerns at the portal entrance before entering this sacred space. Walk gracefully to the center. Open to the highest guidance within. Ground and focus to receive the profound healing there.

Take your time, ask for balance and strength, for your intense mission to Gaea Star. Seek the inherent wisdom of your souls to share your unique talents, with humanity. May this ceremony, shower you with divine love in all ways."

As she extends her wings, fluttering them high and beautiful for all to see, her divine feminine splendor radiates, first in the four directions, then below, and above. She signals to a musician who plays a flute softly. The elders, their llamas and other tribal members unite as a family to form a semi-circle that faces the brigade, with the star children in front of them.

What a magnificent vision – the colorful tribes, llamas, the star children and the rainbow brigade with their angelic guides behind or next to them. It is a wondrous weaving of realms, talents, ancient beings, loved ones, majestic crystals and Gaea Star shining in full moon glory. Yes, an auspicious moment to remember, the beginning of the gathering of the tribes of light.

Then the unique blessings begin. A young girl in a pretty white dress, with colored star patterns, waves a smoking herb around the brigade. She gazes into their eyes briefly, as if seeing into their true essence and sings a sweet melody, that she makes up for each just then.

A shaman holds a crystal wand, decorated with crystal pieces in his left hand, first to the heavens, then to the earth below, and to his heart. He closes his eyes. Upon opening, he holds the crystal wand close while saying in his own language, a blessing for each of the brigade that he stands in front of.

Next, an elder in a royal purple ceremonial dress, unwraps a purple bundle. She takes out a shiny rainbow quartz crystal ball. It revolves in her left hand, swirling with imagery of Gaea Star, her blue oceans and green-brown earthy continents with energy lines encircling about her. They pulsate above, beyond and within her beautiful surface, showing the outline of the grid that generates energy as she sails through the universe.

The grandmother passes her right hand over the crystal ball three times, singing, *"Aheya, Gaea Star, noyana, tia heya, nana hey hey. Oh, oh, blessings for their new lives."* Then she walks around each brigade being, the star children and their angels, holding her crystal ball. It changes into another kaleidoscopic color combination whenever she blesses someone else, flashing white, blue, turquoise, yellow, gold, green and purple rays, like fireworks.

When she stands before Ayalasha, holding the crystal ball in front of her, she looks for a long while. Suddenly the ball transforms into purple light that shoots purple stars all over. The grandmother whispers to Ayalasha, so only she can hear, "My daughter, word is sent to Gaea Star that you are coming. Heed your inner feelings, for they will always lead you to safety and sacred protected places of wisdom. Many are trying to keep humanity afraid, in the dark. Go with grace, stand strong, shine bright." She touches her warmly with love.

Ayalasha takes her hand, saying, "Thank you, grandmother."

They exchange a loving hug. A flute echoes in the distance and birds, whistle softly. It is a precious moment for them.

Two shamans, wearing intricate headdresses and beaded clothing step forward. One, holding a small, wrapped bundle close to his heart, instructs the brigade to blow three times on it. After they impart their breath blessings onto the bundle, he hands it to the other. He holds the bundle up to the sky, the earth and his heart, then rubs it over each of them. They feel the pleasing effect of their heartfelt blessings. The shaman takes the bundle and places it on earth by the entrance of the labyrinth.

Next, a mystical priestess wearing a green robe and a glistening gold crown of stars, smiles lovingly at the brigade as she gently hums, holding her hands in front. She emanates pure healing love without touching them.

Another priestess, in a luminous golden cape, holding an intricately carved crystal staff that dances with sparkling light, speaks. "Achina, great central sun. We seek protection of these light beings on their journey to the blue green Earth, where the pure waters sustain all life there. May your peaceful souls reflect your inner lights and inspire healing ways of love that can truly help to heal the aching hearts of her tribes."

A wizened elder raises his arms, looking up, to say, "To the essence of all there is, from the heavens above, to the realms of Gaea Star, the mother earth, Pacha Mama. We dance and pray for the well-being of these wise ones, who carry our hopes for the restoration of humanity and the protection of her precious sacred lands. May it be so."

A handsome, fit being, with a huge feather headdress and colorful wings strapped on, leaps into the middle, surprising the gathering. As he dances, a helper says, "We commemorate all souls present by dancing to honor the life force that sustains us all."

Drummers and singers chant a tribal song that accompanies his passionate expressive dancing.

Achay, aho, adonai, heya naheyo, naheyo, na achay

We dance in a sacred way, celebrating the beauty of life everywhere

May all beings honor the spirit that dwells so deeply within

May we always remember the source of love, Adonai

Everyone appreciates the moving ceremonial dance. Even the labyrinth crystals flicker brightly in response to the superb, honoring commemoration.

17

THE LABYRINTHINE WALK

Isis signals to light the torches. What an exquisite sight, ethereal ones floating, lighting up the circular design, which creates an array of golden flames flickering in the moonlight sky.

Isis gazes lovingly at everyone. "Star crystals, please begin." Each child takes a medallion on a silvery chain from a twinkling star basket, that one of their mother's holds. They hand it to their chosen brigade member and then hug them. Upon receiving the gift, the members say thank you for the honor to be included in such a loving way. They put the medallions on, adjusting how it hangs in order to see the interesting design up close.

Teladi - Crystal White light

Teladi is delighted to go first, wearing his sparkling medallion. He walks reverently through the labyrinth. Brilliant lights beam out, when he passes a series of white crystals, as if reflecting his white light energy. Upon reaching the center, he stops in between the four crystal pillars.

"Ah, what a powerful, magnesite, crystalline vortex, my favorite, to pray to spirit."

Another burst of white light shoots like rockets into the sky. A voice whispers, "Wise master. We are grateful you were chosen, to teach calming ways of stilling the mind, the first step in restoring the serenity of humanity."

Teladi nods, "Yes, I am pleased to be of the utmost service anywhere." He walks back through, still in a prayerful manner, oblivious to all the crystals that shoot white lights as he passes by.

Rionarta - Red Crystals

Rionarta goes next, walking on until he sees a collection of red crystals that flicker on and off, as if charging for take-off. He stops to study what the interesting array is composed of. "Wow, incredible specimens. I love the glowing, warm energy generators. I wonder what they are."

A brilliant red stone cluster, with a sharp triangular point, sparkles, whispering, "Come close, Rionarta, we have awaited your presence, to impart our crystalline knowledge to you to carry into the realms of Gaea Star. We are composites of starry origins, stones that contain the fiery energies of will, action, focus, manifestation and vitality. We were gathered by the Amenti mineral collectors, eons ago. Our names are many, bixbite, aventurine, vanadinite, zircon, rhodochrosite, zoisite, ruby and blood silvers."

Each stone shimmers in response when the voice says their names. Rionarta listens carefully to remember each one. He touches the smooth, sharp, pointy, reflective and shiny clusters.

The voice responds, "Choose a gem to use. All are suited and ready to reflect their unique powers for the highest healing purposes in the distant realm you are traveling too."

Rionarta senses which one to select, by running his left palm over each. He stops at the triangular red aventurine which drew his attention when it flashed warmly. Next to that one, is a smaller version, flashing red.

He says, "This one, aventurine. My gratitude for expressing clearly who you are. I am willing to be a trusted crystal emissary. Thank you, for my supportive new tool for this adventure."

The red crystals shimmer goodbye in rays of red, burgundy, maroon and rose pink. He holds the gift in his left hand as he slowly returns through the labyrinth.

Kardichay's Meteorites

Kardichay goes next, strolling peacefully into the center. He pauses to attune to the potent energy there, silently asking for guidance for his journey. At first, there's no response. He says, "Thank you," and turns to leave but he hears a strong voice.

"Kardichay of the red fire crystals realm, be seated."

"Of course," he says, immediately sitting on the stone path.

The voice asks, "What do you see?" Kardichay looks around to place where the voice is coming from, but all he sees is an array of enormous round red stones, containing spherical shapes, that swirl and bubble within the stones brightly.

He watches the beautiful striations of the twinkling reds that move like waves, rhythmically to the shore. Scanning his memory to place the stones, he says, "These must be chondrite meteorites, from the far away asteroid belt of Riyancus. I have never seen such large stones." The spheres flash bluish, then reddish colors.

The voice says, "Yes, you're right. They carry the molecular structure of water, thus their spherical shapes. Blasted from realms of ancient stars and galaxies, these meteorites are cherished as the ultimate tool to assist with inter-planetary travel and communication with the wise ones you leave behind.

You were chosen to receive this powerful meteorite due to your extensive crystal knowledge. It is easily programmed to ease travel through the atmosphere of Gaea Star, to facilitate confidence, to remember your divine purpose, and to understand how to maintain the balance of your body, mind and spirit."

Kardichay says humbly. "Wow, I am honored and grateful to work with such a positive communicator. Thank you for this knowledge. How may I obtain one?"

"You are welcome. There is more to learn of their potent energies in due time. Nothing is a problem to manifest, in the lands of the plentiful."

Suddenly, out of the sky, a meteorite streaks in a trail of blazing reddish light to land at his feet. He laughs at how fast it happened. He picks up the stone to examine it closely. "It is the same stone. How can that be?"

The voice responds, "Sometimes there is no explanation for the appearance of all things. This stone asks you to become one with all levels, wherever and with whomever they may be. Leave rational reasoning to accept the essence of complete divine union."

Kardichay brings the meteorite to his third eye. "Yes, I sense the stone's magnetic driving energy will assist my travels. I am ready to maintain connection with my starry origins, as the ambassador of alignment."

"Thank you. Remember we are always with you. Goodbye." Kardichay watches as the shimmering wave stops, signifying that the spirit disappeared. He returns through the labyrinth holding the meteorite. He walks beyond the entrance and places it quietly in his pocket and then smiles at Celestia.

Celestia's Bliss

She is so ecstatic waiting her turn, that she did not even notice what transpired with Kardichay. They exchange loving glances, as she walks through the entrance, and is immediately absorbed in the uplifting, labyrinthine effect that flows over her like an angel's kiss. The choir is singing pretty as she hums along the whole time she is in the labyrinth.

Crystals flicker in brilliant golden hues as she passes by, leaving a lingering light energy for all to benefit from. A cluster of lovely pale blue flowers appear and fall at her feet near the end of her walk. She sniffs them, sighing. "Ah, thank you." She feels blessed by their sweet fragrance - it reminds her of heaven. She places a blue flower in her hair and goes through the portal entrance, smiling at Azul who is waiting to go next.

As each brigade member passes all the way through the labyrinth, they stand by the entrance, touched by their mystical experience. They remain in a prayerful mode to watch the others go by, rich with feelings of lightness of being and honoring respect for the spiritual experience they just encountered.

Azul's Calcite Star Beams

Azul steps to the gate, to admire the towering crystals that serve as the doorkeepers, the sentinels, into the multidimensional labyrinth. He senses their strong energies and the good intentions of those who passed through this ceremonial space before him. Walking calmly to the center, he pauses to set his intentions with a prayer. A forceful wind startles him out of his reverie as it swirls about, with golden white light balls bouncing by and landing playfully near him.

He thinks, *"What is projecting this new wave of energy?"* He looks at the crystals on the edges near him to ascertain if one is generating an energy field to cause the wind to act like that. At first, he sees nothing unusual, but then notices an amber colored cluster that looks like a miniature spaceship with pointy terminations, like teeth at the ends.

He thinks, *"Yes, that's it, projecting through the beam-like ends. Hmm, a powerful ally for sure."* He steps closer, drawn to gently touch the crystal and says, "Who are you? What are your reasons for presenting yourself?" He listens for an answer.

The spirit speaks, "Hello, Azul. I am Calcite Star Beams, an ascension healing tool, to guide your journey. I resonate the higher realms of divine consciousness to help to access your celestial origins, and the patterns of the ancient wisdom of advanced civilizations."

Azul responds, "Thank you, Calcite Star Beams. I am honored you chose me to work with your powerful healing force. I sense your ability to travel through multi-dimensions." He closes his eyes, to unify intensely with the spirit of the crystal.

He hears, "Carry me, as situations may arise when my assistance is needed, especially in setting up crystalline grids during the shadows of confusion, that lie ahead for Gaea Star. Gather as light force groups. Hold clear intentions to connect with positive interdimensional beings to manifest spiritual growth, healing and to foster the highest good where it is needed."

Azul nods, saying, "I understand you are a mighty ally to help rearrange the playing fields of life." As he rubs the calcite, a white light flashes. He is surprised when he sees a small calcite star beam crystal next to the larger one.

He hears, "It is yours, Azul. I am the master of replicating at a moment's notice. Be blessed with the grace of healing love in all ways."

Azul picks it up to hold to his heart, saying, "Thank you, Calcite star beams, for this gift." A white light flashes in response. He returns through the labyrinth holding the star beam crystal, completely immersed in the compelling experience. All the while sensing its uplifting energy.

Lakul's Master Carnelian

Still in a deep place, Azul smiles as he walks past Lakul, who stands solemnly at the portal, breathing in the healing energy there. Lakul closes his eyes and holds his arms up in a prayer to the spirit above. He then moves through slowly, humming with attentive respect until stopping in the center as instructed by Isis.

He reaches in his pouch for the carnelian he found in the cave in Diyanna's gardens. He places it on the altar, next to the shimmering fire as an offering. "Great spirit of the fire and the essence of all things sacred, I await your instructions."

He closes his eyes to pray. He listens and hears whispering words, "Thank you for the gift, Lakul, but it is yours. Bring it to the master carnelian, at the end of the labyrinth, to receive an energetic merging for your incredible journey. We are always with you."

Lakul is surprised, "Thank you, master spirit. I am honored to do your bidding." He returns the carnelian to his pouch and walks ever watchful and slowly back through the circular designs.

"Ah, yes, here it is," he says, upon seeing a large glowing orange-reddish stone along the path. "Hello, Master Carnelian. I take in your powerful orange ray. Yes, what a treasure. Certainly, it is my pleasure, thank you."

He takes out the smaller carnelian, touching it lightly to the bigger one and watches how they glow differently at first. Then their two shades merge into one pure orange ray. He senses the transfer is complete. "I'm grateful for this energetic charge up from you, spirit of the fire within. Bless you."

He puts the stone in his pouch, walks back through the labyrinth, and goes to the side to be alone in his reverie, having encountered a spiritual communion unlike anything ever before. Yes, it certainly takes a huge action to humble Lakul.

Teesha's Sparkling Wand

Teesha goes next, gracefully walking and singing lightly to the center with crystalline lights flashing yellow, as if they say, "Hello, sweet one." When she passes a crystal staff, yellow sparkles, explode from it in all directions, causing her to pause and admire the sparkling rays that paint the sky like fire. "Oh, how pretty, I love you, Miss Sparkles."

The staff flew into the air, and waves as if to say, "Hello, Teesha."

It flies into her hand. She is surprised but holds onto the flashing wand like it's a shiny shell she just found on the shore. "Thank you for this delightful sparkling wand. I love how it paints up the sky." She waves it around with ribbons of pretty yellow rays trailing as she returns swiftly through the labyrinth. Colors rise up everywhere swirling after her.

Mira and Ilanu are excited to meet her as she returns through the entry. They want to check out her new wand, but Initamay reminds them. "Hey, stay focused. Concentrate on seeking the stillness within. Your turns are soon. Mira, you're next." Ilanu and Teesha go off to whisper quietly as they examine the wands' mystical light flashing abilities.

Mira's Papagoite Crystal

Mira stands there, so exhilarated; she can hardly relax into the seriousness of the ritual. She does her best to walk slowly, while absorbing the mesmerizing effect of the labyrinth. At the center, she is awestruck by a white quartz with turquoise and blue flecks with clusters that look like miniature temples. They seem to jump out to her. She knows, they are heavenly jewels, carrying the essence of the divine-casting brilliance in all ways.

She whispers, "Crystal spirit, to your grace, I see into your showy distinct essence. May I ask who you are?"

The cluster with the highest pointy projection, flickers translucent blue rays and then she hears a whispering voice. "I am Papagoite, a celestial unifier of all levels. I reawaken the memories of past lives, to help rediscover the clear path to the soul's true essence, to manifest your divine missions. Carry me to access the highest, most beautiful, loving place within, so you may always sing your soul's song.

I am the truth bearer, bringing you clarity, understanding and the synthesis of all the bodies, physical, emotional, mental, and spiritual. I help you to flow into balanced communication with the higher realms."

Mira touches the cluster gently. A small piece of the crystal falls into her fingers. She looks at it. "Thank you, blue crystal spirit. I will cherish this gift and your knowledge." She puts it in her bag and returns through the labyrinth singing all the way back. She smiles at Initamay as she stands at the entrance ready to go next.

Initamay's Lepidolite

Initamay pauses at the entrance to greet the strong, welcoming intensity of the labyrinth. She takes a deep breath and walks in a prayerful manner, to the sacred center, where she pauses to assimilate the uplifting, inspiring silence. She is humbled by the impact of the many ones who passed through the labyrinth in this same manner. She feels all of their lingering prayers within the sacred design.

As the fire flickers gently amidst the soothing lights of the tall crystals, she is moved to speak. "I am Initamay, my brother, Ilanu's guardian. I am lover of all living elements. I ask for support as we journey into a new life that calls for dedication to inspire a more nurturing way of life on Gaea Star."

A gentle voice whispers, "Hello, green lover of all life. As you leave this labyrinth, seek the wisdom of the lilac crystal that will reveal itself. It is Lepidolite, the peace stone, known to encourage acceptance of your new roles. Be in harmony with all that you do. Many blessings will surround you."

Initamay is touched, "Thank you. I'm grateful for this peace stone to release and feel goodness within."

She turns, breathes deeply, and then slowly returns through the winding path, humming, and watching for the tall lilac stone. As she nears the end of the labyrinth, she senses that she is close and slows down. Suddenly to the left, a tall shiny lilac crystal pillar glimmers purple, blue, and rose. Then all three colors glow at once, as if turning on for her. She watches intently as the pillar flickers.

"Ah, Lepidolite, I see, sense and feel you, like no other stone right now. We are in balance." A warm calming rush of love floods over her, healing and releasing energy within her.

A husky voice whispers, "I am within the center of all that you seek. Take me on your adventure. I will be useful on Gaea Star, when it's necessary to realign energy grids to inspire the nations, with healing waves of loving acceptance for all things."

Initamay smiles, "Oh, of course, Lepidolite. I love filling my medicine bag with potent healing tools for well-being. Thank-you."

"Pop," she hears just then. Something drops at her feet. She reaches for it. "Thank you, beautiful lepidolite, stone of peace. Come with me to share your wise ways on Gaea Star." She tucks it into her pouch and returns through the labyrinth, passing Ilanu, who is surprisingly ready for his turn, even though he happily played with Teesha and her new sparkly staff for a long time.

Ilanu's Magic Crystal Wand

Initamay whispers, "Ilanu, please stay focused. Walk quietly. Pay attention. It's a relaxing and rewarding experience."

He nods, "Yes, I see how "the maze" works. I saw your gift from the lilac stone. Nice, to be precise."

Initamay laughs, for she never heard it called a maze, "Yes, the stone is very pretty, thanks."

Ilanu is so excited that walking slowly while he tries to concentrate is not possible. It's not his true nature, at least not yet. He does not think of the serious reason of why he was there. He is distracted by the flame torches, the crystals bordering the paths and the shiny lights shimmering everywhere, all of which created a mystical, supernatural realm for him to explore.

Isn't being in the present moment all that we are ever asked to be, aware, alive, happy and grateful? Ilanu fully conveys his soul's natural expression, living for the bliss of the moment with joyful enthusiasm and innocence while ignoring the serious, non-believing judgmental ways of many people.

He makes it to the center, pauses briefly to revel in the special feeling of warm comfort he feels there. He then smiles at Initamay and mimes an expression of '*how proud he is to be there.*' She smiles warmly at him, for yes, she is very pleased. He begins his return through "the maze," as he calls it.

But this time, he walks slowly, as there are shiny stones to carefully examine. He says to himself, "Oh, look at the painted pathways and the colorful crystals arranged like rainbow colors. So much to see, so what's the hurry, no reason to scurry?"

"Hey, what was that?" he says, when a crystal wand, he thinks, winks at him. *Really, does that happen*? He stops right in front of it to watch. Yes, it winks again - this time twice. "Hey, master crystal wand, flashing brightly, I see you are fond, in this nightly."

He leans over to touch it and suddenly, the wand flies straight into his hand. Surprised, he catches and waves it around with a smile, until he sees Initamay smiling again, but signaling for him to keep on going now. What a conscious sister she is.

He mimes, "*Alright. Yes,*" to her while saying to himself, "*Best to keep moving, to keep on walking.*" He tries to put the crystal wand back three times, but it refuses to stay by flying back to him each time, as if it wants to be his.

Finally, Ilanu realizes the magical wand must be an awesome gift meant for him. He says, "Thank you, I accept, magical crystal wand. Yes, I know that I will be fond." He holds it close to his heart, saying proudly, "Onward," and points the wand to go back through 'the maze.'

Ilanu loves parades and so steps as if he is in his own parade, waving his wand like a baton, flipping it into the air, and watching it return to him easily, but not in any manner that made sense. He walks differently then when he passed through the first time.

The wand is a funny tool, like a trickster, that fits Ilanu like a glove. "What a perfect treasure," he says, as he strolls through the rest of 'the maze,' and every so often, he flashes the wand. What a pair they are, like two peas in a pod, like thunder and lightning, like salt and pepper, like a rainbow after the rain.

He walks on his tippy toes, as he leaves the labyrinth, hardly touching the ground. Oh, how excited he is to tell Initamay and Teesha who are standing at the entrance. Teesha watched how the wand flew to him, so she wanted to be right there to see it for herself out of curiosity.

Ilanu holds the crystal wand in front of her, and of course, it lights on and off, as if on cue. "Look at this cool crystal wand that came from the middle. It was flying around. It was me it found. Did you see what happened when I tried to put it back."

Teesha says, "Yes, he came to you. I was impressed."

"Yeah, it kept acting like, no, that's not my lair. I think it wants to be my friend. Yes, it's my new friend." He swirls the wand with a wonderful flourish, ending with a bow. "Introducing, Mister Crystal laser wand, of which I am newly fond." He brings the wand close for her to see. It lights up again, as if it heard his nice intro.

Teesha leans in to admire it. "Amazing, a real crystal laser wand, that responds to you like that. I wonder who the maker was to have such magic?"

"Yeah, I wonder too. Hey, maybe they're nearby watching." They look around laughing, but who programmed those wands, is not to be discovered right then, as there is so much fun to enjoy around the ceremonial area.

Teesha waves her sparkling wand in front of Ilanu, saying, "Hey super cool. Let's see what they do together."

He quickly says, "Yes, let's." They go dipping and zooming around with their awesome crystal, sparkler wands, trying not to make too much noise but that's difficult for them.

Ayalasha's Rally from the Faeries

Ashento and Ayalasha stand by the entrance awaiting her turn, wearing their long cloaks, that sparkle brilliantly with stars and crystals. He reaches for Ayalasha to bring her close for a hug and says, "My sweetness, I am only to escort you to the atmospheric portal of Gaea Star where you'll proceed without me. I'll wait for your return, even if it takes eons. You are my great love."

He smiles, looking sincerely into her eyes. She accepts his overwhelming love, flowing deeply inside her heart. He says, "You may not remember me until you awaken to your spiritual destiny. Memories from eons ago will soothe the unfulfilled longings in your heart, helping you to feel our warm connection."

Ayalasha says, emphatically, "Ashento, you are deep in my memory, warm and snug within my heart. I will never forget you. The fulfilling delight of our love is all I need."

They silently gaze into their eyes, hugging, touching each other. The longing to be together is intensely palpable. This last loving moment is the real treasure for them to experience before she departs for Gaea Star.

The Medallion

As they embrace, she notices her new medallion gift from one of the star children, earlier. It is glowing and dangling in front of her. She takes her left hand to bring it close, to examine it, "Oh, it's such a sweet and familiar motif, the rainbow lightworkers symbol with embellishments."

A vision flashes - a long ago memory, of a geometric design. She can't quite remember where it was from. Ashento holds it to study it.

He says, "My sweetness, this is an ancient symbol of the essence of the universe, signifying the inherent patterns of creation. Many cultures have implemented this holy design in their art, temples and buildings, the star beings, Maya, Aztec, Inca, Native American, India and elsewhere. The forces of love gave this to all of you to master self-awareness, to activate the healing force within, to release fears and to unify you as leaders and healers for the greater good of Gaea Star."

She looks at it, saying, "I remember now, the familiar spiral circles, the powerful eight directions, the star within, the rainbow colors, the feathers of the lightness of being, all to remind us of the pure loving divine essence of life. What a beautiful package of spiritual wisdom to accompany us." She places the medallion above her heart, and watches as it sparkles in the glowing moonlight.

It is her turn to enter the labyrinth. She pauses at the entrance, breathing in a pure breath of life, merging herself with the energies of the portal and beyond. She waits until she has unified with the mystically, mesmerizing energies there. She walks reverently as Ashento watches. Every so often, her medallion flashes rainbows rays in the flickering fire light.

After arriving at the center, she sets her intentions. "I seek the wisdom to walk the priestess path of light, as I bear the torch of love for all to see, feel and be healed by. May I manifest the highest, gratifying aspect of my soul's deepest longings on Gaea Star."

She closes her eyes, breathing in deeply, while absorbing the serene comforting energy. A soft wind blows in. Ethereal humming and light chimes sing. Sweet bird songs fill the air. The tall crystal sentinels along the path flash purple rays. Misty rainbows arch above her. Tiny flowers rain down everywhere.

A voice whispers, "My daughter of radiant golden light. We have lived as kings and queens, in many forms, on Gaea Star. Now we are free as the wind, to celebrate, nurture and prosper in the realms of the all-knowing. We honor your dynamic creative efforts. Your strength to cultivate pure love within and how you express your passions, enhances your ability as a gifted priestess of the healing expressive arts."

Ayalasha hears galloping and a whiny. She sees the magnificent unicorns, trotting to the edge of the labyrinth. A bevy of faeries and Emeraldina are flying to where everyone is gathered.

A faery calls, "Ayalasha, all who are going to Gaea Star. Please pay attention to the signs in nature. We'll be the crickets, the birds, the flowing rivers, the sweet, lovely flowers, and the whispering wind. We are in all things - everywhere you don't look."

Ayalasha smiles, "Thank you, unicorns, faeries, winged ones. Yes, I'll look everywhere, for I am your friend in all ways."

Exhilarated, she returns through the labyrinth, playing with the faery kin, who flutter about, dancing, and singing, as she skips through the pretty pathways, with uplifting joy, right into the waiting arms of Ashento. They hug passionately while most of those watching, now realize he must not be going to Gaea Star with the rainbow brigade.

How did that happen? Remember when Isis told Ashento that he was to remain in the high realms to pursue his spiritual studies and be a guide for Ayalasha and the brigade? Everything happened so quickly that there was not a moment to mention this to anyone, or even to process this intense, unsettling aspect before the pressing need to say goodbye at her departure. That is why no words were spoken, only a knowing.

Ayalasha releases Ashento, takes his hand, and turns to speak, to her fellow travelers. "Now that we have passed through the labyrinth, let's sing for our angels. I have the perfect song." She takes out her instrument, hums, then sings.

Back us up oh angels, back us up oh spirit

We're ready, ready to shine

We know you're watching us

We know you're guiding us

We're ready, ready to materialize, on to Gaea Star

Back us up oh angels, back us up oh spirit

We're ready, ready to harmonize

Michael, Gabriel, Uriel, Chamuel, Ariel, Jophiel, Raphael

Azrael, Raziel, Metatron, Sandolphon, Angel Ohm

We're ready, ready for Gaea Star

Back us up oh angels, back us up oh angels

When Angel Ohm's and the archangels' names are sung, they join in dancing. What an unusual sight, to see the normally serious celestial one's dancing and celebrating with all the many diverse beings gathered from throughout the universe.

Since everyone is singing and having so much fun, Ayalasha leads the song through a few more times, to keep dancing and whooping it up. Yes, it is a wild, happy, moment before the brigade departs for the distant realm beyond and for who knows how long.

18

LLAMAS TO GAEA STAR

Just as the upbeat song ended, chanting and drumming is heard coming from behind the crowds. Everyone turns to see who it is. "Wow," Mira whispers to Teesha, "what a colorful procession of the elders."

"Yes," Teesha says, "let's join in." They go to meet Andaluchiya and Ritoyo and their tribe, as they lead their colorful llamas, singing and drumming as one family.

> *Hey yuna hey, hey yuna hey, hey hey hey, hey yuna hey*
>
> *We are all one family of light, one family of love*
>
> *Bringing our llamas as gifts from above*
>
> *To grace life on Gaea Star with love*
>
> *Hey yuna hey, hey yuna hey, hey hey hey, hey yuna hey*

Andaluchiya and Ritoyo welcome the admirers that cluster around the llamas as they walk up. She says, "Michael, we spoke with Ayalasha about gifting these loyal friends to accompany the mission to Gaea Star."

Michael says, "Thank you, they look quite special."

Andaluchiya rubs Ausan's neck and her soft fiber, saying, "Yes, they cheerfully carry burdens, precious water and provide fibers for warmth."

Ayalasha says graciously, "They will be well-received and cared for, in the mountain highlands." She too strokes them as they are now familiar with her touch. Pointing their ears, they extend their long necks to give her a kiss. Ayalasha laughs, saying, "Michael, please meet them. They give whisker kisses."

He goes to the llamas and that's exactly what happens - They lean over to give him a sweet whisker kiss. He laughs. "Ah, yes, they are adorable. Alright, we accept your wonderful gift. Perhaps, Andaluchiya, you and Ritoyo would like to escort them to their mountain home, to seed a new peaceful spiritual life there?"

Andaluchiya, surprised by his offer, translates to Ritoyo. They confer. "Thank you, Michael, but we must counsel before we answer."

He says, "Yes, take a moment to discuss this. The crystalline ship is due to sail very soon. Brigade, pay heed, this is your last chance to say goodbyes to your loved ones."

The highland tribe crowds together, talking in their language. Ayalasha takes the lead ropes for the llamas and signals for anyone to come to meet these friendly ones. Many rush over and express joy at their cuteness and whiskery kisses.

Ashento and Teladi, stand by talking quietly, while the other brigade members chat with friends that seek their attention before they leave for such a lengthy uncertain period.

Lakul, exercising near the edge of the crowd in preparation for the journey, says, "Oh greatness, I'm thrilled to be embodied on Gaea Star, one of my favorite places. Hmm, yes, where one can enjoy the wondrous aspects of humanity. I heard about the great looking women there. Oops." He looks around to see if anyone heard that last comment and sighs, relieved when he realizes that no one did. He resumes exercising since it invigorates and prepares him for anything. He loves to keep his body as a tool ready for action.

Mira is singing lightly, a little overwhelmed by the excitement. Teesha is sketching the highlights of the radiant scene before her for later creative expansion.

"Mira, isn't this experience amazing? I wonder where we'll end up?"

Mira answers, "Does it matter? I don't see what the difference is where we go. I wonder though, how are we going to keep in touch? What do you think we should do to make sure?"

Teesha smiles, "We'll never forget each other. We're so close. Let's always travel together."

Mira sighs, "Yes, I love that, sailing through the universe as one."

Teesha takes her hand, "Let's look at those sparkling lights over there and forget about anything else." Mira nods. They go to see them.

Kardichay and Celestia are feeling their excitement, as they speak with friends, even though she is distracted by the luminous stars and comets streaking by. Seems like everyone is trying to converse all at once. Finally, she takes a moment to say, "I heard Mira and Teesha. Do you think we'll forget each other?"

Kardichay responds warmly, "No, Celestia, that is not possible, given how I feel about you. Of course, we'll remember each other. Haven't we remained fond of one another since we met many years ago?"

She shyly says, "Kardichay, that's sweet. Thank you. There must be a way to remember if we get separated. Maybe a sign in the stars, or the sparkling light in your eyes, that will activate something from deep within and long ago because we don't even know how long this mission may take, do we?"

Azul comes up right then and joins in, "Well, it could take lifetimes, and in that case, we may easily lose track of each other. Yes, the eyes are the sweet windows into our souls. I like that. When we look deeply, we'll feel a familiar response, a knowing. Our new crystals will help us remember too. This mission is a leap of faith. We have to believe that all is for the best. We'll be fine, I feel that for sure."

Kardichay smiles, "Yes, when the crystals flicker, it will be like a light turned on within, shining bright. Awakening our memories of each other, but hey, I don't think we have to worry. We're together for now. Let's believe it's going to be fine."

Celestial says, "Yes, you're right. Well, I hope we stay connected but for now it's a wonderful night to watch the stars. I feel so relaxed after walking the labyrinth, don't you?"

Kardichay says, "Yes, it was powerful for me too."

Azul agrees, "Yes, the energies were different for each of us. I feel prepared and look forward to this new adventure ahead."

Celestia, seeing more friends coming toward her, says, "Oh, I'll reconnect soon. I have to say goodbye." She goes to engage with a small group of well-wishers that surround her.

Angel Ohm's Gifts

Kardichay smiles as he watches her walk off. He says to Azul, "Hmm, she is so lovely. What a blessing that we reconnected for this mission. I saw the crystal starship we're going to fly on behind the platform docks a while ago. Do you want to check out the workings of it? It's not too far. I'm going to go there."

Azul says, "Yes, Celestia is an angelic being and no, I'm staying to relax here for a moment. I need too, it's been a whirlwind." He sits on the ground. Yes, he needs a rest and now is the perfect time.

Just then, Angel Ohm waves to Kardichay to come to her. When he does, she says, "Please bring Rionarta with you."

"Of course," he says to her, and looks around, until he spots Rionarta, laughing as Ausan, the llama, gives him a whiskery kiss. The unicorns are prancing around, with a bunch of little ones on their backs. He goes to him. "Hey Rionarta, Angel Ohm wants to speak with us. Wow, they are so cute."

"Okay," Rionarta says, "coming. Goodbye, furry friends. I love you." As he walks with Kardichay toward Angel Ohm, he says, "Yeah, they're so soft yet, so strong."

Now they go off in the opposite direction of the crystal ship which is shimmering in the distance. Well, that was a close call since Zoz and Keme, are hiding and snoring in the back of it and would easily have been discovered.

For the moment, they're in the clear, but what's to happen when everyone gets on board? Did Zoz think this through? How are they going to remain hidden after they arrive?

Angel Ohm floats to a quiet area near lush trees that are bursting with purple-grape like clusters, flowing to the ground. She reaches into her ethereal gown, to bring out two small shiny pouches and hands them to Kardichay and Rionarta.

She says, "My crystal scholars, here is a gift, a tool that may be necessary to use. I only obtained these. Your departure is looming. Keep them safe, to prevent their use for negative reasons. Please open them. I will explain their purposes."

Kardichay opens the pouch and takes out a large flat quartz crystal. He examines the prominent white streak running through the middle. "These are Faden crystal healers. They have the ability to heal from within their own structure. See the white streak is where it healed its' own break." He shows it to Rionarta.

Angel Ohm says, "Yes, they're helpful to unify and restore balance to the grid of Gaea Star, especially in troubled regions that desperately need realignment."

Kardichay holds it to his heart, "Thank you, Angel Ohm, for giving me this healing crystal. It is in good hands." He returns it to his pouch for safe keeping.

Rionarta takes out a shiny metallic piece from his new pouch, studying it, "A mineral, Titanium, I believe."

Kardichay looks over, "Yes, indeed. It is a rare specimen."

Angel Ohm beams, "Yes, that's excellent. Titanium is a precious metal that will accentuate the rainbow light body, transform technological and medical aspects and help to create healing light tools and structures on Gaea Star."

Rionarta says, "Thank you. I'm honored to carry this transformative gem on our journey. I'm sure it will be handy." He rubs the stone until it sparkles and puts it in the pouch into his pocket.

Angel Ohm smiles. "Go with our blessings. I have a gift for Teladi, so I must find him, before departure." She touches their shoulders in a loving gesture, then floats away, singing lightly.

Rionarta says, "Well, she is sweet. We are fortunate to be part of this grand plan. She gave us potent gifts."

Kardichay agrees, "Yes, she did. I'm glad we're on this mission. We make a good team."

Rionarta, nods, "Yes, I'm pleased to work together." They return to the departure area.

Angel Ohm floats through the crowd until she sees Teladi talking with Ashento. "Excuse me, may I have a moment, Teladi?"

"Of course," he says, "be well, Ashento. I'll look for your messages as instructed. So, until we meet again, may you sail into the realms of the most-high places in pure bliss."

Ashento says, "Thank you, Teladi, I'll shine the light of love from here for all of you to receive." They hug. He goes in search of Ayalasha.

Teladi follows Angel Ohm for a short distance until she stops. He says, "Angel Ohm. What are your thoughts?"

She smiles brightly, "Master Teladi, I have a precious gift, for you to bring to lovely Gaea Star." She reaches into the soft fabric of her gown and hands him another sparkling pouch.

He is surprised and slowly opens the bag, taking out a beautiful, clear quartz crystal with colorful inclusions within it. He looks it over, "Remarkable. A gem of immense powers. I see wings of angels in the phantom minerals that dwell within and feel the loving energy of this radiant quartz."

Thrilled that he knows her gift, she smiles, "Yes, Teladi, you are the master who listens to the deep essence within your soul. The phantom wing crystal helps one to remember the angelic realm is always here in support, especially when the shadowy veils may be difficult to penetrate. Treasure this key crystal. It is only for those who awaken to their divine destinies and seek to restore balance to Gaea Star."

Teladi says, "Angel Ohm, Thank you. I accept this gift, to cherish and use wisely." He holds it to his heart, then looking at the stars, says, "I sense it's healing gentle wisdom." He returns it to the pouch, and hugs her, looking deeply into her eyes. "From my heart to yours, I shall miss you and will think of you fondly."

She is startled by his display of affection. "Oh, I will miss you too, Teladi, and await your heavenly return." What a pleasant surprise they connect in such a loving way. They enjoy their last moments, by being close, smiling at each other and creating a pleasant love sensation that flows out like a misty wave of healing white light all around them. Then with a start, she says, "Oh, I'm sorry but I must go help Metatron prepare the departure activator."

"Oh, certainly. May I join you to be of technical assistance?"

She says, "Yes, I'm sure Metatron will be pleased to see us both, as departure is looming. He is creating something new and special and may need further support to complete the details."

Teladi says, "Then, let us be on our way. We have important matters to do together." She laughs, quite pleased for his company. They walk away arm in arm.

The Elders Join the Mission

Ashento finds Ayalasha playing with her llama friends. Just then, the tribal elders return from discussing Michael's proposal of going to Gaea Star. Mysteriously, he appears in a light mist at the same moment. He smiles, saying, "Andaluchiya, Ritoyo, what is your consensus for the mission?"

She smiles, saying, "Master Michael, Ritoyo and I, are honored to leave our beloved country, to reseed the mountains of Gaea Star with our peaceful way of life, to benefit all of humanity."

Ritoyo, touching his heart, speaks to Andaluchiya. She translates, "We bring compassion and our humble llamas to live simply in community, to inspire those who forgot how to live in a loving manner, which is the only reason for being."

Michael is pleased. "Congratulations. Thank you, for your noble attitude in joining this mission, to awaken the lost souls who forgot their connection to the source of love. Many will seek your wisdom for eons throughout the mountain regions. All right, then, we must arrange the crystalline ship to include you and the llamas. Are they a mated pair?"

Andaluchiya laughs, "Yes, we selected a favorable couple in all ways, fiber, friendship, loyalty and gentleness. Ausan, the female, wears rainbow ribbons, and Cusi, the male, has rainbow tassels on his bags. They are young, healthy and enjoy traveling."

Their tribal family gathers for emotional final goodbyes. It is hard to see them go. They are truly their beloved leaders.

Michael says, "Kardichay, Rionarta, let's confer on the expansion of the crystalline ship." They go to speak with him, a little distance away from everyone.

Kardichay says, "I have an idea to expand the size using crystalline technology."

Rionarta nods yes, "Hmm, are you referring to some sort of replicator device?"

Kardichay smiles, "Yes, I believe that with the new crystals we recently acquired, we may program them to synergistically increase the total capacity bearing space appropriately."

Rionarta laughs, "Well, that's a mouthful. You are always good at long explanations. I follow though, that may work. I guess we need to go see."

Michael says, "Yes, thank you. Please go to figure that out as you know the details. I will check on the brigade."

Rionarta and Kardichay say, "Okay" together. They head toward the crystal ship, talking excitedly in technical terminology.

Michael signals Uriel to him. He flies over. "Please assist in organizing the traveling party."

"Yes, of course," says Uriel. He turns to the crowd. "Attention, brigade, Andaluchiya, Ritoyo. Are you almost ready?" He floats around, trying to count, mumbling about who is supposed to be on board. "Yes, I think we are complete, are we not?"

Initamay arrives, looking around. Guess what? She discovers that Ilanu is not there. She says, "Oh no, not again. We were doing so well in keeping track of him. Where did he go to? I thought he was with the others."

She looks to Uriel, "Excuse me, but we're missing Ilanu. Sometimes I can locate him, with my loud whistling." She whistles twice, but no answer.

Uriel laughs, "Ilanu is being his true self, a happy joyful soul."

Initamay says, "I'll head to the labyrinth, to try there first." Off she goes, still whistling every so often, with no luck though.

PART 9

DISTRACTIONS
BEFORE TAKE OFF

19

UNTIMELY ECOUNTERS

In the meantime, Zoz and Keme, who are still hiding in the crystalline ship, wake up from their snoozing after hearing Initamay's whistling and other voices coming toward them. Zoz peeks out to see. Alarmed, he says "Oh, oh, two guys coming here. I don't have a good feeling. Let's bail, hide in the trees over there until things settle down here."

Quickly scrambling away, they race to the trees, where no one will see them. Once hunkered into the new hiding spot, Zoz says, "Wow, another close call. We need a new plan to get on board, while no one notices. Lets' wait until the coast is clear, nothing we can do until then."

Rionarta and Kardichay, never even notice Zoz and Keme running off. They were so engrossed in discussing how the enlarging plan is going to work, as they walked to the ship. After looking it over, Kardichay says, "Impressive, the entire structure is a crystalline star ship made out of unusual metal, sitting on danburite crystals that enhance propulsion."

Rionarta examines the sides. "Yes, it's remarkable the crystal technology used to create such a vessel. I like the translucent mineral ore comprising the sides. Let's check out which is the best choice for expanding easily."

They circle the entire structure, exactly what Zoz thought might happen. Yes, his plan to get a free ride, as stowaways would certainly have been foiled by those two.

Rionarta says, "Actually, the space is suitable for all of us and the llamas."

Kardichay laughs, "Really? Let's count who's coming. Us, Initamay, Ilanu, Celestia, Mira, Teesha, Azul, Teladi, and Lakul. I assume Ayalasha is leaving in her purple star comet, to give her one last moment with her new love, Ashento, who isn't coming."

Rionarta says, "Yes, that's too bad about their separation, but he'll be guiding us, I'm sure. Teladi will fly in his own incredible crystal rocket creation. Remember, that's how he arrived here?"

Kardichay says, "Right, that's nine then, Andaluchiya, Ritoyo, eleven, and the llamas, so yeah, there should be room. Let's explain that to Michael." They walk back toward the gathering.

"Well, that was easy to figure out," says Rionarta.

Kardichay nods, "Yeah, I like situations simple to solve. I have a strange feeling that where we're headed, things may not fall into place so easily." They disappear up the path.

Keme and Zoz heard everything still hiding under the trees. They smile. Zoz says, "Okay, Keme, now is our chance to get it right this time. I saw large cargo boxes when we left the ship before. Let's see if we can sneak into them until the take off."

Keme says, "Cargo boxes, really? I hope I fit."

Zoz laughs, "Funny. Well, there's no choice, we don't want to be discovered." Crouching they start running to the ship, and hopefully make it without encountering anyone.

Meanwhile, Initamay's search around the labyrinth in hopes to find Ilanu is futile. Miffed that he's missing at this crucial moment again, she thinks, *I need to let go of where I think he may be and follow my feelings. Releasing expectations always works better anyway in his regard. He loves faeries and the elves. That's right, he must be with Verdalon playing by the trees in that pretty cluster."* She walks below the overhanging branches, scanning and calling. Just as she comes out from beneath the branches, who do you think she runs into? Not Ilanu, but Zoz and Keme running to hide in the crystalline ship. *"Oh no. Trouble,"* they both think.

Initamay, surprised by their repeat appearance, is suspicious, and thinks, *What's going on? Why do we keep running into each other? What are their intentions? It's too coincidental."* They stop to try look nonchalant, as if its' perfectly fine to be where no one else is. "Whoa, what are you two doing way over here?" she asks abruptly.

Zoz smiles uneasily, "Hello. We meet again. We were, um, just waiting to watch that unusual ship takeoff over there. We're taking a quick jog and studying the vegetation of the trees."

Just as he speaks, Mister Coole, Ilanu's friend from Diyanna's gardens, hops from a branch, landing at their feet, to stroll silently past them. Zoz thinks fast, saying, "Oh, there he is. We're still observing this cool cat."

Keme quickly agrees, "Yeah. Ah, the trees are unique, and the cat is a rare creature."

Initamay laughs at how Keme chimed in, but she feels wary and not sure of their excuses. Then again, she has more important issues to attend to. She leans to pet Mister Coole. He's cute. *"Hmm, interesting cat,"* she thinks as he purrs, responding to her gentle touch. He seems to turn up in the strangest moments.

Zoz thinking he may have convinced her, says, "I heard calling. Were you looking for someone?"

Initamay now remembers why she was there in the first place, saying. "Yes, I'm looking for my brother, Ilanu. We're going away very soon."

Zoz says, "We haven't seen anyone here. Do you need us to help you find him?"

She smiles a little, "Ahh, that's nice, but no thanks. I'm sure he'll turn up. He always does. I'll head a different way then." She turns to go, then looks back, "I'm Initamay, and you two are?"

Zoz glances at Keme. "I'm Zoz, he's Keme. Have a good trip, Initamay. Who knows, maybe we'll run into each other again."

She says, "Thank you. I plan to, but I don't think we'll see each other again. We're going far away, for a while. Goodbye." She runs toward the crowds, concerned that Ilanu is really lost this time.

Zoz and Keme watch her leave. When she is out of sight, Zoz says, "Whew, another close call. Darn, she is really attractive when she's all riled up, full of action. I like that."

Keme speaks very pronounced. "Excuse me. We're going to help find him. How was that supposed to work?"

Zoz says, "I knew she wouldn't want us to, just a friendly gesture. Keep the peace, a show of support goes far."

Keme says, "She was wary of us. Anyway, how are we gonna hide in that ship with all of them?"

Zoz looks at the crystal ship flickering in the distance, "Look, one thing at a time. Once we're on board, something will come to me. We keep hiding until it lands on Gaea Star, and they depart. I think it will work as the ship is probably traveling at lightspeed. It won't be that long. You're okay, just be cool."

Keme sighs, saying, "The things I do with you - never a dull moment. But this is the last time. I mean it."

Zoz says, "Hey, I'm a man of my word. We have the same plan, just a little later. I think the coast is still clear. Luckily no one is there yet. Come on, let's go. It's our chance."

A Run in With Lucifer

Zoz takes off running, with Keme behind him. Just as they come around the bend, they see the crystal ship in full sight. Oh no, but wait, who do you think they run into? Lucifer. He was on his way back to speak to the brigade with his one more element, remember? They bump abruptly, as his head was down, talking to himself. He was not looking where he was going, since his thoughts were elsewhere. He had finally figured out, what element he was going to offer, as a final sendoff gift for the brigade.

Lucifer looks up surprised and immediately notices their furtive behavior, and ragged appearance. Yes, as a seer, he is aware of all things, positive or negative. He senses something is not good here.

He slowly says, "Well, well, the two of you in the wrong place at the right time for me to meet. So, what is your explanation? Where are you trying to get so quickly ?"

Zoz and Keme try to calm themselves to appear relaxed.

"Wow," thinks Zoz, "we're in a pickle. Hmm, what can I say that he'll believe?"

He looks down and guess who ambles by at the puurfect moment? Mister Coole, that slinky cat, seems to show up at opportune moments.

Keme sees him glance down. He follows his gaze to see the cat is rubbing Lucifer's leg and loudly purring. He says, "Hey, here he is. We were looking for him for our studies."

Zoz rallies behind that crazy excuse, by expounding on it, "Yes, we were sent to observe this cats' behavior here."

Mister Coole is enjoying his new petting buddy, Lucifer, who has returned to thinking about the brigade. He is certain, they must be ready to embark without his last instructions. "Well, alright then, best to slow down. Excuse me, I have to be somewhere very soon." Off he hurries, just like that without even looking back at them.

Zoz and Keme are surprised but relieved, that they somehow managed their way out of the unpleasant potential of failing in their assignment and missing out on the hefty reward from Slake that is driving their pursuing antics.

Lucifer, being preoccupied does not thoroughly check out these two. Even if they did not appear as they should, he lets them get away, without thinking it through. It was the first time in a long while, that he let his guard down since he was on his important mission to get to the launching area before the brigade's departure.

Mister Coole had something to do with that. He showed up, right then, to soothe Lucifer's searching manner. He is soft and gentle, which is what cats are known for, being the true masters of changing frenetic energy. Subsequently one has to relax, to feel their softness and hear their soothing purring, right?

Cats sense energies, and who knows about the loving wild spirit within Mister Coole? He may be playing his significant role in the great plan for all things. As each aspect in life, wherever or whomever, is a part of the grand creation, of the oneness that lies within us. For we are always connected to spirit, to the wondrous force of love.

Zoz and Keme waste no time. They quickly run to the crystal ship before anyone else comes along. Zoz checks the storage crates. They are conveniently empty. He hops in and signals to Keme to get in the other one. He grumbles since he has to squeeze in tight due to his size. He finally gets all of himself in without sticking out.

Zoz reminds him, "Keme, you can fit. Its' only temporary. Come on. We'll be flying at light speed, so lighten up. Stay quiet."

You hear his mumbling. "What was I thinking, getting involved with you again? This is the very last job I am ever doing with you, for sure."

Zoz laughs, "Alright, that's fair. Now settle down. They may be coming. I have to plan what we're doing after we get there." He thinks, *How clever, that we managed to get on board and into hiding. Now what happens after take-off?"*

He hasn't figured that out yet, since he is a man of the moment, as most crooks are. One thing at a time, is his abiding motto. They made it on the ship, that's all he was trying to do.

Mister Coole seems to be following them as he appears at the open door of the ship. Ah, just enough for a cat like him to slink through. He sniffs around and spies the crates. Hmm, perfect, for him to hop onto. Then he jumps to the high rafters above the boxes and settles there as another stowaway. Wonder what his intentions are, for coming along? No one explained to him about the mission. Is he volunteering, or out for a fun adventure? No telling what he's up to. He's harmless, but persistent. None the less, he is going to Gaea Star, uninvited.

Locating Ilanu Again

Kardichay and Rionarta, explain to Michael, that there is no need to enlarge the transport ship. He says, "Excellent. Preparations are almost ready, except for a few details, like our young magician, Ilanu, still missing. Initamay went in search of him."

They laugh. Rionarta says, "Again? He's a real character. We'll help locate him."

Michael says, "Certainly, if you can find Initamay. Last I heard, she went to the labyrinth." They head off in that direction.

Metatron is with Uriel and Chamuel, when Initamay comes rushing by. He says, "Hey, what's the problem here?"

Initamay stops and sighs. "Oh, sorry, I'm rushing. Ilanu is missing. Can't find him anywhere. I need your help, please." Metatron gently touches her shoulder with a concerned look.

Chamuel says, "Certainly, we love to help all who ask."

Metatron agrees, "Yes, Chamuel, by all means." He says to her, "Chamuel sees everything far and wide. He is the one to consult to find lost things."

Initamay is relieved. "Thank you. It is a challenge to be Ilanu's care giver sometimes. He is so like a little boy, quite often."

Metatron says, "We commend your vigilance for his wellbeing. Zestful ones can be impulsive in their enthusiasm for life."

Chamuel closes his eyes, "Now then, let me assist you." He is silent as if listening within. Then he nods as if agreeing. He opens his eyes, smiling. "Ah yes, I see. Well, I have a challenge, Initamay, and a favor to ask of you Metatron."

They are puzzled. "First, due to the brigade, flying to Gaea Star very soon, far from our guiding help, the forces of my inner light, instructed to assist in this way. We are to give the necessary tools for you to find Ilanu yourself, since this may not be the last time he disappears at a critical moment."

Metatron says, "Yes, it's always better to receive knowledge, by assimilating the wisdom from direct experience."

Chamuel says, "Correct, Metatron. You have the helpful tool, that is perfect for Initamay to use now and in the future."

Metatron laughs, "Indeed, impressive, Chamuel. You are always spot on at perceiving, the importance of transforming any problem into a positive lesson. Yes, my crystalline locator is my favorite tool to connect with anyone, wherever."

Chamuel says, "Thank you, then let us begin the lesson."

Metatron reaches inside his cape. Smiling, proudly, he holds up a clear quartz, crystal wand with a three-sided face and a seven-sided face. It glistens in the moonlight. He says, "Divination is the perfect use for this locator. Hold it to your third eye. Ask within for your insight to reveal what you seek. Try this scrying tool to ascertain Ilanu's whereabouts."

He hands it to Initamay. She slowly peers into the mysterious triangular faces, saying, "Thank you. It is clearly resonating a pure healing force. I like it."

"Just a moment," Chamuel says, "before using the divinator crystal, first, release any anxieties. Say, I believe in the power of the great spirit, for I trust in all things. Can you do that right now?"

Initamay nods. She holds the wand close to her heart, breathing deeply, shaking her body, to release concerns. She closes her eyes and whispers softly Chamuel's words. After a few moments, she opens her eyes, stronger and more confident to say, "Yes, I am ready to begin. I completely trust in the spiritual loving essence of all that there is."

Chamuel smiles, "Yes, I see you changed, very good."

Metatron, "Excellent student, you learn so quickly."

She holds the crystal to her third eye, "I ask for clear vision to see Ilanu." At first, she sees a mist, changing into a greenish ray, and then a vision appears – Ilanu is playing with the elf, Verdalon, with other elves and faeries drumming and singing in the forest, which explains why he didn't hear her whistling.

"Oh, thank goodness, I see Emeraldina." She touches the crystal wand, again to her third eye, to send her a telepathic message. *"Emeraldina, please bring Ilanu right away. We're waiting. Take the path out of the forest. Follow the torches, they'll lead to where we are, near the crystalline transporter."*

Emeraldina hears her message. She stops playing with her friends to fly to Ilanu, landing on his shoulder. "Ilanu, you are late for an important date. Come mister, to meet your sister."

Ilanu looks surprised, "Oh, sorry I was having so much fun with Verdalon. Now I must go along, since I forgot, my lot. Goodbye my friend, I hope to see you again." He vigorously shakes his hand and taps him on his tiny shoulder.

Verdalon says, "Alright Ilanu, to you, to you, I bid you adieu, until we meet again in the forest of the morest."

Ilanu laughs. "I'll miss you, but I must be going along. I hope you have a wonderful life, full of song." He waves to his faery friends as he walks with Emeraldina flying nearby. She guides him all the way back to where Initamay, Metatron and Chamuel are waiting.

When they arrive, Initamay smiles, saying, "Thank you, Emeraldina, Metatron and Chamuel." The two archangels beam and give a thumbs up.

Emeraldina laughs, saying, "Yes, he's here for now."

Metatron says, "Please retain the crystal wand in a special place. I see you'll need it where you are going."

Initamay says, "Thank you," and gives him a big hug. She tucks the crystal wand into her medicine bag that hangs over her shoulder.

He continues, "Now I must go to the departure area. We are preparing a special surprise." He leaves, preoccupied, mumbling about his exhilarating project that is to help the starship to fly at light speed.

Ilanu's attention is piqued after hearing their discussion. He blurts out excitedly, "Crystal wand? Is that how you found me? A surprise? Wow, this is exciting. Can I see the wand, please, pretty please? It must be magical, for sure."

Initamay puts her finger to her lips, gesturing to be quiet and wait as the archangels deserve respect. Ilanu stops, nodding yes, while miming, "*Okay, sorry, forgive me.*" He is so good at mime under any circumstance.

Chamuel smiles, "Yes, Initamay, it is only a tool however, to train yourself."

He looks to Ilanu. "Eventually, you will not need to use it, because the gift of vision, will be very clear. When that arises within, pass the crystal wand onto the next soul, who may need it as you did, to reconnect to their inner vision as well."

Initamay says, "Thank you. Chamuel. I am grateful to learn such a useful attribute. I'll cherish this until it flows to the next for their teaching." She embraces Chamuel warmly. He is really huggable, like a warm fuzzy teddy bear.

Now she turns her attention to Ilanu. "At last, you're here. Emeraldina, thank-you for coming so fast. You're a sweety. I think you need to come along, to help look after Ilanu. What do you say?"

Emeraldina flies from Ilanu to land in her outstretched left hand. "Yes, I'm happy to sail with my friends and you, to dance and sing in the magical greenery of glorious Gaea Star."

Ilanu has thoughts for only one thing, another mystical crystal wand to see. "Please, can I see it?"

Initamay is admonishing at first. "Ilanu, you gave me a good scare again, trying to find you. I'll show it to you later. Please stay with us as we are boarding any time."

He says, "Yay, we're leaving soon, under a full moon."

She laughs, "Yes, that's true. Come on, let's get going. The departure area is up ahead over there."

They walk on the path until Ilanu sees the tall flickering torches, the luminous crystalline selenite sentinels, and the ship, shimmering in the moonlight. He says, "Wow. A real ship to sail in. How incredible that we get to be the travelers. How did we win?"

Initamay laughs, "Yes, it is a special miracle." The rest of the brigade are smiling and waving as they get close. They have waited patiently for them to assemble all together.

"All in due time," Teladi said when everyone was still not there. He smiles at Ilanu, nodding as if he knew he was on a fun tangent.

He loves Ilanu. There is no reproaching him. He's just being joyful. Teladi encourages Ilanu to let his bright spirit shine in whatever manner he chooses, as he enjoys his humorous distractions. Ah yes, he remembers how similar he was growing up with his wise grandmother in the forest.

Now the Gaea Star mission is finally ready for departure. Wow, what a long eventful journey for the brigade members, first sailing from their own planets to Star Sirius, then the council meeting, browsing Diyanna gardens, walking the mystical labyrinth and now, here for the final ceremony, to be held in front of the waiting crystal starship. What an immense collection of crystals and statues, and other important looking things to greet the crowd and the brigade.

20

LOVING LAST MOMENTS

etatron comes to see Angel Ohm and Teladi, who are putting the finishing touches on his large project and then covering it with a light cloth. He smiles at them, saying, "Thank you. Yes, we're ready at last for the final lift-off ceremony." Angel Ohm and Teladi look warmly at each other.

Michael strides to the ceremonial area where everyone is gathered. "Ah, I see the brigade is all here," he says. "It is my pleasure to greet the newcomers, Andaluchiya, Ritoyo and their llamas, to the mission." He goes to them, and they sniff his face, gently tickling his chin. He laughs. "What delightful creatures, yes, sweet, indeed."

Andaluchiya says proudly, "Thank you, Michael. Yes, they are gentle, and their packs are full of colorful gifts for our new homelands."

Michael pets the llamas. "Thank you for your thoughtful intentions. I'm sure they will serve and be loved by many."

Family and friends surround the kindhearted pair, to touch them, give hugs, and receive pleasurable kisses, one last time. They are certainly well-loved everywhere they go.

Most are too involved in saying goodbyes, that no one notices what Metatron, Angel Ohm, and Teladi are doing. He is checking with them, asking questions. He even looks underneath the covering and sees everything is to his liking. He says to Michael, "The positive generator is in warmup mode. The arrangement is a significant feat to utilize my soul template to further enhance the velocity of the propulsion for their swift transport."

Michael says, "Excellent. Yes, I'm sure it will be successful, as all of your creations are."

Metatron says, "Indeed, a spirited accomplishment of great magnitude. I see the brigade is all here too." He winks at Ilanu, who mimes an innocent, '*Who me*,' look with a big expressive smile.

Michael says, "Splendid, then we'll begin soon."

Metatron says, "Alright, let's continue our preparations." They walk over to his project to confer with Teladi.

Michael asks, "Master Teladi, you are traveling in your starship, correct?"

Teladi answers, "Yes. I am thrilled to fly to Gaea Star, in my crystalline ship right after the rainbow brigade ship does."

Next, Michael goes to Ashento and Ayalasha, who are holding hands and says, "Ayalasha, are you leaving in your purple star ray?"

She smiles at Ashento, "Yes, I'll sail through the galaxy on rays of purple light, as far as I can, with my love, Ashento."

Mira and Teesha look at each other with surprise when they hear that Ashento is not going. Michael senses the confusion and begins to explain, just as Isis floats up with a pleasant wind filled energy. Yes, she has arrived. He signals to her to speak.

She smiles, saying, "For those who do not know our learned master Ashento is remaining in these high realms to continue his spiritual pursuits. He will be a guiding mentor for Ayalasha and all who need his wise teachings on Gaea Star. It is an important role that is just as essential for him and for your mission to succeed.

Remember you have invisible wings to fly into the golden light to reconnect with the loving essence of all things, not only in creative endeavors but when seeking the truth of who you really are. Ashento, please share a few wise words for the travelers."

Ashento stands regal, breathing in slowly, smiling at his beloved Ayalasha, still holding her hand. "Thank you, Isis. I am pleased to serve as a guiding spirit, for Ayalasha, the great lover of my soul, and for the brigade members that I have grown fond of since meeting them here."

He gazes into her eyes, then turns back, "In accordance with the will of the heavens, I may offer guidance only when sought through prayer, meditation or ceremony. We are one family of love, one family of light. You will never be forgotten or left behind."

He looks lovingly at Ayalasha, "Although I will miss her gentle radiant soul, I am grateful she is chosen, for my sweetness, is truly a wise leader, to bring positive, uplifting, spiritual loving energy to all she connects with."

They gaze in an endearing exchange for all to see. Ayalasha says, "Ashento, thank you, for your love. We will miss you and remember your kindness. May we be reunited as swiftly as the winds of eternity blow."

They embrace close, with some of the others, coming to offer hugs, and say poignant goodbyes. Ayalasha steps away to make room for those lingering to say goodbye to Ashento.

Mira, Celestia and Teesha, go to Ayalasha after saying goodbye to him, to show support at this difficult moment. Nothing is said. They just breathe with her, smiling, sharing love. Such a nice warm feeling happens when women gather together. Yes, it's powerful indeed and moves mountains.

Archangels Parting Messages

Archangel Raphael

Archangel Raphael flows from behind the crowd, exchanging glances, with Michael. He signals him to speak. Raphael rises like the angelic being he is.

"As patron of traveling, I wish to bestow a blessing on this tribe of dynamic souls. May you live in harmony, with peaceful love for all beings, and enjoy a safe, fulfilling journey to Gaea Star."

He floats to the side where some of the brigade, say, "Thank you," altogether.

Archangel Barachiel

Suddenly, a pleasing fragrance of roses permeates the air and then pink, yellow and red rose petals drift over the crowd, much to their delight.

Celestia smiles, "It's Archangel Barachiel, he always appears with roses."

Huge bolts of lightning streak across the night sky, illuminating the picturesque landscape far into the distance, with cracking thundering claps, followed by wild laughter. Then a jolly Santa like being, materializes in front of Azul. He's cute with his fluttering wings crafted out of rose flowers. Azul bows, respectfully.

Ilanu laughs with glee. "Wow, that's the best lightning magic. The way you light up the sky, makes me want to fly, so high. I wish I was in on your secrets. I love the cool things you do for kicks."

Initamay overheard him and says, "Ilanu, he's an archangel, not a magician. That's different."

Ilanu says with a wondering look, "Sorry, sis, I didn't know there was a difference. Isn't it all the same, from here to there?"

Initamay looks at him the same way that he just did. She realizes that what he said, was true. You know when someone even a child, in a matter-of-fact manner, says wise words of truth. Suddenly, you stop in your tracks, humbled by the silliness, of being an adult in this world, which is engulfed with social and political stuff, that is better left unsaid.

Initamay says softly, "Sorry. You're right, Ilanu. Thank you, for helping me remember. Yes, its' all the same, here, there and everywhere. I am deeply grateful for you. I love you, Ilanu."

She surprises him by giving a warm hug. He's used to her, bossy, big sister ways. He thinks, "*I must have melted her heart.*" Then he says, "Gee, thanks. Love you too, sis."

The crowd, awed by Barachiel, go close to him like people drawn to a famous person since most have never met anyone with such a dramatic presence.

"Hello, Barachiel," Michael says, "thank you for your showy arrival. Please share your wisdom with the brigade."

Barachiel laughs, saying, "Ah, yes, thank you. Exactly what I hope to do. Well, well." He turns to the waiting crowd. "Expect a miracle, and a miracle will miraculously appear. Always keep moving along. Do not give up, no matter what. Laughter is the key to longevity. When you see or smell roses, that's me. I'm near and willing to help you, in whatever you need."

He raises his hands to the sky, first together, then opens wide his arms, "Hello, creation above, bless everyone please." Suddenly, another wondrous flotilla of rose petals drifts down. This time, in greater abundance, to everyone's delight, especially for the little ones who are running all over, trying to catch them.

He says, "During a storm, greet the lightning and the magnificent sky dancing." Suddenly, lightning bolts illuminate the sky. Thunderclap's echo, and rainbows reflect off the full moon. "That's me and my awesome friends, Chango, the thunder king, and Oya, the thunder queen, with Iris, the rainbow queen. When we thunder beauty, in a symphony of wonders, put down your cares. Go out to revel in the moment to receive the powerful, positive, vibrational healing."

Lakul loves the outstanding energy. "Come on. Let's revel in it right now." He dances in appreciation of the fantastic sky show as it explodes all over. Ilanu, Teesha, Mira, and Initamay, follow him, laughing in delight.

Barachiel laughs, "Thank you. May everyone enjoy the marvels of nature. Grow roses. Their enchanting fragrance arouses memories of your spiritual origins within the angelic realms, where a part of your higher self still remains. At times, you may feel intense longing to reunite with your fragmented selves.

We are always here, sending you love, cheering you on to reconnect to your divine essence. Thank you, Michael, for this moment to speak to these special souls of light."

What a festive celestial celebration and memorable panoramic sky to enjoy before the brigade departs.

Archangel Sandolphon

Sandolphon and Saraswathi, go near the entrance of the crystal ship to where an altar is arranged. The choir and musicians, dressed in golden robes, carrying crystal and metallic bowls, harps, flutes, bells, and other instruments, follow them to set up for the ceremony.

They go to where Metatron stands proudly in front of a large pyramidal structure that's covered with a billowing gauzy fabric. Palpable energetic vibrations are emanating from it. The bowls are placed on the colorful altar. Large quartz crystals, candles, a basket of herbs, a white pitcher of water, flowers in a painted vase, and smaller crystals are arranged around the bowls in a distinct pattern.

Metatron signals to light the candles. An angel floats over to blow on them. The children, noticing what they are creating, happily sprinkle the rose petals they gathered from Archangel Barachiel all around. They love to make pretty altars as well.

Archangel Ariel, the Lioness

Suddenly, pink rays streak across the sky like a spectacular sun setting. Bells tinkle in the nearby trees from a blast of wind. Beings look with wonder at what is coming. Teesha, who has the ability to see for a long way with her sharp eyes, detects movement. "Look, coming out of the forest, its' a lioness."

Rionarta quickly steps in front, as if to protect the group. There is a hush, a feeling of what is going to happen, as the lioness slowly, gently approaches Rionarta. He is poised in awareness.

Pink rays of mist appear to float down, covering her. In a flash, the lioness transforms into beautiful Archangel Ariel. She calmly observes everyone. Upon seeing Michael, she says, "Oh, Michael, excuse me, I have a prayer for the rainbow travelers."

He nods for her to speak. She says, "Thank you. I am pleased, rainbow ones of light, that you are going to protect the Earth's resources and my wildlife friends. May you be confident and courageous, as you care for Gaea Star's gorgeous but fragile environment. I remain here and will send you hopeful, encouraging support. Call on me when you pray or sing in nature's magnificence. I'll answer in the flowing rivers, and in the gentle winds. Children, can you help me please?"

The children, faeries, elves, and even a cute green leprechaun go to her, as she takes out a shiny rose bag. "It is a special treasure for your hearts to bloom wide open to pure love."

Ilanu, super excited, says, "Wow, a leaping leprechaun. He's no bigger than a fawn." Off he hops, trying to imitate him.

Ariel says to the leprechaun, "Choyka, please pour it onto the cloth." He takes the bag and pours the contents onto the cloth. What do you think came out? Lovely rose quartz gems cascaded into a pile by the crystals. The little ones say, "Oh's and ah's," as they excitedly try to snatch them up.

Ariel says, "Dear little friends, first, please give the rose quartz to the brigade as a gift. They are traveling away today."

The children listen to Ariel, going to the brigade first, who await, smiling with open hands, to receive a pretty rose quartz gift.

They each say, "Thank you," to the little ones who are thrilled to have an important role. A few add, "So pretty, we love them." The children hand out the other rose quartz to the crowd.

Initamay hugs Ariel, "Thank you. We'll seek your wonderful presence in nature, Ariel. We are grateful for your blessing."

Mira goes over too. "Yes, thank you, dearest Ariel, for thinking of us before we leave. Of course, we'll remember you always. We won't forget who we are."

She hugs Ariel. "Oh, my daughters," Ariel says, "release any worries. Your spiritual strength will blossom at the right moment. You will awaken to your destinies, that we are certain." The archangels, nod in agreement. The others in the brigade go to hug her too.

A warm loving feeling permeates within the crowd, the archangels, the faeries, the llamas, grazing nearby and the unicorns who trotted up with the royal faeries. This is the precious last moment before they depart, leaving behind so many loved ones.

PART 10

THE DEPARTURE

21

METATRON'S GRID

Michael faces the gathering. "Brigade, we are opening the portal to energetically assist with your swift journey from Sirius Star to Gaea Star. Sandolphon, prepare. Angel Ohm, please release, the vibrational activators."

Sandolphon and Saraswathi walk with the choir and musicians to the front of the ceremonial area. They begin tuning for the opening song.

Angel Ohm floats up. Waving her crystal wand, she touches the billowing gauzy fabric draped over the pyramidal form as Teladi watches proudly. The fabric transforms into a golden mist that lifts and glides away, revealing a metallic geometric grid that pulsates with rainbow colors shimmering throughout. Huge white columns rise high in the four directions on the outside of the grid. They are flanked by more selenite crystals that look like protective guards.

A large white pyramid is glowing within the center of a series of circles interlocked by lines and triangles. Immense crystals are placed at strategic points in different colors and compositions.

The brigade is incredulous at the unusual geometric art structure. Kardichay says, "Wow, a unique, impressive creation, Metatron."

Rionarta says, "Yes, remarkable. It looks like a crystalline template for a powerful energy generator."

Metatron is beaming as he stands next to the grid. Angel Ohm continues waving her wand around the structure, while Teladi is deep in a focused meditation next to it.

Celestia says, "Metatron, I feel vigorous pulsations from this beautiful power center. Please explain the layout of the crystals."

Initamay says, "Yes, please do, it is fascinating." The rest of the brigade are curious and quickly come to see the intriguing structure up close.

Teesha says, "It's a fantastic design, I'll draw it, so I won't forget it. We may need to recreate it on Gaea Star someday."

"Thank you," he says, "but be brief as liftoff is imminent."

She says, "Sure, that's easy." She takes out her pad to sketch since she does that quickly.

Metatron looks to Michael, "Is there time to explain the significance of this grid?"

He nods, "Yes, an explanation is relevant and essential for the success of the journey, is it not?"

Metatron says, "Alright then, let's begin with," he stops talking as if he is in thought.

Mira says to Teesha, "Please note his comments, okay? We want to remember every aspect of this grid. I think it's important."

Teesha says, "Of course. I love to be a scribe. I'll finish drawing after, to set the design." She flips the page to take notes.

Metatron reverts from his thinking reverie, with a start. "Yes, I see. My spirit within, asks you, the brigade, to select a place where you are drawn to, on the grid. Spread out, surround it with yourselves, because the circle must be continuous. Please attune within, in preparation for the journey. I will explain as we proceed."

The brigade nods to his request. They each select a different point to encompass the circle, except for Teladi who was already meditating at his chosen spot. Most of them understand the relevance of the grid in being an integral part of the ceremony before they leave, possibly for a long time.

Everyone, except Ilanu. He is captivated by the wonder of the design and how it pulsates so brightly. He keeps walking around it, occasionally bumping into a brigade member since he is not paying attention. He is talking to himself, counting the stones, the points and the intertwining circles.

Metatron waves to let him be as he loves Ilanu and wants him to connect in his own unique way to the grid. He is aware that each has a lesson to learn from this special grid creation.

Metatron signals Angel Ohm to go to Teladi. She flows over to gently touch him to awaken him. He returns right away, smiling, looking to see what is going on. She whispers, "Excuse me, Teladi. Metatron wants us to help the brigade connect to the grid and to explain the details."

"Oh, certainly," he says, looking to Metatron, who nods.

Angel Ohm says, "This is a template of a light activating chariot that enables attunement and connection to the sacred universal energies that exist everywhere." She looks to Teladi.

He understands her look and says, "Please breathe deeply. Let anything that no longer serves you drift away. The journey that lies ahead, requires activating our light bodies. Go deep within. Release. Surrender to the oneness that we are. Let us become as rainbow rays like the golden sun." He attunes also.

Lakul sets an example of loosening up by shaking, huffing out and taking in fresh air. He is always the first to release any unwanted stuff, for he loves to be free and clear. After each of the brigade follow his example, they relax into concentrating silence.

Angel Ohm waves her crystal wand around the grid and the pyramid within the center. Suddenly melodic tones emanate from within it, causing the brigade to return to their senses to look at what is making the tones, although nothing is obvious as to the source of the sounds. She says, "Thank you, star travelers, for attuning, please stay with me now for our discussion."

She goes to a blue grey flattish, tabular crystal that is imbedded into one of the overlapping circles, to say, "Can you sense its significant emanations?"

"Yes, I do," Celestia says, after going close to listen within.

She hears, "My daughter, I am Celestite, your guardian angel."

She laughs, "Hello, thank you. Glad to meet you Celestite. You are a delightful guardian." She faces the group. "I love this heavenly crystal. It's Celestite, my guardian angel."

Teesha says, "Wow. Really. Outstanding, so pretty."

Mira laughs, saying, "That's sweet. Celestite will be helpful on Gaea Star since it seems that many beings have forgotten about their angels."

Ilanu says, "Hey, that's, cool. Let's figure out this tool."

Kardichay is mesmerized by the superb crystals and where they're placed in the grid.

Metatron says, "Kardichay, you're near the white sentinels. Do you know what they are?"

Kardichay touches an opaque pillar, saying, "Yes, it's selenite, the great activator and harmonizer. I sense the instantaneous energy current, the vigorous synthesis between everything utilized in creating this intense powerhouse of energy."

"Thank you, I'm pleased that you appreciate the inherent reasons for their use." Metatron looks to Rionarta to ask, "You are within the center, near the pyramid. Do you know what it is?"

Rionarta scans the glistening pyramid. Breathing deep, he says, "It is apophyllite, a resonating vibrator to activate one's light body to easily sail through interdimensional realms. An excellent intention as it transmits the healing essence of the universe."

Metatron nods, "Brilliant. Thank you. Now, Celestia, you chose the white columns. Do you understand what they are?"

She answers, "Thank you, Metatron for using such magnificent crystals. I'll attune to these." She closes her eyes to sense the pulsating columns, breathing deeply. Opening her eyes, she says, "Yes, I sense the serene radiance of scolecite, flowing with loving vibrations that awakens and aids our journey through the realms."

Metatron nods, "Very good. Everyone is acutely aware. Now for the stones within the grid." He pauses, noticing Teesha still writing quickly. "We must speak slow for our diligent scribe." She smiles and keeps writing.

He asks, "Azul, can you ascertain the crystal that you are resonating with?"

"My pleasure," he says, as he touches a green stone with indentations, and then drift offs. He returns, smiling "I hear, 'moldavite.' It is an inspiring gem emanating spiritual lightness of being from the stars."

Metatron waves to Angel Ohm to speak. She nods and says, "Yes, that is right Azul. Thank you. It was an honor to use potent crystalline vibrational stones to create energies for this travel generator."

Metatron smiles, "Thank you, Angel Ohm. Lakul, please explain your crystal connection." He is leaning on a tall white crystal rising high on the sides of the grid.

"Certainly," he says, "I chose this due to the expansive resonation of its energetic quality. It's familiar but I'm not sure what it is. I'll ask."

He breathes in and seeks his inner vision. After a moment, he opens his eyes, to say with clarity, "Ah yes, natrolite. A favored mineral that comprises our communicators, due to its' strong light beam energy, empowering, transforming, excellent for soul travel and sensing the angelic realms that resonate within. Yes, we are love filled oneness, and to the stars we shall return. I am revved up now."

Angel Ohm waves her wand as if saying, *"Yes, thank you."* Lakul grins, putting his thumbs up.

Meanwhile, her wand caught Ilanu's attention. He mimes, *"Can I please see your magic wand? Pretty please."*

"Yes, my dear," she says as she flows to him. He is surprised when she hands him the wand. "For the one who plays with magic. Let it teach you, for she has many lessons."

"Thank you," Ilanu says as he bows, bringing up a flower, just like he did in the chamber meeting when he demonstrated his talents to the assembly.

She takes it, and sniffs it, saying, "Thank you, a beautiful Star Lily, my delightful favorite."

Ilanu excitedly waves the wand which catches Initamay's attention. She was still connecting to the crystal energies in the grid. She gestures to keep the wand low and be quiet.

He agrees by miming, "*Oh, yes, sis, I am mum.*"

Without being asked, Initamay says, "Angel Ohm, I feel pleasant, pulsating angelic energy and calming earthly strength here. I'll ask within." She runs her fingers over a shiny quartz, breathing in, shaking to relax and attune to it.

After a few moments, she says, "Angels are singing, "*elestial.*" I sense ancient wisdom of the universe. It inspires one to immerse in the living essence of all things."

Angel Ohm nods, "Yes, the power of elestial helps to connect with earth star energies also."

Mira, who is close to Initamay, says, "Oh, sweet angels, I want to hear." She goes to the elestial to listen and says, "Yes, a choir is singing a heavenly melody." While humming along with the singing, she notices a lovely crystal and says, "Oh, that's pretty, the starry lines are like golden trails of light."

Angel Ohm says, "Mira, please tell us what you feel."

She nods, breathing deep, listening intently. After a moment, she opens her eyes. "It is a transforming stone of light that helps to sail beyond perceptions into the oneness of creation, to see and feel our true selves." She sings a melody, "*Star ray, tay ay a, hay ya, hay ahay, oh, oh, star ray.*"

Angel Ohm says, "Mira, thank you, that's a pretty melody. The lovely stone is a *'star ray,'* and is called astrophyllite on Gaea Star."

Mira touches the stone as she sings *'star ray'* softly, causing it to shimmer brightly.

Teesha is a speed writer with perfect recall memory and even sees the colors of melodies. She is nearly caught up with noting down what everyone said so far.

Mira notices, "Wow, Teesha, you're good. I didn't know you were fast at writing everything down. Do you hear colors or see them in the melodies of life, too?"

Teesha smiles as she shyly says, "Thank you. Mira. Yes, I see colors in everything, even in the music. We all have different talents that we excel in, right? I don't know too much about crystals but I'm sure someone will explain to me later."

Teladi interjects, "Yes, of course, Teesha in due time." He is standing nearby in front of a white stone. "Metatron, I so enjoyed helping to set up this incredible masterpiece. It is an impressive cohesive merging of geometric shapes, lines and stones." He touches the white stone. "I believe this is a phenacite, a third eye opener, a light body activator to access pathways to our vibrational currents."

Metatron says, "Thank you, correct. You are most welcome, Teladi."

Angel Ohm says, "Yes, Teladi, thank you. Metatron chose these stones for their energetic assistance for smooth lightship travel and to help the brigade attune to their inner soul's light as they encounter the multiple changes in their new realm."

Teladi says, "True. No doubt, this will be known forever as Metatron's cube. May I charge a crystal with the essential blueprint of this design, for future use, perhaps?"

Metatron says, "Yes. I hope this harmonizing grid will be useful when the shift occurs, causing vast changes for Gaea Star."

Smiling at Angel Ohm, Teladi reaches into his bag and retrieves her crystal gift with the angel wings, to her delight. He touches several stones and holds it to the elestial crystal, until he senses the transfer of energy is complete. He starts to take the crystal but leaves it as if listening to a voice within.

Nodding, he says to the elestial, "Ah yes, I see." Turning to everyone, he says, "Metatron, the elestial spirit asks the brigade to select one of their special crystals, to do the same, to connect with the grid stones, in order to impart their powerful knowledge into their crystals, to spread their esoteric wisdom throughout Gaea Star."

Angel Ohm says, "Yes, I love that idea."

Metatron agrees, "Of course, we share every tool that will help to raise the healing vibrations. Please align with your favorites to endeavor the success of the mission. That is vital to us."

The brigade reach for their special crystals and then with them, touch the ones they are drawn to in the grid. Each crystal reacts differently to theirs. Some shimmer while others flash, hum or blink. Teladi goes back into meditation to sense the compelling energies of the nearby crystals.

Ayalasha takes out her amethyst wand that she used when calling in the purple ray to sail like a comet to Star Sirius. She holds it in front of a brilliant amethyst projecting high. "Yes, I sense the divine connection with the rays of purple light. May we always listen to their guidance that flows, unimpeded wherever we go."

A purple ray flashes from her wand to the one she touches, causing a brilliant violent flame to burst out, then it changes into a radiant glowing ray that circles around her and the brigade. Each reverently receives the violet flame with their hands.

While everyone is busy connecting their crystals to the grid crystals, Ashento goes to the front to stand in direct alignment with a towering transparent crystal. He closes his eyes to attune to the glistening crystal that has an angular chiseled top and four linear sides with milky white inclusions within them.

He hears ethereal whispering, "My son, we are pleased to assist in your role as guiding your rekindled twin flame, Ayalasha. May you open your heart ever wider, to embrace pure divine love in all things, as your sweet love embarks on her journey without you. All will be well. Thanks to your noble devotion and support from these heavenly realms. I am Danburite, utilize me when you seek to commune with the ones of Gaea Star."

Ashento says, "Thank you master danburite. I feel your powerful uplifting wisdom. I will flow into my role of service with ease. You have made it lighter to soar unattached and free."

Removing his cape, he assumes a strong stance as if to align with the grid. It is clear now to see how his tattoos are similar to the grids design. The crystals in the grid, pulsate and flash, and then suddenly his colorful tattoos swirl and radiate rays of blue light.

He looks as if he's generating great spiritual power. If anyone had a doubt as to why he was chosen to be the guide from the celestial realms, it was now obvious. Yes, he is truly a regal master of his body, mind and spirit in all ways. Ayalasha gazes lovingly at him. She senses the amazing spiritual experience that he chose to keep silent about.

Angel Ohm says to the elders as they stand next to their llamas, "Andaluchiya, Ritoyo. Are you drawn to a crystal in the grid?"

Andaluchiya translates to Ritoyo. He looks, then points to a tan and black stone that sits on the edge as supporting energy. She touches it. He nods yes, that one.

Angel Ohm flows over to look, asking, "Does anyone know what this is?"

Rionarta goes close. "I believe it is Chiastolite, a grounding mineral. Ritoyo chose wisely. It is helpful for protection, calming strength, a perfect balancer for our travels."

"Yes," Angel Ohm says, "thank you, correct. Andaluchiya, how about you?"

She walks around the grid until stopping in front of a crystal, flashing gold, blue, green and violet rays. She gazes at its mysterious energy until saying, "This one that shimmers pretty rainbow reflections right there."

Angel Ohm asks, "Kardichay, do you know this one?"

He comes to look and says, "Yes, it's Spectrolite, a powerful enchanting crystal that generates energy to travel freely through the realms. Shamans and healers love to work with this valuable tool as it radiates the spirit realm and the rainbow light body. See how it reflects so beautifully."

"Thank you, Kardichay," she says, "and to you Andaluchiya, for connecting with such a helpful crystal."

Metatron says, "To everyone, I'll cherish your special affinity to these stones. They were chosen to enable your crystalline ship to travel effortlessly through the galaxy corridors with powerful propulsion, in the highest regard for your well-being."

"Yes, may it be so," Angel Ohm says. She warmly gazes at Teladi as they stand close, mingling their energies with pink rays emanating. What a peaceful loving moment for such sweet souls.

The grid is actively blinking, as if charging up. Colorful lights radiate in concentric circles around it slowly. Then they speed up, causing many of the circles to rise high above while still casting out rays. All the points of the grid are flashing, as if stimulated by everything around it. You see the great impact it has already, even before their crystal light ship is activated completely as the etheric impression of the grid rises like a holographic template to hover over the gathering in the night sky.

Michael signals Sandolphon and his musicians and choir to come forward since it is now time to begin the final ceremonial send-off.

22

OPENING THE PORTAL

Sandolphon says, "Thank you, Metatron, Teladi, and Angel Ohm for beginning this final ceremony with your remarkable energizer grid. It has set the tone for the success of this flight. Everyone, please come near, bring your attention to the ceremonial area."

The star travelers walk from their places along the grid to assemble where he pointed to. When their rearranging is complete, he turns to the waiting crowd to speak.

"Hello, rainbow crystalla brigade, what a wonderful blessing you received from all the wise ones and this generating grid. My deep gratitude for choosing to leave your realms to embark on this healing mission. We also thank the many who came to give you such a loving send-off to Gaea Star."

The wise elders from the Bochuti realm, Fayonalia, Nepthytoka and Amsinia come to take places near the altar. Sandolphon bows to them, saying, "Welcome wise elders from Bochuti. We are pleased for your participation." They pick up instruments to play along with.

He nods, saying, "Before we begin, we need to check if the course coordinates are properly set."

Demeclis, the platform builder comes over to say, "Sandolphon, I'm happy to assess that."

Waving his hand, Sandolphon says, "Yes, please, show a few of the brigade the ship's operating capacity."

Demeclis agrees, "Yes, good idea. Kardichay, Rionarta, Azul, Initamay, please come with me." They glance at each other, for that's not something they expected, but they willingly follow him, realizing it's important to learn this new method of space travel, as things change rapidly in this technology.

Sandalphon says, "This is our latest generating concept. It is necessary to create the sufficient energy to travel at light speed. Once the proper energizing, transmitting level is attained, and all points are set, then the crystal ship will fly swiftly to Gaea Star."

He looks to Saraswathi. She speaks, "Yes, first, we place rose oil into the percolator. Celestia, please take this vial to pour into the dispenser, in front of the ship. You'll see where it is, as the fragrance is wonderfully strong there." She takes a quick sniff since she too loves roses in all forms.

Celestia is happy to fulfill her wishes. She takes the rose vial and gently sniffs the fragrance, sighing with delight from the joyous feeling of pleasure as well. She follows after Demeclis and the others who went to set the coordinates.

Meanwhile, musicians sit next to the singing bowls, and the crystals on the colorful cloth. They lightly pass a wood mallet along the edges of the crystal bowls, making a deep toning resonation. The choir harmonizes their heavenly voices, creating an ethereal synthesis of singing voices, bowls and instruments.

He gestures to Saraswathi. Smiling, she says, "Thank you, dear ones. We are pleased to harmonically activate the crystalline star ship with nurturing toning vibrations that tap into the sacred spheres of music. Let's open the portal, by humming and singing with the majesty of the crystal toning bowls. While we wait for the return of the others, it is essential that everyone attune to this musical, healing vibration, to begin to activate the light bodies of the travelers, and their crystal star ship."

Sandolphon says, "We ask that you please sit down to help align with the forces of light, to assist their lightspeed travel. It is good to breathe deep and slow, releasing concerns for the brigade's well-being. They will be protected and supported while on Gaea Star."

The crowd is excited to be drawn into this unusual light activation as the pleasing music plays. Everyone finds a place to sit. The more minds and hearts that tune into these healing sound frequencies, the easier it is to activate the profound effects in manifesting a successful crystalline light speed flight.

Sandolphon directs the four when they return from the front of the ship to stand by its entrance. Saraswathi says, "We are ready now, Metatron. Please lead the visualization."

Metatron steps up, holding a large crystal point in his left hand, saying, "Yes. Thank you. Let's now begin opening the portal. We ask the forces of loving light, to activate the rainbow light portal with my *"visualizer."* May we all join our hearts and minds, concentrating with clear intentions, visualizing that our star travelers arrive safely and swiftly, with no concerns to Gaea Star. Brigade, please use your crystals in the same manner."

Again, they stand proudly and bring out their special crystals to hold in front of them. It is certainly an unusual dazzling collection of shimmering, flashing pulsating crystals and wands.

Those assembled relax into a quiet meditation, while the Bochuti elders and others, gently tap the crystal bowls, gongs, and inscribed metallic bowls as they sing, soft, mesmerizing tones. The choir sings harmonies, raising their intense focalizing sounds higher and higher. Their angelic wings flutter with the echoing rhythms, ringing throughout the area.

The altar crystals and those in or near Metatron's grid, along with the ones the star travelers are holding, glimmer lights softly. Brilliant colorful rays shoot high into the sky, forming a radiant rainbow, over the crystalline ship, which is now glowing ever brighter. Everything is blending together with profound pulsations.

Rionarta says, "Wow, exciting. I love it." He is still observing the grid and its numerous vibrating crystals. He hopes to remember how to reconstruct this impressive grid on Gaea Star someday.

Michael walks up, waving his golden blue sword at the shimmering opening. Gabriel flies up and gloriously blows three loud blasts on her trumpet. Instantly the crystal ship starts to shimmer faster with a gentle humming, whirling sound as if it is preparing for takeoff. The brigade is excited to sail into the unknown, very soon on this wild adventure.

Almost All Aboard

The doorway is illuminated by encircling crystalline rays. Then it dissolves, revealing an opening into the ship.

Ilanu gleefully says, "Oh cool. What a high magic tool."

Michael says, "All right, Andaluchiya and Ritoyo, this is the moment for departure." They are sitting and watching the activities by their llamas as they graze.

Michael continues, "Teladi and Ayalasha will be traveling to Gaea Star on their own devices. Everyone else, please proceed to the entrance of this ship. Blessings on your journey. Our prayers are with you."

Andaluchiya stands, "I see. Thank you. We are blessed to go to the land of the blue waters." She speaks to Ritoyo. He rises and prepares the llamas for entering the ship. He smiles a warm farewell at his beloved tribe, for he is their grandfather elder. They wave their last goodbyes. Some are rather tearful, but most are proud to see them going on such a noble mission.

There is last-minute shifting as the group assembles into a line, first Rionarta, then Azul, Lakul, Mira, and Teesha, holding hands, and Celestia with Kardichay. They are all smiling and looking at each other with excitement.

Mira says, "Goodbye, Teladi and Ayalasha."

Teesha adds, "Yes, blessings for a safe journey."

Celestia says, "Good luck. We'll see you there."

Initamay is lightly holding onto Ilanu for safe keeping. He has the nerve, right then, to say, "Hey, sis of whom I am fond, can I see your wand?"

As if he does not have enough wands to play with already. Remember he has the one that came to him in the labyrinth and the wand that Angel Ohm just gave him.

Initamay says, "No, wait, until we get settled in the transport. We need to stay focused on sailing through this together this time with no incidents. Ilanu, please."

Ilanu says, "Okay, sis. Yeah, I want to see how we travel so fast. I certainly do not want to be the last."

Bringing up the rear, are Andaluchiya and Ritoyo, holding hands, walking with their llamas who are not phased at all, for going on such a trip.

The rainbow brigade members are grateful and courageous to embark on this amazing journey, together. They wave goodbye to those standing nearby. It is a poignant moment for those watching.

Lakul is singing, *"Here we go to the land of the colorful rainbow, oh yeah."* He is breathing deep and shaking to prepare for the speedy trip.

Archangel Jophiel floats up, signaling for them to enter. One by one, or two by two, they step inside the clear walls and look around silently in awe of the beautiful crystal lines of the powerful energy pulsating ship.

Rionarta walks immediately to the front of the ship to see the rose oil gizmo, as he has never seen this type of generator in action. Azul is rubbing his hands with a few of his special crystals.

When almost the whole group has passed through the entrance, the elders, and their llamas, start walking through the opening. Some of them keep waving to their loved ones watching.

Michael, Metatron and the archangels stand by with Teladi, Ashento and Ayalasha, the unicorns, royal faeries and their friends, to observe their take off. Once it departs, they plan to leave as well.

Lucifer's Last Element

Suddenly there's a commotion in the crowd, as if someone is trying to push their way through to the entrance of the ship. It's Lucifer, rushing up with an air of great importance. Yes, he is rather late as always. We wonder why it took him so long to get there after he ran into Zoz and Keme back on the path. Remember they ran and squeezed into the crates where they have been hiding for a while now.

Lucifer must have had an unusual session somewhere along the path, where he stepped out of time and into another reality, which he is well versed at. He is also a shapeshifter and well-seasoned time traveler. He is brusque as he pushes his way through the crowd, saying loudly, "Excuse me, pardon. Please let me pass. I have an important reason to speak to the brigade." He finally arrives a bit breathless near Michael.

"Oh, at last, Michael, excuse my tardiness, as I had to ponder the most beneficial aspect to add to the brigade's mission. I ran into a few issues. Never mind about that right now."

Michael is surprised and says, "Yes, Lucifer, what is it? The modules are activated for the ship to disembark any moment now."

Lucifer says, "Yes, right away then." He steps to the ship's entrance, saying in a booming voice, "Light workers, star brigade, please return to the entrance. I am here to present your final instruction."

Those inside, upon hearing his words, look surprised at each other, but quickly walk to the doorway, to stand by the llamas, who were not all the way in yet. When everyone is reassembled around the doorway, Lucifer solemnly says, "Rainbow brigade, you will not remember the divine aspects of your missions on Gaea Star. The veils of illusion may hide this truth for lifetimes. To awaken to who you truly are, you will have to tap into the treasure-filled, loving light that lies nestled within your hearts and souls. Then, your spiritual awakening will set you free forever."

He steps back, disappearing into the mists that surround the shimmering crystalline ship. The brigade has no time to think or discuss what Lucifer said, as the ship is whirling faster. Then it transforms into an impressive rocket crystal star ship.

Michael says, "A fond farewell, rainbow brigade. May the forces of light guide you always. Please return to the ship's chamber. Hold clear your intentions to travel with the speed of rainbow light. Enjoy your new life."

Without any further actions, they return to the inner main area, except the elders and the llamas who are waiting until the others settle down. Within a flash, the shimmering doorway disappears, and crystal lights spray in all directions. In a burst of luminous light, the starship blasts off into a brilliant rainbow comet that streaks across the night sky.

Lucifer's face is in the light of the sparkling mists left behind, silently watching as the comet sails off, trailing rainbow light. He nods as if he knows something they don't.

Sailing Through the Universe

Andaluchiya and Ritoyo lead the llamas to a spot in the rear of the ship next to the boxes that Keme and Zoz are hiding in. The peaceful pair take the unusual position called kush, with their feet tucked beneath them, and their heads up. Once the flight is moving along, they may even hum, showing how easy it is for llamas to be comfortable traveling even under strange circumstances.

The brigade is thrilled to be flying quickly in deep space. Most are focusing on the scenery whizzing by out the windows of the ship. No one seems phased by Lucifer's last comments as it is so exhilarating to be in this moment, not worrying about the future.

Ilanu is glued to the largest window, watching the galaxy zooming by, trying to count them gleefully. "One, two, kazillion, I can't count. I wonder how many they will amount. At last, we're so far above, I cannot even see the lands I love."

Initamay laughs. "Yes, Ilanu, there are stars, planets and worlds speeding by." She is relieved that Ilanu is in front, safe and happy. It was a real challenge to keep him present and on time. She relaxes for now, even though she is bursting with excitement for what is looming ahead for all of them.

She whispers softly as she fingers a pretty beaded necklace, "Dear Creator, source of light, I express my gratitude for everything that has transpired for me and everyone on this journey so far. May we always be guided by your love."

Mira and Teesha are sitting close, enraptured with the starry views, whispering about the trip. Mira says, "We're going to be together. I feel and know it. We have our love to support whatever we do or where we go." She hums a light melody.

Teesha sighs, "Yes, so true. Hopefully we'll always be on the same path." She takes out her pad to sketch the inside of the ship. She is happy to outline the interesting things until the opportunity to paint them comes along. Yes, there is much to note.

Lakul is stretching as usual, while watching the stars zing by. "Ah, we're on the way to the green lands and blue waters. Here we come Gaea Star, ready or not."

Rionarta is with Celestia still observing the rose oil gizmo. They are breathing the rosy fragrance wafting out the top, smiling, and so grateful for this special moment. After that, she joins Kardichay and Azul as they check out the inside of the ship's unusual shiny structure.

Azul, running his fingers over the glistening sides, says, "I wonder how they shimmer so brightly."

Kardichay says, "I believe it is due to the crystal minerals imbedded within the metallic composite. They create a remarkable property called birefringence, within the molecular component that splits the atoms into differing rays, causing the shimmering appearance when the light energy passes through." Azul just nods, he is always impressed with Kardichay's knowledge.

Rionarta says, "Yes. It looks like it may also be due to the minerals that are embedded within it, calcite, fluorite, galena or spar."

Kardichay nods, "Yes, those crystals are excellent when given the proper settings, to generate energy. They are certainly the main factors comprising the inner workings of this ship."

Azul says, "Thank you both for the helpful explanations."

Celestia agrees, "Yes, I love the profound wisdom you two have. Let's take a moment to attune to the high energy coursing through this ship, please." They silently agree by sitting, breathing deeply, and going within, together.

Meanwhile, back in the storage area, Keme and Zosakel are still in the boxes. Zoz peeks out to see if the coast is clear. *What the heck,* he thinks. He's startled by the furry llamas sitting there, chewing peacefully. Their ears perk forward when he popped his head out, but luckily, they did not react strongly to draw attention to them. He quickly put his head back and whispers, "Keme, those furry creatures are out there near us chewing. We need to figure something else out, but for now we're staying put."

Keme laughs, "Are you kidding? Wonders never cease. I'm feeling scrunched right now. I can't even move."

"Yeah, me too, but we have to wait until I think of what to do. We're moving fast though, so it's not going to be very long anyway."

As far as Mister Coole is concerned, he is perfectly content perched high in the rafters, watching in silence as cats always do, with his teeny tail flitting back and forth.

Andaluchiya is quietly knitting a woolen hat while Ritoyo is peacefully napping near their llamas.

The Last To Embark To Gaea Star

The unicorns and royal faeries watch the rainbow trails as the crystal ship disappears in the distance. Queen Oonalia says, "Rayanca, are you ready? Our moment to leave has arrived. We promised to be there together."

"Yes, we are," says Rayanca. It certainly looks like it as he and Luina are stomping and quivering with anticipation. The royal faeries fly to their upper necks, to nestle into their lustrous manes. Each unicorn extends out their magnificent wings. They rear up together to smoothly fly off in a rainbow, arching across the sky. Everyone waves, cheering goodbye.

Teladi grins as he observes the rainbow trails of the ship and the unicorns.

"To the realms of Gaea Star, I now fly." He reaches for the angel wings crystal gift from Angel Ohm.

She comes close, "Goodbye, my wise friend, Teladi. May the blessings of the light-filled essence of love, guide you always. We wait your return."

Teladi gives her a last hug, "Thank you, Angel Ohm. I will remember your kindness." They embrace with sweet loving energy.

He breaks free with a pat then, holding the angel wing crystal high, he says in a strong manner, "I call my crystalline star ship." In a flash of white light, it appears with its four carved angelite crystal pillars looming, brilliantly luminous and glistening. He nods, smiling, "Ah, thank you for your swift response."

As he enters within the four pillars, he turns, saying, "I am off to assist in the restoration of humanity through the reawakening of love for all things. Blessings to those that remain in harmony, in these high realms. We will miss you. It is so."

He turns back and with his crystal wand, taps the pillars, which fire from within, transforming into a solid crystal rocket, that blasts up, and streaks away in a blaze of white light trails. Angel Ohm waves and sighs as she watches him disappear.

Ayalasha says, "Ashento, now it is our turn to go," and then she says to the crowd and the archangels, "I am leaving Star Sirius, but part of my heart remains here amidst such caring, loving souls. I will miss all of you. I promise to shine my love through the darkness that is shadowing Gaea Star right now."

Several beings comment to her. "Thank you, Ayalasha, for taking on this mission."

"We are here in support, for as long as it takes."

She responds, "I thank each of you with my love."

Ashento and Ayalasha look at each other. He asks, "Are we ready to activate our light bodies?

She sighs, touching his handsome face, softly, saying, "Yes, my dear, I am ready to fly, but my heart, already yearns for your presence."

He touches her gently, on her hair and cheek. "Oh, my sweetness, we are always together, united in our deep love eternally, no matter where we are. Let's begin our departure."

She reaches into her cape for her beautiful amethyst quartz crystal wand. Holding it to the stars, she says, "As the priestess of the purple ray, I awaken you, ray of love, to carry me to Gaea Star." A swirl of purple immediately encases her in a luscious royal hue, fit for a priestess of the most - high.

Ashento merely says, "Blue ray, I am ready for your cascading presence to let me sail through the universe with my sweetness." Swiftly, a serene wave of blue light encircles him and then swirls around Ayalasha's royal purple ray.

The two dazzling rays meld into a brilliant magenta ray that looks exactly as when they were flying to Star Sirius center, moments before they met. The radiant magenta weaves a cocoon of sparkling light until their activation is complete.

In a sudden burst, the colorful rays shoot off, splitting into two comets, flying side by side into the night, with their double helix tails twirling together like eagles mating high in the sky. Slowly dissolving into waves of light, their comets streak on by leaving intense magenta trails fading in the distance. What an astonishing departure of so many beloved beings before the crowd.

Ashento's luminous face appears in his blue light body next to Ayalasha. "My sweetness, this is my goodbye prayer to you,

"You are forever woven into the tapestry of my soul

Out of the blue and the purple rays

we traverse through the heavens

flying as stars in glowing arcs

crossing galaxies and light years

on missions of love and unity

onward to Gaea Star Crystal

Our effortless flight slows

as one journey ends, another begins

Just ahead, there she is, floating in infinite space

Our precious, precious, Gaea Star

Our divine missions may separate us

You may forget me, but I will never, ever forget you

as our spirits are united as twin flames in eternal love."

Ayalasha is touched, "Thank you. Ashento, I will love you forever. I await the moment of our divine celestial reunion."

As they rapidly approach the blue green planet's revolving orbit, Ashento says, "My sweetness, this is where I must leave you. Goodbye, oh my great lover."

Ayalasha says to her beloved, "Ashento I love you, goodbye. I will miss you and will never ever forget you."

Lovingly, he says, "My sweetness, I'll hold you forever in the depth of my soul." He looks at her passionately one last time. Then his brilliant blue comet blasts off as a powerful rocket booster, careening into space, dissolving into blue trails while Ayalasha's purple comet continues sailing toward the glowing, glistening Gaea Star.

Sailing just in front of her are the majestic unicorns with the faeries nestled in their manes, and in the distance, the rainbow crystalline ship, speeding along. In the rear is Teladi's crystal starship, soaring briskly, flashing white light.

Everyone on board the crystal ship seems to be settling into the flying experience, thrilled for the new mission and unknown adventure that is looming ahead for them on Gaea Star.

Lakul is meditating. Ilanu is waving Initamay's magic wand that she finally gave to him. Teesha is happily sketching the events from the ceremonial site, the best she can remember. She already finished outlining the details of the inside of the ship.

Ilanu mimes to her, "Hey, come to play, oh yay."

"Yes, coming right now." She says, finishing with a quick flourish. Of course, wands take precedence over drawing since they are her favorite crystals to play with.

Mira and Azul are enjoying the fascinating vista of the galaxies whizzing by the window. It is the first time they can observe the starry space so easily.

Mira says, "We are flying faster than the stars, wow." Azul nods. He is taken with the celestial beauty of the realms speeding by. He loves the perfection of the universe, in all of its' oneness.

Initamay is happily relishing the rose fragrance emanating from the gizmo up front. She is studying how it powers the ship. Celestia is sitting, enjoying the trip, smiling at Kardichay every so often. He is not noticing as he is in the pilot seats, now with Rionarta, keeping close attention on their propulsion and studying the technical aspects of the cockpit area, for future use, perhaps.

At last, they are close enough to see the swirling atmosphere of the blue-green planet, the luminous, Gaea Star. She appears so beautiful and alive. Colossal rainbow crystals are rising from the top of her perfectly round shape. Several of the brigade say, "Oohs and ah's," at her lovely sight and hold each other with anticipation as they begin to enter her atmosphere easily.

Isis flies by in her majestic rainbow-winged glory, watching the scenario unfolding. She whispers, "Yes, it is done. The mission to awaken humanity on beloved Gaea Star is flying into her reality. The Creator fulfilled a promise to assist the tribes of light as they transform into human life.

Blessings, rainbow brigade, for your new life on Gaea Star. You are not separate. You are always part of the source of love and light. You will be supported in all that you do. You will find each other and remember your missions of love. May you share the great joy of love, treasuring the one and all."

Isis flies away leaving a rainbow light trail. All that remains is the glowing Gaea Star slowly revolving, ready to receive the dynamic rainbow brigade, the mountain elders, their llamas, the unicorns and the royal fairies that all came along in a wonderful show of support for such a noble mission.

They are happily streaming to the lovely blue green planet of waters, with their hopes and dreams fully charged for the wonderful escapade that is beckoning. Love overcomes all with gentleness and compassionate caring.

The End

EPILOGUE

August 7, 2018

Transforming a screenplay into a novel, requires filling in details and giving thoughts to the characters. It took longer than I imagined when I began in 2017. I'm glad to birth this after carrying it within for years. What a pleasure to cocreate with Ashento and weave in new aspects, crystals, and characters with divine messages of love. Dwelling in the celestial realms, with the light workers, archangels, and the Sirius council, fostered a dramatic contrast to the absurd shenanigans in this world now.

Often, I randomly opened to a page in a crystal reference book or to a page number I heard whispered. It was always the perfect crystal for that part in the story. It was uncanny how it happened. I love writing at my cozy workspace that overflows with crystals, plants, flowers, and statues with the view of the brook winding along through the grassy meadow and forest.

I love the ritual of writing by eleven, with a goal of finishing a chapter daily. I found a rhythm, even with everything that goes on at Singing Brook farm on a busy workday, or with housemates and their children making distractions.

December 4, 2018

As the warm sun streams in, the first draft is done. What an incredible learning this past year. I'm grateful for persevering. I did not realize that the book 1 story was to evolve into only taking place in the celestial realms. Book 2 is the escapades of the brigade after arriving on Gaea Star. I knew it was going to become a trilogy. Every day is a creative undertaking as I receive inspiration from everywhere.

January 20, 2019

What a ride for this world during this tumultuous year, with the political mess, pandemic, and wearing masks. Staying home was easy as I have worked from my own spaces since moving here in 1992, quite content to create in this peaceful serenity. I'm completing my eighth musical CD with Bob Sherwood, "Release."

April 26, 2019

Things take time. After sending this to the publisher, I had to reformat the text, which meant another chance to reedit it. I recall last night at 11:11 p.m. when I heard noises in my kitchen. It was a black bear snorting at the bird feeder. I tapped on the window, but she was not fazed. 11:11, a bear blessing. Happy for the magic and mystery of nature that aligns with me.

October 2020

The Gaea Star Crystal, book 1 was published this January. Now I'm enjoying crafting the adventures of the rainbow brigade on Gaea Star as book 2. Publishing and marketing companies are calling to make this into a successful novel or movie, but nothing has fallen into place yet. I'll never give up as the theme of saving earth's precious resources is unfolding daily all over the planet. This is a momentous year of great change. Nations are struggling to achieve balance. Many are striving to protect and honor the mother earth and her people. Does the delay in giving this message to the world have to do with the shadow side desperately trying to stop the wave of awakening souls from reestablishing the essential belief that love overcomes all chaos and that all lives matter?

What a grand story we are in as the plot thickens. When will we live in harmony? Many are standing in long lines to vote as if their lives depended on it. Beings are courageously seeking positive change to transform this ailing society. Yesterday, the Republicans stacked the Supreme Court in their favor. This is an intense moment as Americans choose to stand for truth, love, compassion and acceptance. I wake up with a new song.

Oh, yeah, let the rains come and wash it all away

Purifying the air, the water, the fire, and the earth

Purifying her people all over again

Yes, let's begin again

Oh, yes, right here in the mists

In this moment of great change

Come on now, breathe in a slow deep one

Yes, for it is real, we are stars

and to stars we shall return

Let's loosen our wings to float up and up

into the realms of love ever higher

Many people are striving to overcome the imbalances, the primary reason the lightworkers came here. Yes, it takes a while to get it right. Let's release all that binds and set our dreams to sail through spiritual creativity, living once and for all in peace.

November 3, 7, 18

Election Day. Are we rising and choosing the path of compassionate love? Only the next few days will tell. We have high hopes for the healing of humanity. It has to start one step at a time, so let's choose the vibrations of loving life in all ways.

At last, the election outcome is determined. We have a new president and the first woman vice president. Perhaps they will restore trust, and healing, which is so needed during this intense time. Most of us are breathing with relief, that the balance has shifted. The light is shining brighter even if the old administration does not accept the results, with angry disruptions.

The uncertainty of the transition to a new government is hotly disputed. It feels like we are edging closer to living with light-filled loving awareness. Yes, the energies are shifting, uplifting and soothing the aching hearts of humanity.

I am inspired, to write a new chapter, Metatron's Grid. I love the esoteric meaning and design of his creation.

December

Winter descended. Sending out this manuscript was not to be, due to technical issues. I had to relax more than once rather than panic when I thought I lost the text. Completion takes time. At last, redone with inspiring support from the unseen ones. I pray for the well-being of everyone for the new year.

A powerful full moon, the thirteenth of this intense, dramatic year. So many lives have passed. Book 1 is opening its' wings and sailing beyond my home. I am grateful for all that has come to me.

June 11, 2022

Summer, finally about to republish this book, with many new changes. Book 2, *Entering the Portal*, of the *Gaea Star Crystal* trilogy is also due to come out with a fabulous colorful cover by Nina Rossi.

May we live in peace, for love is the only sweet feeling deep within our hearts, that heals and overcomes everything.

May the tribes of humanity awaken, opening their hearts to live in unconditional, loving harmony.

May we remember that we are radiant orbs of golden light and set ourselves to fly as high as we dare to, into the universe on wings of loving light.

Much love to all, Mariam.

ADDENDA

ARCHANGELS IN ORDER OF APPEARANCE

Archangel Michael is the Prince of the Archangels with his legions of blue lightning angels. He passionately serves all humans in need of aid or protection in crisis. He imparts clear communication, helping to create a strong foundation to set your highest intentions to harmonize your life. He is the dynamic leader of the Rainbow Brigades, those helpful Lightworkers, who came to Gaea Star, (Earth) to help humanity awaken to the loving essence of their true spiritual selves.

Archangel Gabriel, revered as the messenger of revelation, with her golden trumpet and white lily flowers, is the bearer of good tidings. She imparts divine blessings, encouraging insight, wisdom, mercy, motivation, and overcoming fears. Ask Gabriel for confidence, to release writing blocks and to master the art of teaching and sharing knowledge. She is the protector of childbearing, fertility issues, and child rearing.

Archangel Metatron, called the angel of life, is one of only two archangels believed to have lived on Earth. He was the prophet Enoch before ascending to heaven and becoming an Archangel. He is revered as the guardian of the sacred geometric symbol, the Tree of Life, Merkabah, or Metatron's cube. It is a compelling three-dimensional design, formed out of triangular shapes, circles and lines - a dynamic blueprint, a template of an etheric vehicle powered by universal energy.

This ancient design signifies that everything is all one and always moving with centrifugal force, generating positive energy, protection, creativity and inspiration.

Connecting with Metatron helps in developing your spirituality in the quest to improve one's life. He records good deeds in the Book of Life or the Akashic Records and loves children of all ages. Ashento's colorful tattoos are based on the design of Metatron's cube.

Archangel Sandalphon is the angel of music, the spiritual brother of Metatron. He helps to access spirit through the music. It is believed he was the prophet Elijah on (Earth) Gaea Star, who sailed to heaven on a chariot of fire light, drawn by winged horses. He inspires self-assurance and focused clarity to tap into your talents and passions through creativity and music, to serve humanity and lovingly care for Gaea Star's natural beauty.

Archangel Ariel, the lioness, patron of all animals, is the fierce protector of Gaea Star's precious environmental resources. She provides insights on survival necessities, food, shelter, housing, and oversees the harmonious order of the planetary bodies, such as the sun, moon, and the stars.

Archangel Jophiel is the patron of artists. She encourages you to enjoy the beauty in life, by releasing chaos and negativity. She loves to organize places or situations that are in disarray, to gain a different perspective to change your attitude for the positive.

Archangel Chamuel is the peacekeeper, who sees and knows all things throughout the universe. Call on him for strength, to overcome adversity, to allay fears and dissipate negative energies. He helps to find lost objects, including loved ones and helps to improve love relationships.

Archangel Uriel is the angel of wisdom and service. He is the patron of the arts and sciences and loves to solve problems by shining the light of wisdom through the shadowy aspects of life. He inspires you to clarify and make decisions, stabilize emotions, recognize danger, heal loss of self-respect and awaken your true spiritual purpose. He helps access the gift of prophecy, or psychic abilities through visions, dreams and insights.

Archangel Raphael is the patron of physical and emotional healing, and safe travel. Ask him. He works with Archangel Michael to restore peace and harmony and to relieve pain and injuries, addictions and cravings.

Archangel Raziel is the angel of mysteries, who helps to gain a deeper understanding of the essence of creation. As the holy writer he imparts the esoteric secrets of spirit and the wise scriptures. He inspires a deepening of faith, and a renewed belief that all things are sacred, by stimulating ideas and focused concentration. He loves to activate your psychic abilities such as clairvoyance and clairaudience, to enable hearing messages from spirit and ones' intuition.

Archangel Azrael is the angel of transitions, that oversees the crossing over of souls into the spirit realm. He helps with loss, grief and assists counselors and ministers to help with emotional and physical changes, by smoothing out difficult issues.

Archangel Lucifer, according to many, was not the fallen angel as some believe. Known as the light bearer, he inspired independence and progressive thinking, by acknowledging freedom of will and choice. He was a true rebel who wanted to show how to rise above the seductive pleasures of earth life and aspire to create a more harmonious spiritual existence.

Archangel Barachiel is the chief of guardian angels and patron angel of blessings, good fortune, marriage and family life. He is the joyful one, usually preceded by lightning and roses falling from the sky. Ask him to achieve successful endeavors, to release blocks to access your abundant self. He is the master of making good things happen with a real sense of humor as well.

CHARACTERS IN ORDER OF APPEARANCE

In the Beginning

Celestia - angelic child, rainbow brigade member

Mira - angelic child, rainbow brigade member

Azul - angelic child, rainbow brigade member

Isis - Egyptian Goddess

Gaea Star - Spirit of Mother Earth

Alaria - Angelic Choir

Archangel Michael

Archangel Gabriel

Response to the Archangel's Message

Kardichay - Red ray, rainbow brigade member

Priestess Marsoula - From Alay Lana, the temple of Mercury

Rionarta - Red ray, rainbow brigade member

Carmina - Student in Rionarta's Temple grid

Lakul - Orange ray, rainbow brigade member

Teesha -Yellow ray, rainbow brigade member

Initamay - Green ray, rainbow brigade member, Ilanu's sister

Emeraldina - Emerald faery

Ilanu - Green ray, rainbow brigade member, Initamay's brother

Ashento - Blue ray, master spiritual teacher

Ayalasha - Purple ray, rainbow brigade member

Tofal - Ayalasha's partner on the purple ray planet

Lartimus, Ishima - Ayalasha's horses

Teladi - White ray, mystical wizard, rainbow brigade member

Azrael - Student of Teladi

The Dark Side

Zosakel, (Zoz) - Hired by Slake, to thwart the mission

Keme - Zosakel's side kick

Slake - Boss from Marcon

Along the way to Star Sirius Center

Aloha Plumerias - Fruit cocktail women

Purple Faery

Piano Player - Merkabus driver

Tela - Aloha Plumeria Greeter

Bella - Director, Joyous Bubbles Spirit Care

Miyah - Assistant, Joyous Bubbles Spirit Care

Aronsky - Child on the Lotus Merkabus

Silvery Faery Nymphs -The water gardens

Painty the Turtle - The water gardens

Demeclis - Landing Dock Builder

Star Sirius Center

Angel Ohm - Metatron's assistant

Gandhi - Indian leader, tapestry room

Salvador Dali - Artist

Georgia O'Keefe – Artist

The Council Chamber

Metatron - Archangel in charge of the meeting

Archangels - Ariel, Jophiel, Chamuel, Gabriel, Uriel, Raphael, Raziel, Azrael, Sandolphon, Lucifer

Spiritual masters - Maitreya, Kuan Yin, Yogananda

Saraswathi - Hindu goddess of the arts

Lakshmi - Hindu goddess of abundance

Ganesh - Hindu god of abundance and overcoming adversity

Native elder and child - From the Amazon jungle

Vestara - Being from Pleiades

Ikabayo - Being from the planet of Unaikota

Fayonallia, Nepthytoka, Amsinia - Elders from Bochuti

Diyanna's Gardens

Mister Coole Cat

Lady Bug Angel

In the Alaymytia Faery Realm

Oonalia - Faery Queen

Tubaiyo - Faery King

Rayanca, Luina - Mighty unicorns of the forest

Grandmother Utawa -Teladi's grandmother

The Labyrinth of Crystalline Light

Andaluchiya, Ritoyo - Elders from Recuayo

Ausan, Cusi - Llamas

Two little girls that love the llamas and unicorns.

Verdalon - Green rhyming elf

The Final Ceremony and Departure

Many wise elders and helpers - Imparting blessings at the ceremony

Archangel Barachiel - Patron of lightning, roses, joy

Archangel Ariel, - Patron of animals and protecting Gaea Star's environment

Choyka - Leprechaun, Ariel's forest friend

CRYSTALS IN ORDER OF APPEARANCE

Key wisdom - 7, Hobiton asks Okemo to find to help Gaea Star.

Selenite - 32, 132, 223, 234, 237, Celestial temple, Dianna's garden, final ceremony sentinels, Kardichay connects with in Metatron's grid.

Cinnabar quartz - 38, Kardichay's gift from Priestess Marsoula.

Giant rubies - 38, Red mineral display.

Black tourmaline - 38, Rionarta's gift from Carmina.

Orange quartz - 39, Surrounding Lakul's exercise area.

Yellow citrine - 40, Teesha's crystal.

Green apophyllite – 41, Initamay's gift from the faeries

Green magnetite- 42, 60, Ilanu's magic powder.

Amethyst - 46, 241, Ayalasha's wand to fly to Sirius, in the grid.

Laser quartz scepters - 47, Teladi's crystal rockets.

Magnetic mineral ore - 49, Slake gives to Zozakel.

Crystal solar panels -54 , On Star Sirius rooftops.

Red banded Jasper – 79, 86, Gems imbedded in the portal archway.

Rainbow fluorescence quartz - 86, Near the portal archway.

Petalite, (Lithium) – 86, Kardichay, Celestia connect with it.

METATRON'S CUBE OR GRID

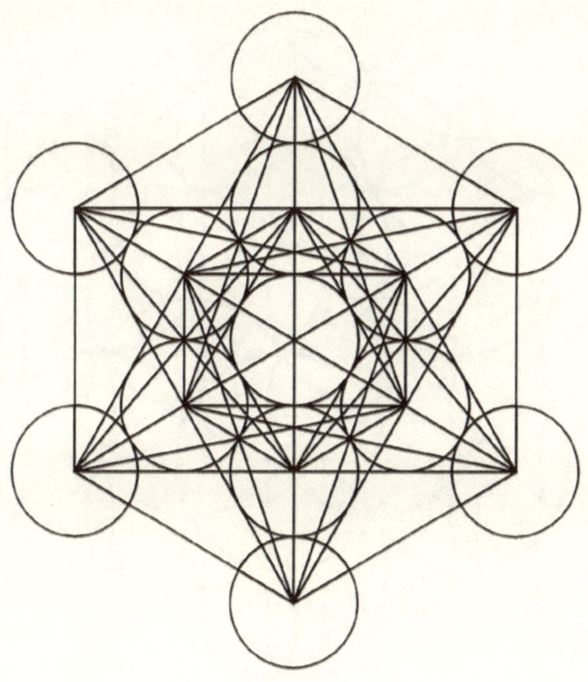

FLOWER OF LIFE GRID

REFERENCES

Airaudi, Oberto and Ananas Esperide, Text, Poetry by Oberto, Airaudi, 2006. *Damanhur, Temples of Humankind*, Cosm Press.

Carey, Ken. 1988. *Return of The Bird Tribes*, Unisun.

Conty, Patrick. 2002. *The Genesis and Geometry of The Labyrinth*, Inner Traditions.

Erasmus, 12th Century. *Book of Wisdom*.

Farndon, John. 2006. *The Complete Guide to Rocks & Minerals*, Anness Publishing Ltd.

Godwin, Malcom. 1990. Angels, *An Endangered Species*, Simon & Shuster.

Melchizedek, Drunvalo. 1998. *The Flower of Life*, Clear Light Publishing.

Melody, 1993. *Love is in the Earth*, Mineralogical Pictorial.

" " 1995. *Love is in the Earth*, A Kaleidoscope of Crystals.

" " 1996. *Love is in the Earth*, Kaleidoscopic Pictorial, Supplement A.

All three books, Earth Love Publishing House.

Permutt, Philip. 2007. *The Crystal Healer*, Cico Books.

Simmons, Robert and Naisha Ahsian. 2005. *The Book of Stones*. Heaven and Earth Publishing.

Simmons, Robert. 2009. *Stones of the New Consciousness*, Heaven and Earth Publishing.

Sperling, Renate. 1994. *The Essence of Gemstones*, Bluestar Communications.

Waldherr, Kris. 2006. *The Book of Goddesses*, Abrams Books.

Zerner, Amy & Monte Farber. 2009. *The Shaman's Guide to Healing Crystals*, One Spirit.

Of course, I also used the incredible world wide web, a brimming treasure trove of excellent information, colorful videos and remarkable photos. What a blessing to have this resource to use. I remember when I wrote papers with bulky outdated encyclopedias.

Now, we can soar into the realms of so many interesting lives, events, crystals, minerals, countries, songs and countless inspiring books.

I am grateful, for coming such a long way, in advancing our lives, for the better, which benefits all of humanity.

ABOUT THE AUTHOR

Mariam Massaro is a dynamic visionary, author, singer, songwriter and musician who loves to weave inspiring messages of love and peace. Mariam founded WiseWays Herbals in 1988, an herbal medicinal and natural body care product line, distributed nationally and internationally. She co-founded the Blazing Star Herbal School in 1983. Both are still flourishing after thirty-four years of educating and providing herbal products for well-being.

Mariam is also a midwife, ceremonial minister and the creatress of the Gaea Star Goddess Show, the Gaea Star Band and co-host of the Gaea Star Crystal Radio Hour. The popular Dreamvision7 webcast with over 500 shows and thousands of listeners created with Bob Sherwood, Craig Harris, and special guests since 2012.

She is also a flamboyant performer, costumer and author of *The Gaea Star Crystal* screenplay based on her original 1999 story, *"Rainbow Crystals of the Earth."* She cocreated her first CD, *"The Gaea Star Crystal, Awakening the Tribes of Light"* as the movie soundtrack in 2009. The trailer made from their independent filming of the *Gaea Star Crystal* received the Best Trailer award in the Hollywood and Vine Independent Film Festival in 2012.

She is the proprietor of the Singing Bridge Performing Arts Lodge and Airbnb lodge in West Cummington, Ma, which offers an artsy creative space for events, live music, swimming as mermaids, and hikes.

Mariam is a devoted yogini and loves living on her peaceful organic herb farm with her friendly llamas and cool cats in the hills of western Massachusetts.

ALSO, BY THE AUTHOR

*B*lessed by Light Filled Love, The Celestial Teachings of Ashento, Spirits of the Sun, reprinted 2021, is a compelling autobiographical story of Mariam's awakening as a creatress of the arts after meeting her twin flame, Ashento in a dream while alone in the forest on her first vision quest. Ashento is a spiritual master from the seventh celestial realm who is dedicated to guiding humanity with his loving wisdom to help restore harmony to Gaea Star, our Earth. Mariam hears his powerful inspirational messages through his voice, whispering to her. Their souls have remained united in love, for eons.

The Gaea Star Crystal, book 2, *Entering the Portal, 2022*, Spirits of the Sun. This rich new novel is the continuing saga of the fascinating adventure of the rainbow brigade, (lightworkers), unicorns, and royal fairies who sail at lightspeed from Star Sirius on an important mission to Gaea Star, (earth) to save her precious resources and restore harmony for humanity. The star travelers are invited to pass through the portal of illusion into the realms of the fairies, crystals and beneath the earth.

Songs of Spirit, Spirits of the Sun, 2014. The lyrics to Mariam's CD's. Seventy-seven original, uplifting, empowering songs celebrating life. Available from mariammassaro.com.

Mariam's Music

Gaea Star Crystal Radio Hour,

Streaming 24/7 on dreamvisions7radio.com

11 am, 11pm, Thursdays, Fridays, (EST)

CD's, or music downloads - mariammassaro.com. or streaming on Spotify or Pandora.

1. Gaea Star Crystal, Awakening the Tribes of Light, 2009

2. Gaea Star Goddesses, (Celebrating the Divine Feminine) 2011

3. Smooth Sailing Love Songs, 2013

4. For the Children, (Delightful Happy Offerings), 2014

5. Best of Gaea Star Crystal Radio Hour, 2013

6. Vision Quest, (Mariam's Medicine Path Journey), 2014

7. Who We Are, (Gaea Star Crystal radio hour tracks), 2015

   Applehead/ Sony Records.

8. Release, (Uplifting originals) 2021

Contact Info

email – mariam@wiseways.com

Blessedbylightfilledlove.com

WiseWays Herbals website - wiseways.com.

mariammassaro.com

thesingingbridgeperformingartslodge.com

Facebook - facebook.com/mariam.massaro

Spreaker.com/user/gaeastarcrystal

Youtube.com/gaeastarcrystal

Video - www.vimeo.com/36481222

(Live at the Academy, Gaea Star Goddess Show), 2011